T0059495

continued . . .

STATE OF THE ONION

"Pulse-pounding action, an appealing heroine, and the inner workings of the White House kitchen combine for a stellar adventure in Julie Hyzy's delightful *State of the Onion*."   —Carolyn Hart, author of *Laughed 'Til He Died*

"Hyzy's sure grasp of Washington geography offers firm footing for the plot."   —*Booklist*

"Topical, timely, intriguing. Julie Hyzy simmers a unique setting, strong characters, sharp conflict, and snappy plotting into a peppery blend that packs an unusual wallop."
—Susan Wittig Albert, author of *Holly Blues*

"From terrorists to truffles, mystery writer Julie Hyzy concocts a sumptuous, breathtaking thriller."
—Nancy Fairbanks, bestselling author of *Turkey Flambé*

"Exciting and delicious! Full of heart-racing thrills and mouthwatering food, this is a total sensual delight."
—Linda Palmer, author of *Kiss of Death*

"A compulsively readable whodunit full of juicy behind-the-Oval Office details, flavorful characters, and a satisfying side dish of red herrings—not to mention twenty pages of easy-to-cook recipes fit for the leader of the free world."
—*Publishers Weekly*

Praise for the novels of Julie Hyzy

"Deliciously exciting."   —Nancy Fairbanks

"A well-constructed plot, interesting characters, and plenty of Chicago lore . . . A truly pleasurable cozy."
—Annette Meyers

GRACE
INTERRUPTED

JULIE HYZY

BERKLEY PRIME CRIME, NEW YORK

THE BERKLEY PUBLISHING GROUP
Published by the Penguin Group
Penguin Group (USA) Inc.
375 Hudson Street, New York, New York 10014, USA
Penguin Group (Canada), 90 Eglinton Avenue East, Suite 700, Toronto, Ontario M4P 2Y3, Canada
(a division of Pearson Penguin Canada Inc.)
Penguin Books Ltd., 80 Strand, London WC2R 0RL, England
Penguin Group Ireland, 25 St. Stephen's Green, Dublin 2, Ireland (a division of Penguin Books Ltd.)
Penguin Group (Australia), 250 Camberwell Road, Camberwell, Victoria 3124, Australia
(a division of Pearson Australia Group Pty. Ltd.)
Penguin Books India Pvt. Ltd., 11 Community Centre, Panchsheel Park, New Delhi—110 017, India
Penguin Group (NZ), 67 Apollo Drive, Rosedale, Auckland 0632, New Zealand
(a division of Pearson New Zealand Ltd.)
Penguin Books (South Africa) (Pty.) Ltd., 24 Sturdee Avenue, Rosebank, Johannesburg 2196,
South Africa

Penguin Books Ltd., Registered Offices: 80 Strand, London WC2R 0RL, England

This is a work of fiction. Names, characters, places, and incidents either are the product of the author's imagination or are used fictitiously, and any resemblance to actual persons, living or dead, business establishments, events, or locales is entirely coincidental. The publisher does not have any control over and does not assume any responsibility for author or third-party websites or their content.

GRACE INTERRUPTED

A Berkley Prime Crime Book / published by arrangement with the author

PRINTING HISTORY
Berkley Prime Crime mass-market edition / June 2011

Copyright © 2011 by Julie Hyzy.
Cover illustration by Kimberly Schamber.
Cover design by Rita Frangie.
Interior text design by Laura K. Corless.

ISBN: 978-0-425-24190-5

BERKLEY® PRIME CRIME
Berkley Prime Crime Books are published by The Berkley Publishing Group,
a division of Penguin Group (USA) Inc.,
375 Hudson Street, New York, New York 10014.
BERKLEY® PRIME CRIME and the PRIME CRIME logo are trademarks of Penguin Group (USA) Inc.

PRINTED IN THE UNITED STATES OF AMERICA

10 9 8 7 6 5 4 3 2 1

For anyone who has ever opened heart
and home to a stray

Acknowledgments

Special thanks to my fabulous editor, Emily Rapoport, and to Michelle Vega, Kaitlyn Kennedy, and Erica Rose at Berkley Prime Crime as well as to my marvelous agent, Paige Wheeler. You are all a dream to work with and I thank you for your enthusiastic support.

Thanks, too, to my blogmates at www.MysteryLovers Kitchen.com, and at www.KillerCharacters.com. What fabulous groups of people! So much fun. I count myself lucky to be associated with these great authors.

I have to thank one individual in particular for his help with this book. Our good friend Jerry Rodell (who also happens to be my pledge-father from ages ago), is an active and avid Civil War re-enactor. He provided a steady stream of facts, pictures, and websites, as well as an in-depth knowledge of re-enacting I could not possibly have found elsewhere. Any and all errors (and variations due to creative license) are mine entirely. Thank you, Jerry. And a special thank-you to his wife, Denise, for the girly info . . . especially about the Soiled Doves. Loved that!

My family means everything to me, and I want to take a moment to thank my wonderful husband and kids. Love you, Curt, Robyn, Sara, and Biz. One of our new additions to the family makes her debut in this novel as "Bootsie." Hope you enjoy meeting her.

Thanks to Mystery Writers of America, Sisters in Crime,

and Thriller Writers of America. I especially want to thank readers who "friend" me on Facebook, post reviews online, and e-mail asking how soon the next book will be out. You make this job a joy. Thank you all, from the bottom of my heart.

Chapter I

THE TWO WOMEN GLARED AT ME WITH SUCH sizzling fury I was afraid their eyeballs might catch fire. Flanked as they were by a pair of our manor's elderly security guards, they appeared harmless enough, but both were so visibly agitated it was hard to be sure. They shifted their weight and met my gaze as the guards, Niles and William, explained the situation and handed me the women's photo IDs. I took an involuntary step back in case either of the two in custody decided to take a swing at me.

We faced each other in Marshfield Manor's West Salon, a high-ceilinged room on the mansion's first floor. In the midst of a major refurbishment, the room was off-limits to visitors. Painting scaffolds blocked butternut bookcases, café au lait walls, and even one of the floor-to-ceiling windows. The two massive billiard tables that hadn't been removed were covered with protective canvas duck. Since it was Friday and near quitting time, the painters and carpenters had taken off for the weekend, leaving the West Salon empty and quiet. I was pleased that our two security guards had opted to escort our unwelcome visitors here. This way our conversation would not disturb lingering tourists taking a final circuit of the mansion.

Casting a wary glance at the women, Niles did most of the talking. "We tried to tell them—politely, y'understand—that the south grounds were off-limits but they drove straight down there anyway. When we caught up with them on foot, they started beating us up."

"That's a lie," the shorter one, Rani, said. Slim yet curvy, she watched for my reaction with the alertness of a cat ready to pounce. At first I guessed her to be Hispanic or Italian, but based on the surname from her ID—Ogitani—I thought perhaps there might be some Japanese in her blood. She wore her dark hair pulled back into a severe ponytail—sleek, like a panther. She ran an appraising gaze over the two men, as though sizing up dinner options.

William fingered his jacket where the sleeve had been torn from the shoulder. "They ruined my uniform."

Niles pointed in the general direction of Marshfield Manor's far southern grounds where a group of Civil War re-enactors were establishing a campsite. "The guy that they're after is the one I feel sorry for."

I wondered how our two security guards had managed to corral these women and herd them back here. Rani was clearly a tough cookie. I, too, felt sorry for the guy they were after. "Who exactly is this Zachary Kincade?" I asked.

Rani took a step forward. "Zachary Kincade is a world-class jerk. I can only hope one of his Civil War buddies plants a musket ball into his brain." With a malicious grin, she turned to her companion. "Or better yet, aim lower. That would be fitting, don't you think?"

The other woman, Tamara, didn't answer. Although she also wore her hair pulled back, hers was washed-out blonde streaked with gray. Sporting heavy eye makeup, crimson nails, and three silver chains hanging from her thick neck, she kept her hands shoved into her pockets, edging away as she eyed the door.

Neither woman looked like the type to trespass on private property simply to pick a fight. They were both in their mid-thirties and—if their clothes were any indication—financially well-off. They wore almost identical outfits of easy, comfortable pants and tops in solid black. Most pieces bore recognizable logos. Everything, including their black leather ballet flats, appeared brand-new. Like they'd prepared ahead for a stealth maneuver. Attempting to parse what I knew with what stood before me, I was reminded of a puzzle game from the Sunday papers, "What's Wrong with This Picture?" which I'd played as a kid.

"We have an agreement with the re-enactors," I began. "They are not to be disturbed at all today. Not until their camp is set up and their—what's it called?" I turned to Niles but remembered before he could chime in. "Living History, that's it. Once their Living History is established on Monday, manor guests are welcome to visit during designated hours of the day."

"No, no, no," Rani said, "we don't care if they're *ready*. We're marching down there and we're confronting him *now*." She offered a sly smile. "But I imagine he's expecting us."

Niles cleared his throat. "We contacted Mr. Pierpont when these ladies first arrived on the grounds. Mr. Pierpont assured us that Mr. Kincade does not wish to be disturbed."

Rob Pierpont was our principal contact and top brass of the re-enacting crowd. He'd proven to be easy to work with but had made the pointed request for privacy for the first few days, explaining that while the group was setting up they didn't want outsiders watching. Claiming it would ruin the effect of walking into a real 1860s Civil War campground, he'd said, "This is almost like an amusement park exhibit. No kid wants to see the fuzzy cartoon character with his head off, and no Civil War aficionado wants to see the Confederate battle flag atop a plastic cooler. It's the same thing."

I'd promised him we would comply. To the women, I said, "You can come back Monday . . ."

"No," Rani said. She barked a laugh. "We are not giving him time to weasel away. Listen, the only reason we agreed to come up here with these bozos"—she swept an arm toward Niles and William—"is because they told us we could talk with you. We figured a woman would understand. Be reasonable here. We're paying guests. We have every right . . ." Her voice had begun to rise as she spoke. Taking a deep breath, she calmed herself. "I just think it's pretty convenient for Zachary to disappear whenever he needs to. This time he's safe behind castle walls."

Not exactly accurate. Our Civil War re-enactor guests were camping *out*doors, as far across our expansive grounds from these "castle walls" as one could get, though the description of the manor was apt. The 150-room mansion was both a major tourist attraction and world-class museum. Its gorgeous furnishings and historically significant artifacts were what kept our docents busy every day of the year except Christmas and Thanksgiving. More than 500,000 visitors came through the manor's front doors annually to follow the self-guided tours. Manor docents and paid security manned key positions throughout the home, ready and eager to answer questions.

Outside was another story. Although we had a four-star hotel and several recreational facilities on premises including a horse-riding stable, most of the land had been left in its natural state. We rarely rented out the forest and grounds that lay to the far south of the property but my predecessor, Abe, had made an exception for this group. Months before I started working at Marshfield, Abe had agreed to this weeklong re-enactor encampment. A Civil War buff himself, he'd been eager to talk and learn from the participants. So eager, in fact, that he'd rented the week out to them at a price that just covered our maintenance costs. I felt a pang of sadness at the thought of Abe missing out on the event he'd been looking so forward to. His murder, just a few floors above where we stood, was still a raw wound around here. One from which we might never recover.

Instinctively I glanced upward. Although I'd originally been hired to take Abe's place when he retired, his sudden death had thrown me into the role unprepared. Other staffers and the manor's reclusive owner—Bennett Marshfield—had been equally unprepared for me to take over. It had been a rocky road thus far. For all of us.

Right now, however, I needed to flex my authoritarian muscle. The two women in front of me were itching for a fight. I cleared my throat. "Since this isn't an emergency, you have no real business here. I'm going to have to ask you to leave."

"Come on," Rani said, wheedling now, "you're a woman. I'm sure you've met your share of idiot men."

One particular idiot man came to mind, but I couldn't see how that made a difference. Before I could cut her off however, she went on, "Zachary Kincade is a class-A scumbag. The top—or bottom, if you will—of the pile. The worst."

"I take it he's your ex?" I said.

"I would never have anything to do with a lowlife like him."

Tamara decided to join the conversation. "He broke up with our friend Muffy."

"Muffy?" I repeated.

Rani took a breath and rolled her eyes. "Blame her parents, okay? They should have had dogs, not children. The poor girl never learned life skills. You know, the kind of savvy you better have if you don't want the jerks of this world twisting you into knots. We tried to warn her about

Zachary . . ." She stopped herself before going further, then worked up an unconvincing smile. "Listen, all we want to do is teach him a lesson. No permanent damage." She seemed to weigh her words, then amended, "Well, nothing life-threatening, at least."

"I'm sorry," I said again, though not sorry at all, "I'm going to have to ask you to leave. Now."

Rani gave a "you-aren't-the-boss-of-me" head waggle. "We're hotel guests. We paid for two nights' stay. You can't kick us out."

Of course I could. This was private property and I had every right to kick her out on her well-dressed little butt. I almost blurted that aloud but just as the words were about to fly from my mouth, diplomacy wrestled me into submission. Again. Once, just once, I wished for the freedom to sacrifice tact and say exactly what was on my mind instead of bending over backward to keep guests happy. But that was my job and I was good at it. "Your entry fee grants you admittance to the house and the gardens."

She held a finger up to correct me. "House and grounds."

"Except this weekend," I said evenly. "When you arrived at the front gate, you were informed that the south end of the property would be off-limits to guests until Monday." Drawing on Pierpont's analogy, I added, "Think of it like an amusement park—when a ride is broken down, they tell you that at the door. If you weren't willing to accept the terms, you should have turned around and gone home."

"I was never told that the grounds were off-limits."

She was lying. We both knew it.

"Perhaps I could interest you in a rain check for another time when the grounds are reopened for day visitors."

Tamara's eyes grew wide as she sidled closer to her friend, elbowing her. Focused on me, Rani didn't notice. "It has to be done today," Tamara whispered.

My stomach gave a hard little lurch, like it was attempting to drive my body into action. Not before I had all the facts. "What do you plan to *do* to Zachary Kincade?" I asked.

"That's none of your business," Tamara said. Visibly uneasy until this moment, she lifted her chin, fixed me with a solemn stare, and shoved her hands even deeper into her pockets. I swore she grew two inches taller. But there was no way I was backing down when the safety of our guests was at stake. I straightened to my own full height. Barefoot I'm five-foot-eight, at least six inches taller than Tamara. With the heels I wore today, I towered over her like an Amazon woman.

"I cannot allow you access to the re-enactors," I said, "especially when you pose a threat to their well-being."

"Who said anything about a threat?" Rani shouted, contradicting herself. "Look at us. We're just a couple of harmless women. We just want to talk to him."

Harmless? Not these two. I could see it in their eyes. When I continued to refuse their request, they launched into a verbal attack on me. Lifting my walkie-talkie, I spoke briefly into the handset, all the while wondering about their quarry, this Zachary Kincade. Who was he? The likelihood of my meeting the man was minuscule, but I couldn't help but be curious.

The response I waited for sang through my radio. Turning to Rani and Tamara, I gestured toward the nearest door. "One of our shuttles will be here in a moment to escort you off the grounds. I'll see to it that your entry fees are refunded."

Rani stomped her foot. "You are *not* kicking us out."

"I'm afraid I have no choice."

Four more security guards swarmed the area and Tamara let out a panicked yelp. Eyes wide, she scanned the room as though looking for a friendly face. There were none. "He texted Muffy," she yelled in desperation. "He broke up with her via text."

I'd heard worse. And although I felt sorry for Muffy, whoever she was, her love life and that of Zachary Kincade were not my concern. I was pleased to see Terrence Carr join the crowd. Tall, black, and with movie-star good looks, our head of security quickly took control.

"Let's go, ma'am," he said to Rani. As he moved to take her arm, she jerked away.

"You don't know what we're dealing with here," she said in a low voice. "If you knew, you'd drag that wretched waste of humanity in here and let us take care of him."

I couldn't help myself. "All this because he broke up with your friend?"

"Via text," Tamara said.

"Listen," I began.

Rani's voice was a growl, "You don't understand."

"Then explain it," Terrence said.

Rani's eyes narrowed. "You're just like him. Attractive, strong. And you think you're God's gift to women, don't you?"

"Only to my wife, ma'am." Whenever Terrence smiled, which wasn't often, he dazzled. This time was no exception. Rani tried unsuccessfully to stifle a little gasp of surprise.

Composing herself, she dragged the back of one hand across the side of her face as though smoothing an errant hair. The two women were no match for the team and they knew it. "I can see we're getting nowhere here," Rani said. "Come on, Tamara, let's go."

"We intend to escort you off property, ma'am," Terrence said, all business once again. "Make no mistake about that."

"As delightful a prospect as that may be," Rani dripped sarcasm, "we are not criminals. We've done nothing wrong, and we are certainly capable of seeing ourselves out. Come on, Tamara. We're finished here."

"No," Tamara said with vehemence. "He can't get away

with what he did to Muffy. I'm not leaving until they bring Zachary in here and we finish what we came to do."

Terrence and I exchanged looks. A female officer near Tamara took a step forward, surreptitiously dragging a set of handcuffs from the back of her belt. Tamara caught the movement and jumped backward out of the officer's reach. "Get away from me," she screamed. Fists still jammed in her pockets, she searched the room, clearly looking for a means of escape.

"Let me see your hands," Terrence said in a low voice. "Pull them out slowly."

Tamara backed up another step.

The room fell silent. The only sound was Tamara's breathing coming in shallow, frightened gasps.

I heard footsteps behind me. People running. It sounded like three at least, pounding the floor and coming to a sudden stop. A man's amused voice: "I just knew it had to be you two."

I turned. Zachary Kincade—who else could it be?—stood behind me, mirth crinkling his eyes. I had about two seconds to assess the subject of this skirmish. About forty-five years old, Kincade was wearing contemporary army fatigues. Exceedingly well. Tall, with a full head of dark hair, a neatly trimmed beard frosted with gray, and a smile like George Clooney's, he held his hands high as he laughed. "Why am I not surprised?"

Behind him, Rob Pierpont was dressed in full Civil War regalia. I'd met the short, portly fellow several times. Pale and doughy, he too wore a beard, but his was far less dashing. I suspected he'd grown it to hide a double chin. Or maybe all male re-enactors were required to sport facial hair. Who knew? The plethora of decoration on Pierpont's uniform proclaimed his considerable rank. At the moment, however, you'd never guess it by his demeanor. Pouting like an angry four-year-old, Pierpont tugged at Kincade's shirt. "Zachary, this is a mistake," he said.

Behind both men were two additional security guards. Wasn't this a party?

My mini-assessment time came to a shattering halt as Tamara's face grew red. She practically vibrated with fury. It was like watching Mount Tamara, seconds before hot lava spewed from the top of her head. I took a preventive step toward Kincade just as she let out a shrill cry. She charged the man, pulling her hands from her pockets, gurgling a feral scream.

"She's got a gun!" I shouted.

Terrence didn't need the warning. Already in motion, he raced to intercept. She nimbly sidestepped his grab as Rani attacked Terrence, first using what looked like a karate maneuver, then jumping onto his back and smacking him repeatedly in the head. All the other security staffers raced forward but not before Tamara got close enough to raise her weapon.

Not a gun. A Taser.

I dashed into the fray. Just as Tamara pulled the trigger, I shoved her sideways. The weapon's two electrodes shot forward into empty space. Like dud fireworks, they extended their tethers and dropped listlessly to the floor without so much as grazing their target.

Security took Tamara down, elbows and knees hitting the marble floor in a muffled *rat-a-tat-tat* of bone-jarring thuds. Terrence wrestled himself away from Rani and handcuffed her, all the while shouting directions to his team. Zachary Kincade had leaned out of the way when the Taser fired and burst out laughing. His guffaws were coarse, unpleasant sounds that reminded me of angry ducks squawking. Except ducks know better than to let their mouths hang open. Whatever attraction he might have possessed was gone in a quack.

Damp and wide-eyed, Rob Pierpont ran a handkerchief across his pasty forehead, looking ready to go into cardiac arrest. As security regained control, I sidled up to him. "You okay?"

He nodded but the sweat dripping down the sides of his face contradicted him. Rob Pierpont barely topped five-and-a-half feet and looked more like a conquered Napoleon than a general in the War Between the States. From our brief conversations leading up to this week, however, I knew that in the real world he was a partner in a Florida accounting firm and that he was looking forward to his impending retirement. "More time to devote to my Civil War hobby."

"I'm so sorry about this," he said.

"Not your fault."

Zachary moved in and crouched next to Tamara, who was restrained facedown on the floor. "You just couldn't let it go, could you?"

Tamara called Zachary a very bad name.

Terrence signaled to his team. "Get him out of here. He's just making things worse."

"Do you know what all this is about?" I asked Pierpont.

He lifted his shoulders. "Zachary can be a trouble-maker, I'll give you that. But until these two women made it to our camp, I had no idea it was this bad."

"How bad is it?" I asked.

Zachary called to Pierpont as he was led away. "I'll meet you out back," he said, pointing, as though we wouldn't understand what he meant.

Pierpont suddenly looked much older than his years. "These ladies didn't tell you?"

"They said he broke up with their friend via text."

"That's not exactly the whole story. Zachary didn't *directly* text the woman he was engaged to . . ."

"Engaged?" I was aghast. "He broke off the *engagement* via text?"

Pierpont winced. "Last Saturday, fifteen minutes before the wedding was to begin, with everyone gathered at the church and his bride-to-be waiting in the wings, he mass-texted the entire bridal party to let them know he changed his mind."

"That's despicable."

Pierpont shrugged. "That's Zachary."

Chapter 2

I KNEW TERRENCE WOULD BRING ME UP TO speed later. Right now, I decided to escort Pierpont out. The poor man was visibly shaken and I wanted to ensure he had transportation back with someone to keep him company. Even if it was only Zachary. "You sure you're okay?" I asked again as we left the West Salon and took the long corridor toward what had once been the servants' back entrance.

He squared his shoulders and gave a little huff, settling himself. "Much better now," he said. "Thank you. Our re-enactments are generally very exciting but it's a controlled environment. This was so . . . savage."

"You've been involved in re-enactments for a long time?"

"My father got me started. Years ago." His eyes took on a faraway look. "Back then, we were so much more authentic. No plastic coolers or blow-up mattresses in our tents. When we roughed it, we roughed it. It was more real."

"I think I'd be a terrible re-enactor," I said. "I'd want to bring my blow-dryer."

"Some women try to sneak them in. But I'm way ahead of them. That's why your property here is so perfect for our run-through. No electricity unless someone brings a generator. No running water nearby. That would be farby."

"Farby?"

He nodded, warming to his subject. "Conventional wisdom says it comes from the phrase: '*Far be* it for me to criticize you' when re-enactors catch anachronisms in one anothers' costumes. For instance, Velcro. There was no Velcro in Civil War times, right?"

"Right."

"Hence, Velcro is farby. Zippers are farby. So are cigarettes that you don't roll yourself with the proper components, and any type of synthetic fabric."

I tried the word out again. "Farby."

"That's what you want to avoid at all costs. Nobody wants to be known as a Farb. I avoid it, always. In fact, participants like me are considered 'progressive' in that we believe in complete authenticity and try to fully immerse ourselves at every opportunity."

He continued as we walked, explaining the camp's reporting structure and how long it took to set up a Living History. I knew that they'd set up this weeklong encampment to run drills and work out the bugs in preparation for the group's big outing at Gettysburg in July. According to Pierpont, that was the year's main event and a chance to re-create that historic battle.

At the exit, I pushed open the back doors and stepped outside, taking a deep breath of the warm afternoon air.

"Beautiful," he said, surveying the south grounds.

That was an understatement. "It is."

I didn't mind making small talk with Pierpont, nor accompanying him out back. When I'd been called to the West Salon to meet with our intruders, I'd been on my way outside anyway. Jack Embers, the manor's landscape architect, had asked me to meet him near the entrance of the hedge maze to discuss a couple of gardening issues.

Jack and I had been playing date-tag for the past several weeks. We had originally planned to go out together—without my roommates this time—back in April. But situations had conspired to prevent us from keeping our plans. I rubbed my right arm, remembering my terror the night Abe's murderer had finally been apprehended.

Since then, Jack and I had tried and failed to set up another date. Spring was a busy time for Jack anyway, but he'd recently taken on a new responsibility. His younger brother, Davey, had joined the firm. More important, he'd rejoined Jack's life. From the little I'd learned, twenty-seven-year-old Davey had "issues" and hadn't yet found his way in the world. After several brushes with the law, Davey had promised his family he would change but needed help to do so. He'd moved into Jack's home about a month ago and all Jack's free time had been taken up by his little brother.

I'd met Davey a couple of times. Except for his beard and slighter build, he could have been Jack's twin. Well, except for Jack's scar, that is. An uneven white line sliced across the left side of his face. I wondered if I'd ever find out where that scar had come from.

"There he is," Pierpont said, interrupting my reverie and picking up his pace. "Kincade!"

Zachary Kincade leaned against a stone wall, chatting up one of our female groundskeepers. A youngster, barely twenty-two, she looked relieved to see us. The moment Kincade's attention was pulled by Pierpont's call, she waved to me and scurried off to tend to a distant flower bed.

Kincade ambled over. "I'm sorry about the trouble back there," he said, indicating the mansion with a dispassionate glance.

"I thought you'd be down at the police station, giving a statement," I said.

"Not pressing charges," he said. "What's the point? They had their fun and have been escorted off the grounds by your efficient security team. I'm not worried. Those girls don't have the guts to try again."

I wasn't so sure, and said so.

Kincade smiled. "I appreciate you worrying about me. But I'm a big boy." He held out his hand. "And you are? You have me at a distinct disadvantage here."

Pierpont gave an exasperated sigh. "This is Grace Wheaton. She's in charge. She's the one to contact if we need anything."

Kincade and I shook hands. "Nice to meet you," he said.

Pure reflex and good manners combined to make me smile and say how nice it was to meet him, too. But when I got my hand back, I resisted the urge to wipe it down the side of my skirt.

"In charge?" Kincade said, eyes brightening. "So much power in such a lovely package."

What era was this guy from? "Let me arrange for transportation back to your camp," I said, calling into my radio for a shuttle to be brought around back. The estate provided free transportation between the hotel and the manor, and between the manor and a remote parking lot. We'd recently expanded that lot to accommodate visitors whose numbers we expected—and hoped—to grow over the next several years.

Part of my job was to boost our image, increase tourism, and establish the Marshfield brand. No small feat—any of them. But before we could expect hundreds of thousands of new tourists to flock to our doors each year, we needed to make certain we had infrastructure issues settled first. Parking lots and shuttles weren't sexy upgrades, but they were important pieces of the whole. Fortunately my boss, Bennett, owner of this palatial estate, agreed with me. Just wait until he heard about today's excitement.

Kincade had to be almost fifteen years older than I was,

but as he moved in closer I caught the smolder of interest in his eyes. Ugh. He reached again for my hand. "I hope you're planning to visit our camp," he said in a low voice. "I'd love for you to see me in action during one of our battles."

I yanked my hand back. "Thanks, but I think I've had enough of your battles for one day."

"Ooh," he said, making his lips all pucker-y. Moving close enough for me to see the yellow flecks in his brown irises, he curled his mouth into what he probably thought was a provocative smile. This treatment might work on a lot of women, but I wasn't one of them. Not any longer at least. "You don't really believe what those ladies said, do you?" he asked softly. "No one really understands me, you know? I try to be a good guy but all I ever get . . ."

His attention shifted to just over my shoulder. For a split second, I wondered if it was a ruse just to get me to drop my guard and turn, but Kincade's body language suddenly shifted, too. No longer relaxed, no longer focused on me, his posture grew rigid and his eyes wide. He whispered under his breath, "How the . . . ?"

I turned to see what had grabbed his attention. Jack and Davey were about twenty feet back, headed toward us. Jack was in the lead, carrying a clipboard. He saw me. "There you are," he called, waving hello with his free hand. Davey followed, a couple steps behind him.

I felt a rush of air as Zachary Kincade bolted past me. He took Davey down in a flying tackle, Davey giving a *woof* of shock as they hit the ground, their bodies skidding hard against the uneven brick pavers. Grappling, the two combatants grunted and rolled while Pierpont and I shouted. Jack dropped his clipboard and jumped in to wrestle the two apart. Davey, having quickly recovered from the surprise of being attacked, fought back with fierce desperation.

I froze to the spot for three heartbeats before I thought

to call for help. As I spoke into my radio, I realized I'd
registered the look of utter surprise on Davey's face. I got
the clear impression he'd never seen Kincade before. But
Kincade obviously had an ax to grind. In fact, he was
grinding right now. Using his body to keep Davey immobi-
lized, he smashed the younger man's face sideways into the
ground with one hand while punching him with the other,
shouting something about "a long time." Davey managed
to pry an arm out from beneath Kincade and grabbed at his
attacker's shirt, straining to pull him off.

Next to me, Pierpont threw his hands up. "Oh, oh, oh!"

Unable to get between the two, Jack wrapped himself
around Zachary's back, struggling to immobilize the man's
arms. Though still punching and grunting, Kincade was
tiring. He wasn't able to both fight Davey and fend off Jack,
and the moment Jack wrestled Kincade into an armlock,
Davey writhed away and leaped to his feet. Blood dripped
from his now-crooked and obviously broken nose. "What
is wrong with you?" he shouted, wincing as he wiped his
face with the back of his hand.

Security came running. Behind them, a flock of nosy
tourists huddled around the near corner to watch the mess.
They were certainly getting an eyeful.

I offered Davey a tissue from my pocket which he ac-
cepted. Jack, meanwhile, had pinned Zachary Kincade's
arms behind him and was shouting close to the man's ear.
As security took over and dragged Jack away from his cap-
tive, Pierpont, who had been stricken silent after his outburst, hurried over to me to apologize. "I am so sorry. I
don't know what got into Zachary." He turned to his com-
rade, repeating Davey's words. "What is wrong with you?"

Rubbing his hand across his cheek and flinching, Kincade sat on the ground with one knee up and one arm
draped across it—the picture of relaxation. Except, of
course, for the blood dripping from his lip. With Terrence
off escorting Rani and Tamara to the local police, our

overtaxed and undertrained security guards looked at one another as if to say, "What now?"

Kincade stared up at Jack, then looked to Davey, then back again. Squinting, he seemed to see Jack with new eyes. He wiped his lip and asked, "I got it wrong, didn't I?"

Ignoring him, Jack made his way over to Davey, whose nose was beginning to swell. Jack took Davey's head in both hands and examined his brother's face. "It's broken, bro," he said. "We're going to have to get you to the emergency room."

Zachary Kincade shouted from the ground, "It's you, isn't it? Not him. *You're* Jack Embers."

Jack spun. "Do I know you?"

Kincade spit blood onto the ground next to him. "You shaved your beard," he said. "Now I see. I forgot to take the years into account. Your brother looks just like you did back then."

Jack stared wordlessly.

Kincade pushed himself to his feet and waved the security staff away. "Don't worry, I'm done. Getting too old for this garbage anyway." He brushed himself off and stepped forward. "You don't remember me, do you?"

Jack took his own step forward, inserting himself between Kincade and Davey. A protective move no one missed. "No. Should I?"

"My name," he said, "is Zachary Kincade."

Jack paled.

Hatred burned in Kincade's eyes. "Thirteen years ago, you killed my little brother."

Chapter 3

OUR SECURITY STAFF ITCHED TO TRUNDLE
yet another guest off to the local police station, but Davey
refused to press charges. Jack pulled his brother aside; I
was close enough to overhear. "He attacked you," he said.
"He should be arrested."

Davey's mouth set in a determined line and his eyes tightened against the pain. "No, Jack," he said, his voice low and
intense, "I want nothing more to do with that family, okay?"

"But the police need to get this on record," Jack insisted.
"We have to document this. You know what happened last
time."

"Just drop it."

"Davey . . ."

"I'm not pressing charges," Davey shouted. Then more
quietly, he added, "I need to get to the hospital, okay? Like
right now. I'm not feeling so good."

Jack threw a scathing look at Zachary Kincade but
Davey gripped Jack's shoulder, dragging back his brother's
attention. "Let it go, bro. We all need to let it go."

Pierpont was buzzing around Kincade, alternately asking how he was feeling and chastising him for his behavior. "What on earth were you thinking? What do you mean about your brother?" He pointed at Jack. "What are you saying? What did he do?"

Kincade didn't answer. Instead, he consulted with the police long enough to confirm that no charges were being brought against him. He turned to me and winked. "One good turn, eh?" Addressing Pierpont, he said, "Let's get back." Without waiting for his colleague to answer, he set off walking. It was a long way to the re-enactors' camp. Pierpont scuttled after him, and managed to convince him to wait for a ride.

Jack watched the whole thing before shaking his brother's grip from his shoulder. "Fine."

I was desperate to know more about Kincade's accusation—and especially why Jack hadn't denied it—but didn't want to intrude on such a tense family moment. At times like these, I call upon my organizational skills to see me through until I'm able to think straight again. Keeping busy keeps me sane, so I radioed for a shuttle to pick up the re-enactors and for a golf cart to take Jack and Davey to their car. The moment Kincade and Pierpont were gone, however, I couldn't stop myself. "What was that all about?" I asked Jack.

He waved me off. "Not now."

I didn't know how to take that. "Later, then?"

He sighed. "Not tonight." Without facing me, he added, "Looks like I'm canceling again."

Davey sat on the ground. Using two fingers from each hand, he applied gentle pressure to the sides of his nose.

"Don't do that," Jack snapped. "Wait for the doctors to examine you. You might knock something out of place."

Davey gave a humorless laugh. "Yeah, because everything is in perfect place right now." Blood dripped into his beard and wound its way through to fall on his pants leg, but Davey didn't seem to notice. Then, as though he'd finally processed the prior conversation, he looked up. "You two have a date tonight?"

Jack crouched next to his brother. "We'll reschedule."

"No, that's stupid. Keep your date. I'm not a kid. I can handle this by myself."

"I'm not about to leave my little brother alone in an emergency room with a broken nose. Let's go."

His use of the words *little brother* coming so soon after Kincade's claim made for an eerie echo. Was I the only person here who didn't know what was going on? Exactly what had happened thirteen years ago?

The golf cart pulled up and I gave the driver instructions as Jack and Davey settled themselves. Jack never made eye contact with me. Not even when the golf cart pulled away. Not even when I said, "Call me later, okay?"

CONFUSED, AND MORE THAN A LITTLE BIT hurt at Jack's brusque dismissal, I headed back to the house intending to write up reports on the afternoon's events and get myself ready to go home. Where Kincade went, chaos wasn't far behind, apparently. That was evident to me even after just meeting him. I wasn't thrilled to have trouble like him remain on property for the coming week, but I reminded myself that more than two miles separated the encampment from the main house. Kincade hadn't had a chance to repeat his invitation for me to come visit him. At this point he probably preferred I stay far away. That would keep us both happy.

Before I opened the servants' entrance door, I glanced back. Only a few security guards stood where Kincade and Davey had gone down in a tangle of arms, legs, hatred, and anger. What did Kincade mean when he said that Jack had killed his brother? I knew so little about Jack Embers. But I intended to find out more as soon as I could.

My office was on the third floor of the mansion's west wing. The double disturbance this afternoon had kept me here well past my usual quitting time. But without a date to look forward to tonight, I saw no rush to leave. It would be a quiet house until my roommates got home. Scott and Bruce wouldn't close up their wine shop until after nine at least. The only thing that waited for me right now was an empty refrigerator and a thick pile of bills.

Frances, my able yet incorrigible assistant, should have taken off an hour ago. I opened the door to the anteroom that served as her workspace, and jumped.

"What has been going on down there?" she demanded. "What's with all the excitement? Who were those women with the Taser? Whose nose got broken?"

"Geez," I said, backing away from her. In hindsight, I realized I should have anticipated this. Frances was the nosiest person I'd ever encountered and there was no way she would have left the manor if there was dirt to be dished. The woman survived on a steady diet of gossip. No exaggeration. Not for the first time I wondered what, or who, waited for her at home. For all her eager chatting about others, Frances was vigilantly closemouthed when it came to her own business.

I was about to give her a quick cursory rundown when Terrence burst in. "What happened now?" he asked. "I just heard that victim in the first scuffle was the perpetrator in a *second* altercation. Is Embers okay?"

Frances perked up. "Jack Embers?"

I didn't like the gleam in her eye. She'd warned me before that Jack was "trouble," but I hadn't taken her up on her offer to tell me all she knew about him. In the short months I'd been working with Frances, I'd learned that if you didn't live according to her strict personal code, which apparently changed from situation to situation depending on who was involved, there was something urgently wrong with you. I bet she got a lot of enjoyment talking about me behind my back.

"Jack's fine," I answered. "His brother . . ." I faltered, ". . . had an accident."

"What about you?" Terrence asked. "Were you hurt at all? How's your arm?"

"I'm fine," I said. "I wasn't touched."

"We don't want you getting hurt again."

I'd been injured some weeks prior, during a do-or-die altercation just one floor above. "Thanks, Terrence," I said, massaging my arm. Although my bandages had come off a while ago, the memory would remain forever. I had a new-found respect for the dangers police detectives faced every day and vowed never to get so personally involved in that kind of situation again.

"Good to hear," he said, then pointed to my office.

"Thanks for staying late, Frances," I said to my assistant, "I'll see you Monday."

She made a noise, but didn't argue. I led Terrence into the next room and shut the door. We both waited to start talking until we heard Frances leave.

When I first started working here, this spacious room had been Abe's office. Frances and I had shared the ante-room she now inhabited by herself. I knew she wasn't thrilled by the fact that I'd taken over this gorgeous space, but I didn't waste time worrying about it anymore.

I took my seat behind the giant oak desk as Terrence settled himself across from me in one of the two red leather wing chairs. He stared out the mullioned windows at the final rays of sunshine peeking around fast-gathering storm clouds. People tended to stare out the windows here; I couldn't blame them. The stunning southern view grabbed me every time I walked in.

Terrence hitchhiked a thumb back toward Frances's office. "How do you put up with her?"

"She comes with the territory," I said. "Bennett decreed that Frances can't be let go or reassigned until she's ready to retire. She's been with the manor for almost forty years." I lifted my shoulders. "And she's good. I mean, really good at her job. Granted, if she were to leave tomorrow, the place wouldn't fall apart, but we would definitely be in for a long, bumpy ride without her."

He squinted toward the wall, as though he possessed X-ray vision. "I don't know . . . she seems more work than she's worth." Snapping his attention back to me, he said, "So what happened out there?"

I brought him up to speed, and when I told him about Kincade's pronouncement that Jack had killed his brother, Terrence scowled. "What did Jack have to say?"

"Nothing. He didn't answer. But when Kincade identified himself, Jack recognized the name."

"You sure?"

Nodding, I continued. "He seemed shocked. Upset." I told Terrence about Davey's reluctance to press charges and his comments alluding to events that had happened in the past. "There's history there, but I don't know what it is."

Terrence didn't either. He and I were both still relatively new hires at the manor. We were an influx of "new blood" designed to help bring the old beauty into the twenty-first century and we had our work cut out for us. Emberstowne was a peaceful little hamlet with Marshfield Manor its crowning jewel. Increased tourism would provide jobs, thereby helping everyone in town, and we were charged with making that happen. We both possessed energy, verve, and determination. What we didn't have was the down-home knowledge—the flesh-and-blood history—of Emberstowne's inhabitants.

Although I'd been born here, I'd grown up in Chicago and then spent several years in New York. I'd returned to Emberstowne to care for my mom, and when a spot opened up at Marshfield Manor for an assistant curator and estate director, I'd jumped at the opportunity. Sometimes I wished I'd lived here all my life. Sometimes I wondered why I stayed.

"What happened with the two women?" I asked.

"The local PD took them both home. They called the husbands home from work to take responsibility for the women. Both men had no idea about the mission their wives were on."

"What about Muffy?" I asked. "Did you meet her?"

Terrence rubbed his face. "Yeah, she was at the one woman's house, waiting to find out what happened. Pretty little thing. Few years older than her friends, I'd guess. She seemed really upset by the whole situation. More upset that we knew that she'd been jilted than about her friends getting into trouble, if you ask me."

"But Kincade isn't pressing charges, so they're not really in trouble anymore, are they?"

He made a so-so motion with his head. "They could nail the blonde one for concealing her Taser but that's just a misdemeanor charge."

"So all's well that ends well?"

He gave me a skeptical look. "Not as long as that Kincade's walking around here. That guy's a bundle of trouble."

"Yeah," I agreed. "I'll be happy when he's gone for good."

Chapter 4

FAT GRAY CLOUDS HUNG HEAVY AND LOW,
warning of storms to come. As I drove home, I contemplated
how the weather might affect our Civil War campers. For the
most part, they'd picked a pretty good week for their drills.
Except for the rain predicted tonight, the seven-day forecast
called for warm temperatures and mostly clear skies. As
long as they lived through tonight, they should be all set.

I often stopped at my roommates' wine shop, Amethyst
Cellars, on the way home, but my instincts kept me moving
tonight. As I drove past, I tried to catch a glimpse inside
but it was too dark to see. A crack of lightning, a burst of
thunder, and suddenly raindrops fat as poodles began making giant *splat*s against my windshield. I flicked on my
headlights and twisted on the wipers. By the time I eased
around the next corner, however, the drops had morphed
into buckets of rain that pummeled my windshield, making
it impossible to see even with the wipers on full speed.

When I made it to Granville, my headlights traced a
watery path across the front-lawn fence of my Victorian

mansion home. Well, mansion was a misnomer. Compared to Marshfield Manor, this house would barely qualify as servants' quarters. What it lacked in stately elegance, however, it more than made up for in lived-in charm. It was all mine—an inheritance from my mom.

I wished, not for the first time, for an empty garage where I could actually park my car. My roommates and I had promised ourselves that this year we'd clear out all the junk in our two-car detached garage, but so far all we'd done was stand in front of the mess, stare, and say, "Next week, for sure." Next week never came. The path to hell is paved with good intentions, they say. And the path to my back door would be paved with puddles tonight.

I noticed movement behind the fence, low to the ground. Probably a fox, or maybe a rabbit. It didn't move like a rabbit, but heck, in this pounding rain the poor thing's goal was to find shelter, not frolic in the grass. It wasn't fit for man nor beast out here tonight, and I felt sorry for the little critter, whatever it was.

I pulled onto the driveway, up past the bump where the concrete had cracked and shifted like tectonic plates. The bump always reminded me that the driveway was due for repair. Way overdue. Just about everything in the house was ready for renovation. The structure was old and my mom had let things deteriorate. Simple maintenance was no longer an option. Full overhauls were needed in every corner and I had no money for any of it. The money part of our inheritance had gone to my sister, Liza, who had quickly blown through it all. Had we worked together and pooled our resources, who knows? But cooperating with me had never been Liza's style. Wherever she was right now. My sister. I sighed.

Dark clouds. Dark moods. I needed something to lighten my spirits and I knew I wasn't going to get it out here.

I turned off the car and took a moment to gather my purse and umbrella as I plotted the quickest path to the back door. An awning there provided some protection against the elements, but in a deluge like this, every second counted. I pulled out my keys and prepared to sprint.

Just as I was about to open the car door, movement caught my eye again. This time it appeared as a shadow racing past me on the driver's side. Whatever it was had decided to take shelter from the storm beneath my car. Fine and dandy for the critter, but what if it was a hedgehog, or raccoon? I was wearing a skirt—which left my legs bare. The minute I stepped out of my car, the hungry beastie might spy my ankle and think: "Dinner!"

Taking my chances, I spoke to my undercarriage guest. "Hope you stay dry under there, buddy." I grabbed my belongings and opened the door. Rain sliced in sideways, drenching me in the second it took to *whoosh* my umbrella open. With my left hand clamped around my purse, I raced for my back door only to have the wind whip the umbrella inside-out above my head. A noise like *"eeee"* burst out from somewhere deep inside me as the cold water soaked through my clothes. There were only about fifteen steps to the safety of my stoop and back-door awning, but they were the longest fifteen steps of my life. I hurried to stand beneath the shelter, relieved that no creature had jumped out to attack me.

Lightning zinged across the sky, backlighting massive rain clouds. A second later, thunder cracked so close and so loudly I dropped my keys. In the breathless quiet before the next reverberating boom, I stooped to pick them up.

That's when I heard it.

A sad, elongated cry. Kind of like Chewbacca from *Star Wars*, except much higher pitched. Coming from underneath my car.

Not a hedgehog, not a fox.

Crouched as I was next to my wrought iron railing, I had a clear view of my car and the tiny head that poked out from beneath. A cat squinted against the rain, then pulled its head back under the car far enough that I could barely make out the white tip of its nose and white underside of its chin. It meowed again, asking for help.

The poor little thing. I wondered who it belonged to.

"Hang on a second," I said, picking up my keys and unlocking the back door. I dropped my belongings inside, grabbed the closest handy item to serve as a makeshift umbrella—a plastic bowl from the countertop—and braved the elements. The cat backed up as I approached.

"Here, kitty," I said, hoping those were the magic words to encourage feline cooperation. Of course, if *I* were huddled alone against the rain and some giant stranger with a bowl on her head called to me, I might not be so willing to oblige.

I crouched down at the passenger side, but the cat backed up farther to where I couldn't see it anymore. Dropping to my knees on the driveway I tried again. "Kitty?"

Two eyes glowed back at me.

"Come out now. I'll take you inside where it's warm."

Unconvinced, the cat didn't budge.

The plastic bowl was doing a nice job of keeping the top of my head dry, but the rest of me would need to be wrung out pretty soon. Temperatures were dropping, the rain was pelting, and I shivered as water sluiced down my back. "Come on. Please? Otherwise I'll leave you out here and you won't like that."

The cat knew I was bluffing. I could tell by the way she blinked.

"Okay, fine. I'm serious."

I got up and headed to my back door, thinking maybe my leaving would inspire it to emerge. I'd never had a cat before—my mom was allergic—so I wasn't quite sure what psychology might work. In the meantime, back in my kitchen where it was warm and dry, I hurried to the refrigerator to grab a bowl of milk. That's what cats liked, wasn't it?

No milk.

I checked my supply of half-and-half. Only enough for about two more cups of coffee and I didn't want to part with it. What else, what else? I pulled open the small condiment drawer and found a gold mine. Cheese. I grabbed a chunk of Muenster and headed back outside, trusty bowl back atop my head.

A car sloshed by, its headlights tracing across my lawn, across me. The neighbors already talked—single girl living with two men in a house that desperately needed repair. What would they think of me kneeling next to my car in the rain, wearing a bowl for a hat? But there I was.

"Kitty," I said coaxingly, "this is for you."

I broke off a small piece of the cheese and reached in. The cat backed up again.

"We're not going to get anywhere if you don't trust me. I'm not here to hurt you. I just want to find out who you belong to."

Maybe it was a feral cat and maybe I had no business feeding it. But something told me to keep trying. Lightning zinged again, and I felt the rumble of thunder through the ground. The cat felt it too, because it picked up one paw, and inched backward.

I dropped the cheese crumble as far in as I could reach. Then I waited.

The cat stared at me, then looked at the cheese. Even in the low light under the car, I could see its whiskers twitch as it caught the scent. The cat inched forward, watching me constantly. Finally, it snatched the cheese and started to chew, never taking its eyes off me.

Little by little, feeling like Elliott in the movie *E.T.*, I dropped tiny bits of cheese in a path that brought the cat closer. I knew I had just a single shot at grabbing it. If I didn't get a good hold, we'd be back to square one in a hurry.

My legs were soaked, my back was heavy with rain, and

I realized that the bowl I held tight made for one less hand I could use to nab the cat. So what if the last few square inches of my body were to get wet? I put the bowl down, gently, and tried not to wince as water saturated my head.

I placed another cheese crumble about five inches beyond the shelter of the car. The cat would have to come out in the rain to get it. I had my doubts. And even if it did emerge, I knew the moment it felt the first raindrop, it would hightail it back to relative dryness. My one shot was a slim one.

The cat eyed the last crumble.

"No risk, no reward," I said softly.

Still under the car, but at the very edge, the cat looked up at me. I sat very still. "It's okay," I said. "Cheese. Right there. Just for you."

The cat eyed the cheese, looked up at me again. This close I could see that it was a black-and-white kitten, mostly black with a white belly and chin, and its front paws were white at the very tips. "Come on, honey," I said, blinking through the water pouring down my face. "I'm getting really wet here and this isn't a whole lot of fun."

The cat inched forward again, then jumped back as though startled. "No," I said, "don't, don't, don't."

I swear the cat heard me that time, because it moved forward in a belly crawl, its eyes on the prize. "That's it," I said, "that's a good boy . . . or girl."

At that moment the wind shifted. That was all the cat—and I—needed.

It pounced.

I grabbed.

In a long moment of terror where it squawked and screamed and clawed, I managed to get to my feet without dropping it. I held the cat as far from my body as possible. I had on a new sweater today and although it would probably shrink three sizes from being soaked, I would prefer if it didn't get snagged, too. My bare forearms bore the brunt of the kitten's desperate wrath. "Just a half second more," I said as I ran up the back steps and through the open door. Triumphant, I kicked it shut behind me.

Inside, the cat leaped from my grasp, racing out of the kitchen and into the dining room before I could call for it to stop. Not that it would have listened. The little thing was spooked, to be sure.

The puddle at my feet was growing bigger by the second. I peeled my skirt from my legs, grimacing at the sucking sound it made. I'd left the bowl outside but I wasn't about to rescue *that* now, too. I'd find it later. Maybe. Right now I needed to get out of my wet clothes. "Hey, cat," I called. "I'm going upstairs to get changed."

No answer. Not that I expected one. I followed its path into the dining room and made a slow circuit of the area. Not here, but a soft thump from the next room gave me a clue. I peered around the corner into the living room just in time to see it disappear under my sofa.

"Give me a minute, okay?" I said. "I'll be right down."

I threw my wet clothing over the side of my bathtub and donned a pair of pajama pants and oversized T-shirt. Still chilled, I finger-combed my hair, pulled on a pair of fuzzy socks, and made my way down the stairs, quiet as a mouse. "Kitty," I called in my most coaxing voice. "Kitty?"

I got down on all fours and peered under the sofa again to find that the cat had backed up all the way to the wall. "I'm not going to hurt you."

The cat's pupils were wide. They glowed, reflecting the adjacent room's lights. "Come on out, honey. I need to find who lost you."

We both heard the back door open. The cat's head jerked upward and it seemed momentarily confused as to what posed the greater threat: the big person on the floor, or whatever was now banging and calling from the kitchen. Two voices, animated, loud.

I straightened and said, "I'm in here."

Bruce led the way into the living room, Scott close behind. Both surfer handsome, Scott was blond, tall, and probably one of the most trusting individuals I'd ever met. Bruce was shorter and had a more muscular build. By nature a nurturing individual, he also had a slightly more cynical view of the world.

"What are you two doing home so early?" I asked. "And make sure you close the back door. We've got a cat in here."

"Did you say 'cat'?" Scott asked.

I'd returned to staring under the sofa as my roommates' footsteps creaked across the wood floor. Bruce got down next to me and peered, too. "She meant to say 'kitten'."

"It won't trust me," I said. "And I don't want to reach under and grab. It might bite."

"Did you try feeding it anything?" Scott asked.

I sat up on the back of my legs to tell them about my success with cheese and we decided to try again. While Scott went to the kitchen, Bruce gave my hair a once-over. "It looks like you just stepped out of the shower. You're totally drenched. How long were you outside like that?"

"Felt like forever."

"I'll bet. And you're still cold, aren't you?"

I admitted I was.

"You're going to get sick," he said.

"You don't get sick from being cold or wet. You get sick from germs."

Bruce was shaking his head. "Mark my words. You'll see. Tomorrow you're going to come down with a nasty cold."

"No way."

I was spared further argument by Scott's return. He'd pulled out four different varieties of cheese. "Is it a boy or a girl?"

"Haven't figured that one out yet," I said, giving the plethora of cheese a perplexed look.

"I didn't know what kind the little kitten would like. Gruyere, Brie, Asiago, Muenster . . . what do you think?"

We put a small crumb of Muenster just under the sofa and then littered a few more out in the open. "Let's back up," Bruce said. "Give the little thing some space."

We shuffled to the opposite side of the room to wait and watch.

"You've had cats?" I asked.

Bruce nodded. "But it's been a while. The kitten is scared right now. No idea where it is or what we might do to it."

"I should ask the neighbors if anyone lost a cat," I said.

A huge clap of thunder shook the house, rattling the windows and making my feet rumble.

"Not tonight you're not," Bruce said. "It's not a fit night out for woman . . ." he pointed to me then to the cat who'd finally poked its head out. "Or beast."

Keeping a wary eye on us, the cat crept forward and picked up the next crumb of cheese, chewing excessively before eyeing the next piece, which was considerably closer to where we stood. We all waited, and I for one, held my breath.

"It's a tuxedo cat," Bruce said quietly.

"A what?"

"See," he said, keeping his voice low and slowly raising his finger to point, "black and white, like it's wearing a tuxedo."

"It's really cute," I said.

The cat must have heard me because at that moment it stopped eating and looked up. It opened its mouth and let out a despondent little cry that again reminded me of a tiny Chewbacca. Encouraged, I slowly lowered myself to the floor and crossed my legs, striving to appear less intimidating.

"Good," Bruce said under his breath as the cat took another cautious step toward me. "It's sizing you up."

The cat made its way, one silent, guarded step after another, until it stood right next to me. I barely breathed.

Then, in what seemed to me a decisive, no-turning-back-now move, it jumped into my lap and didn't squirm away when I touched it.

Emboldened, Bruce and Scott sat next to me on the floor. Bruce picked up the cat's tail and gave it a quick perusal.

"It likes me," I said as I found a sweet spot behind its ears and started to rub.

"*She* likes you," Bruce corrected.

"You sure?"

He nodded.

"She's purring," I said in amazement. "Can you believe it?"

"Looks like she's adopted you."

I shook my head. "This is somebody's cat. Look how pretty she is. How clean. I bet a family lost her."

Scott chimed in. "No collar, and she's clearly a kitten. I'd say no more than two or three months old. I bet she was dumped."

"Dumped?" I said, aghast. "How could anybody dump a sweet thing like this?"

The cat circled in my lap, rubbing against the insides of my legs before finding a comfortable spot and settling in.

"Happens," Bruce said.

"Still, I'm going to ask the neighbors if anyone is missing a kitten. Tomorrow," I quickly added when they both looked alarmed. Changing the subject, I asked, "So you never answered me. How come you two are here so early?"

Bruce got to his feet. "The store lost power. We've got the emergency generators going. In fact, we brought home a few treats. They won't keep until tomorrow so we might as well enjoy them tonight."

Treats indeed. The cat allowed me to pick her up, and I cradled her in my arms, carrying her into the kitchen. The boys had brought home a half-dozen chocolate-covered strawberries and three slices of chocolate-chip cheesecake.

"Oh, yum," I said. "This is the perfect way to enjoy a stormy evening at home. Particularly after the stormy afternoon I had at work." I told them about Rani and Tamara, and their elusive quarry, Zachary Kincade. "What a piece of work," I said. "Supremely confident and ridiculously stuck on himself."

"An irresistible combination," Scott said. "A lot of women go for that."

"This one doesn't."

Bruce smiled at me. "You're not most women."

Scott pointed to the kitten. "And what about our newest female in the house? What should we call her?"

"I'm sure she already has a name," I said, stroking under her chin. She raised her head as though begging: "More, more." She had a patch of white on the right side of her nose and a completely white chin. Her whiskers were white, too, contrasting sharply with the pure black of her face. Such a cutie. Purring again. "We can't name her. She belongs to someone else."

"I'm thinking she belongs to you," Bruce said. "Hmm . . . what would make a good name? She's got those cute little white tips on her front paws."

"And her back legs make it look like she's wearing white hip boots," Scott said, both of them totally ignoring my protests about naming a pet that didn't belong to us.

Bruce snapped his fingers. "That's it. Boots!"

Scott nodded. "I love it. We'll call her Bootsie."

"No, no, no," I started to say, but they cut me off.

"I'll pick up cat food tomorrow morning," Scott said. "There's that new boutique pet shop just a few doors down from ours. But right now, she needs a litter box." He looked around the room, spied our dishpan in the sink, and emptied it of its few remaining drops of water. "This will do. We needed a new one anyway. I'll shred some newspaper and set it up for our little Bootsie."

Bruce had already dropped to his knees. "The poor

thing needs water," he said, digging through the bottom cabinets. "There's that little blue bowl in here some- where . . . ah!" He emerged with the item in hand. "Do you think she'd prefer pink?"

"I think she'd prefer to go back to her family," I said. "Maybe there's a little kid crying right now because she's gone. I'll have to take her back, wherever it is, tomorrow."

"Bootsie" took that moment to rest her nose in the crook of my elbow with one white-tipped paw draped over my forearm, totally relaxed. I craned my neck to look. Her eyes were closed.

My two roommates exchanged a look. Bruce grinned. "Yeah. Uh-huh."

Chapter 5

BOOTSIE DISAPPEARED WHILE I WAS PREPARING for bed. She'd proven adept at using the makeshift litter box, a fact I pointed out to my roommates. "See? Somebody trained her."

"Nope. Just instinct," Scott said.

I already had my sleepwear on, so after taking care of the basics I quickly drifted off, knowing it was the weekend and I didn't need to set an alarm. At about two in the morning, I awoke to a sudden weight shift on my bed and I jumped up, belatedly realizing it was the kitten coming to visit. "You scared me," I chastised her. My door was slightly ajar—I must have not closed it all the way. Either that or little Bootsie here would make a phenomenal cat burglar.

She didn't seem to mind my complaint. I turned away from her to resettle myself and get comfortable. The moment I quieted, she climbed over my back and curled up under my chin, purring like a little engine against my chest. I thought briefly about fleas, but was too tired to worry about it. My last waking thought was that she belonged to somebody and was probably perfectly clean.

My cell phone rang just after five A.M. Bootsie was still curled up next to me—neither of us had moved. "Sorry, kiddo," I said, reaching over her to grab the instrument and glance at the number on the display, certain it was going to be a wrong number. It wasn't.

I sat up to answer, dislodging the cat. She yawned, but otherwise didn't seem to mind.

"Grace Wheaton," I said, donning my professional persona despite the fact that I was wearing wrinkled pajamas and my hair was matted and smashed against the side of my face. I pinched my nose hoping to clear it. My head felt heavy and full. Congested.

"Grace, this is Terrence." There was a lot of noise behind him as though he was out in the middle of a crowd. People talking. Someone shouting.

Terrence Carr calling me at five in the morning? I tried to blink away the blur that seized my brain. "What's wrong?" I asked. "What happened?"

"You better get down here. I need help holding off the press." To someone else he said, "You'll have to wait."

"Talk to me, Terrence."

"Not now. Too many ears at this end. Just get here ASAP."

"Do I have time to shower?"

I heard him grumble. "Make it fast."

I did.

Bruce and Scott usually left for their shop early on the weekends, so they were already awake. "What's going on?" Bruce asked as I raced into the kitchen to grab a handful of almonds, which would serve as breakfast. "Want coffee?"

I sneezed. "No time," I said. "Marshfield needs me."

"This early?"

I sniffled, then sneezed again. Instead of answering, I nodded.

"Told you you were going to catch cold, didn't I?"

"You were right," I said, my *r*s sounding like *w*s. My nose started to run and I dashed to the nearby washroom to grab a tissue. I blew my nose, then blew it again. Returning to the kitchen, I said in a clogged-nose voice, "I gotta go. Sou-ded like some kide of emergency."

"You got it bad," Scott said. "I hate head colds."

"Me too." I started out the door, then stopped. "Whad aboud da cat?"

Scott raised a hand. "I'll get her settled in here while Bruce holds down the store. I'll make sure she has food, water, and a proper litter pan."

"Thakes guys," I said, needing to blow my nose again—desperately. I stomped back to the washroom and came out with the entire box of tissues. "I'b takig this wid me."

"I think you'd better."

The interminable ride to Marshfield gave me time to wonder what could have happened that required my presence so early, much less on a Saturday. The tension in Terrence's voice had been unmistakable. With a rush, I remembered Kincade's vicious attack on Davey. I hoped there hadn't been another incident. I hoped Davey was okay. Swallowing around a lump in my throat, I realized I was more worried about Jack. When Davey had refused to press charges against Kincade, Jack had been livid.

I pressed the accelerator, pushing the limit and hoping there were no police lying in wait for speeders. They were notoriously active on this particular stretch but I got lucky and didn't get caught. The roads were quiet and I made excellent time. Just before I pulled up to the gate, however, I realized why there hadn't been any cop cars on the road. Most of them were right here.

My first thought was for Bennett. Though healthy and active, he *was* over seventy years old. Could he have fallen ill? Hurt himself? My heart thrummed a crazed beat in worry.

A tall, uniformed cop of about fifty ambled over, his

arm extended, palm out. I threw my car into park and rolled down my window.

"Sorry, ma'am, no one is allowed in just yet," he said before I could open my mouth.

"I work here." When he didn't seem impressed, I added, "I'm in charge of the place. Terrence called me."

A quick, appraising glance. "Your name?"

I told him. Evidently Terrence had left word to allow me in, because he waved to one of the other uniformed officers to move the squad blocking the entrance. "What happened?" I asked.

He grasped his belt and hoisted it upward, eagerness blossoming across his fleshy face. "Y'all haven't heard?" He lifted his chin to the south. "Some sort of Civil War games going on, you know about that?"

"Yes, yes . . ."

"Well seems that somebody down there got themselves killed."

I gasped so hard my throat hurt. "Who?"

"Can't say for sure, ma'am. Just that somebody sliced the victim up good."

"Do you mean someone has been murdered?"

"That's what they're saying, ma'am."

I shifted my car into drive, tapping my left foot impatiently as I waited for the slow-moving squad to get out of my way. The almonds in my stomach tumbled all over each other, first in relief that it wasn't Bennett and then again in worry, thinking about Jack. I'd been here less than a year, and this was our second murder on the premises. This couldn't be happening. Not again. "Please, no," I whispered aloud.

"Sorry to have to be the one to tell you, ma'am," the cop said, his expression belying his words. "Maybe you'd best stay up here with us for a while." He raised his hand again, to signal the other officer to move the squad back.

I wasn't about to wait one more minute. "Can't, sorry," I

shouted out the window as I hit the accelerator. I didn't even wave thank-you.

A little more than two miles later nearing the encampment site, I eased along the winding road, making a wide arc to allow for any cars coming the other way. The road here was narrow with low-slung trees forming a lush overhead canopy. The early morning sky was still gloomy, and passing beneath the dusky green branches darkened my way as much as it darkened my mood. I tried ignoring the anxiety twisting my stomach into knots. Didn't work.

Just around the next bend I caught sight of a white-and-blue fender. Another squad car. That made four already. Emberstowne was not a major city, which meant we had a limited police force. Just beyond that squad, another—from a different municipality—sat perpendicular to its neighbor. My gut gave another hard twist.

I rolled to a quiet stop, parking so that two tires rested in the marshy grass and two remained on the road. I alighted and was greeted by the woodsy fragrance of a campfire whose smoke twisted skyward just beyond a copse of trees. As my feet shushed through the damp grass, I shivered against the morning's chill and zipped up my open sweatshirt. Soft noises in the distance grew louder and eventually voices became more distinct.

At first I thought I was approaching a party rather than a crime scene—so many people. But even though there was much conversation, the mood was somber. Uniformed officers were attempting to corral a group of men, women, and children, encouraging them to "calm down." Most of these folks were dressed in Civil War–era garb. Some of them appeared oddly calm as they shuffled past, clad in woolen sleepwear with blankets and shawls tight around their shoulders. I scanned faces looking for Pierpont, but received only curious stares in return. The campfire that had lured me crackled in the nearby clearing, its bright flames dancing quietly, desperately, as though trying to

coax cheer from the gloom of the damp morning and the
overwhelming gray of the day.

There were more people gathered in this part of the estate than we'd ever had here before. And not just people—
animals, too. Chickens scurried between moving feet.
Nearby roosters crowed. Horses were tethered in groups
along the camp's perimeter. The stately animals shifted
and shook their heads, looking as though they'd much
rather be galloping through fields instead of tied to makeshift posts. A police officer to my right rested a hand on a
soldier's musket. "I'm sorry, sir, but you'll have to hand
that over."

About fifty feet away from me another officer shouted
into the crowd, his words dissolving into the open air, his
hands upraised as though to quell the group's rising indig-
nation. "I know the weapons aren't loaded with real bul-
lets, but you know as well as I do that blanks aren't 100
percent safe. Please place all weapons on the ground and
step away from them. Please do so very slowly."

I hurried toward a cop who looked like he might be in
charge but just before I reached him, he got into a shouting
match with a man dressed in Union blue.

Were they *sure* this had been murder? Could it have just
been an accident? I hoped so. Maybe the cop out front had
gotten the story wrong. I glanced around, hoping for clues
that the victim was still alive. I kept telling myself there
had just been a terrible mistake, until I caught sight of a
nondescript van, pulled very high up on the far southeast-
ern rise. The coroner's van. Its tracks sliced straight and
deep through the middle of the encampment.

Tents, in neat rows, stretched out on either side of the
central campfire. These were not the cheerful blue, green,
and tan sporting goods–store tents that stretched across
plastic and relied on nylon to stay upright and dry. These
were old-style, drab tents that might have been white a long
time ago, but were now dingy with use and splattered with

mud. Most sagged. Some bore bright patches of white that spoke of careful repair. Canvas doors flapped in the lonely wind. There were hundreds of tents, large and small, but all of them were nearly identical in style. I thought about how uncomfortable I'd been last night outdoors rescuing Bootsie. The people out here in these cloth tents had surely fared far worse in the terrific overnight storm.

A few re-enactors had clearly given up the idea of costuming and donned heavy, zippered jackets. Too many conversations were going on at once and I couldn't make out what any single person was saying. Children—some of them babies—were whining and crying. I had no idea so many kids would be involved. Dozens of them clawed at their mothers' voluminous skirts, complaining about being cold and wanting to go home.

It made the most sense to head toward the coroner's van. On the way, I hailed another officer. "Where can I find Terrence Carr?" I asked him.

He gave me a quick once-over. "Are you Miss Wheaton?"

I nodded.

Like his brother in blue at the front gate, this cop looked like he'd been on the job for at least twenty years. He settled into lecture mode, tilting his head southward. "You heard what happened back there?"

I didn't want another slow explanation. I had the basic facts: Someone had been murdered but the most important question had yet to be answered. "Who was it? Do you know who died? Have you caught the person who did it?"

"I don't know the victim's name, miss. They didn't provide none of that information yet. And from what I been hearing, we don't have no idea of who did the killin'. Not yet. But nobody's been questioned neither. We're just waiting on orders here."

People streamed in and out of one of the giant central tents, hands clasped around steaming tin cups. That had to be the mess, I assumed. There wasn't enough wind to keep flags snapping, but when the breeze fluttered past, the flags' corners lifted long enough to identify the Union flag to my left and a Confederate flag to my right.

The officer pointed to a rise just past the last row of Union tents, not far from the coroner's van. "Mr. Carr is back there with the detectives right now, miss. Would you like to wait here with us until he returns?" He pointed to a man emerging from the mess. "You could get yourself some coffee while you wait. I'm thinking about getting some. The folks here told us to help ourselves."

"I think I'd better go find Terrence," I said. "He's expecting me."

"I'll take you."

I waved to encompass the crowd. "You have your hands full. But thank you."

The hems of my blue jeans were soon soaked from the damp grass and my gym shoes streaked with green as I made my way toward the low hill in the distance. Not another single soul stopped me nor questioned my reason for being there and for that I was grateful.

The rise was much farther south past the last line of tents than I'd originally guessed. The combination of my quick pace, the wet ground, and the incline made my thighs burn with exertion. My shoes made squishy noises as I climbed. Perspiration gathered at my hairline and when a sharp wind sliced past, I shivered again.

This time, however, it wasn't just the morning's chill.

As I cleared the top of the rise, a flock of birds rushed skyward in a flurry of rustling wings and panicked cries. From my perch at the apex, I looked down into the ravine below. Up until that point, I'd been holding my body tense but the view below caused my limbs to weaken. I had been telling myself that another murder *hadn't* occurred under my watch. But the small group huddled around a motionless blanketed form dispelled any hope.

There were seven people—not counting the deceased—

gathered just inside a wide swath of trees. Terrence was the only black man in the group, and I raised my hand in greeting as I made my way down. He didn't see me. Pierpont had his attention, talking and gesticulating wildly while the others looked on. Two of them were our local detectives Rodriguez and Flynn. I'd worked with them when Abe had died and I desperately hoped they had a better handle on this situation than they'd had on the last one. They weren't bad at their jobs, they just weren't experienced in murder investigations. About ten feet inside the tree line, two other men worked around the body, taking measurements and photos. They picked up small items with tweezers and gingerly placed them into plastic containers.

The final man in the group was actually a woman. Roughly forty years old and solidly built, the clothes she wore rendered her shapeless. With a wide, round face, and close-cropped black hair, it was no wonder I mistook her for a man at first. By her stance and positioning, I gathered she had accompanied Rodriguez and Flynn.

There weren't many murders in Emberstowne. *At least not until I got here*, I thought. And even though Rodriguez was far more seasoned than his young counterpart Flynn, neither had dealt with enough major crime to become crack detectives. They simply hadn't had the opportunity. I supposed we should be grateful for that.

I half-walked, half-slid the last few yards. When I reached bottom, still about thirty feet from the group, I looked back up the way I'd come. For a person intent on murder, this was a perfect location to do the deed. Unless someone happened by at just the right moment and stared directly into the trees searching for movement, the crime would have been committed completely out of sight.

Terrence spotted me and waved me forward to join the small group. "The press hasn't gotten wind of this yet," he said without preamble. "But they will soon. Too many people already know what's happened." He flicked a glance up the hill. "Couple of my guys are waiting for me to tell them what to do. Glad you're here, Grace. I'll let the detectives fill you in and I'll catch up with you later."

"This is just terrible, terrible," Pierpont said as Terrence left. I swore the little man actually wrung his hands. His gaze kept drifting toward the covered body in the wet grass. "I can't imagine who could have done this."

I had to know. "Who was killed?"

Rodriguez answered me. "Zachary Kincade. Mr. Pierpont here has made a positive identification." The well-fed detective raised tired eyes. "I understand you met the deceased yesterday as well."

I had a thousand questions running through my mind but I was prevented asking any of them by Flynn's interjection. "We want to talk to you about the attack yesterday."

"You mean those two women and the Taser?"

Flynn looked at me like I'd grown a plant out of the top of my head. "No," he said with poorly concealed impatience. "I mean the fight between the victim and your gardeners. I understand threats were made."

"Davey didn't press charges."

Flynn made a noise that sounded like a snort. " 'Course not. Not if he planned to take Zachary out later."

"Wait, wait," I said. "This is all moving too fast. You suspect Davey?"

"You got it. His brother, too. From what I hear, murder runs in the family."

"What?"

Rodriguez placed a restraining hand in front of his partner. "Let's not get ahead of ourselves, amigo." To me, he said, "We need you to handle the press. Tell them that someone has died, but don't use the word *murder*. Don't lie, okay? Just don't say much. If they ask too many questions, just tell them, 'No comment.' Got it?"

"Hey . . . guys?" a woman interrupted, clearly peeved to be left out of the conversation. Her lips tight, she waved Rodriguez and Flynn back and extended her hand for me to shake. "Name's Ginger, but everybody calls me Tank."

"Tank?" I repeated. That was a horrible nickname.

"I guess I have a tendency to roll right over people," she said with a wink. "That right, guys?"

Rodriguez didn't answer. Instead, he said, "Your boss, Marshfield, donated a nice chunk of change to the PD to help improve the department after Mr. Vargas's murder." He tilted his head toward Tank. "She's from up north."

"Michigan," Tank added. "I'm here for the next few months to work with these guys and whip the department into shape." She clapped her hands together gleefully. "This is exactly the kind of situation we need for training."

"I don't imagine Mr. Kincade would agree with you," I said.

Tank's eyes narrowed. "True enough," she said, clearly surprised by my asperity. "But there's no changing the fact that he's dead. Now it's up to us to set things right. If we all work hard and smart, we will bring the guilty party to justice. And we'll do it fast."

"The officer at the gate said Zachary had been stabbed," I said. "Who found him?"

"Guy by the name of Jim Florian. And yeah, stabbed." She lifted her chin toward the evidence technicians. "They'll probably give us an idea of how many times."

More than once? I cringed.

"You say the uniforms told you?" Rodriguez rolled his eyes and said, "We warned them to keep it quiet for now. We need to keep details out of circulation."

Flynn kicked a rock, sending it skittering into the ravine.

"Part of the risk you run when you involve uniforms," Tank said. "When the call came in, *we* should have gotten here first. Half the department had tromped through the crime scene already. Didn't they, Rodriguez?"

Unable to meet her glare, the older detective gave the briefest of nods.

"They're like little kids," she went on, "everybody wants to see the dead body."

The blanket covering Kincade's still form was a pale shade of gray. Blood had soaked through the blanket on the left side of the corpse and I couldn't quite tell which way it was facing. "Why did you cover him? Won't that interfere with the collection of evidence?"

Balancing on the balls of his feet, Flynn practically danced his impatience, but it was Tank who answered. She waggled her index finger to indicate Pierpont. "One of his guys covered him up before we got here."

"Jim Florian," Pierpont said. "It bothered him to leave Zachary alone like that. And to be honest, it bothered me, too. I think I'm going to be ill." He backed away from the group and started toward the ravine.

Even though he was heading the opposite direction of the corpse, Flynn shouted, "Don't go anywhere near the body." Under his breath he added, "This is all messed up enough already."

Pierpont made it about fifteen feet before he was forcefully and noisily sick.

Rodriguez leaned close to Flynn's ear. "Settle down. We've got work to do." To me, he said, "You've got a big job on your hands, Ms. Wheaton." He gestured back toward the encampment. "We need to question each and every one of these folks to find out what they might have seen or heard last night." Heavy sigh. "It's going to take a long time, but at least they're set up far enough away from the crime scene that we won't have to relocate them."

Tank waited as Rodriguez reasoned their next moves aloud. He kept chancing glances at the woman as though seeking her approval as he spoke. To me, he said, "My partners and I will be in touch soon and we promise to update you, so you don't have to go off on your own trying to solve this and put yourself at risk. Understand?"

I was about to defend myself, but this was neither the time nor the place. "You know where to find me."

As I made my way back up toward the encampment, I realized that the damp air had cleared my nasal passages and the head cold that had wrapped its fingers around my sinuses earlier had loosened its grasp. I took a deep breath unwilling, though ready, to face the world with another murder on our hands.

Chapter 6

DESPITE THE FACT THAT SATURDAY WAS A DAY off for Frances, I decided to call my assistant and ask her to come in. We could use all the help we could get.

I let the phone ring fifteen times before I hung up. No answering machine. "Darn it," I said aloud. It was still early. Maybe she was sleeping in and had turned off the ringer. But these days who didn't have an answering machine?

I took a deep breath and blew it out, slowly. The next task on my to-do list was one I deeply dreaded, but I picked up the phone again and dialed Bennett's private line. He answered immediately. "Gracie!"

"Did I wake you?"

"Are you joking?" he asked jovially, sounding as fresh and alert as if it were two in the afternoon rather than eight in the morning. "Do you think I sleep the day away?"

Any other time I would have laughed. Bennett picked up on the fact that I hadn't.

"Why are you at the manor today?" Concern lowered his voice. "Isn't this your day off?"

"There's been a"—I stumbled over the words—"an incident."

"What kind of incident?"

"May I come up?" I asked.

"Of course. In the study."

Although there was a hidden panel in my office that opened to a stairway leading directly to Bennett's private quarters, I opted to take one of the staff staircases instead.

I approached his study with a peculiar sense of déjà vu. This was where Abe had been killed, and now it would be here where I broke the bad news that Marshfield Manor had suffered a second murder on its famous grounds. Bennett's portly butler smiled hello as I entered. He held a silver coffee server in his white-gloved hands and an expectant look on his face. Two breakfast settings had been laid out on the low center table. Fresh cinnamon scones were arranged on a plate of pale pink china, their fresh-baked scent filling the air. A selection of cantaloupe, blackberries, and strawberries sat on the silver tray beside them, accompanied by a tiny pitcher of cream. "Good morning, Miss Wheaton," the butler said, stepping forward. "May I pour you a cup?"

My stomach growled my answer. I hadn't had anything but that handful of almonds more than three hours ago. I could sure use a jolt of caffeine. "Thanks, Theo, that would be nice."

Bennett's study was a bookcase-lined, sun-kissed room of overstuffed furniture and carved oak, and always smelled faintly of pipe smoke and coffee. Bennett waited on the small persimmon sofa at the center of the room, with his back to the windows. He patted the cushion next to him and I sat. Theo came around to pour, making sure to add a small measure of cream to both cups. Bennett and I took our coffee the same way, and there was something very comforting about having the manor's butler know that.

The decision to return to Emberstowne to care for my mom in her last few months had changed the trajectory of my life. When I'd relocated here to be with her, I'd hoped and believed that my relationship with my fiancé, Eric, would survive the temporary detour. It hadn't. In fact, it had failed. Spectacularly.

When Mom was in her final days, my sister, Liza, had finally breezed in. Liza stayed long enough to say her good-byes, collect her share of the modest inheritance, and breeze back out—with Eric in tow. Last I had heard they were out west, married, and probably broke.

I wished them both all the happiness they deserved.

Their abrupt departures combined with the loss of my mom had left me in a terrible place emotionally. I had no family beyond an aunt in Florida, who called from time to time to ask how Liza was doing. I no longer belonged anywhere. I no longer belonged with anyone.

Making Emberstowne my home had been a challenge, but it was starting to feel right. Although my house needed constant repair, and although I needed to take in roommates to keep myself afloat financially, it was home. Scott and Bruce were the best things to happen to me in a long time and I appreciated their company even more than I did their rent check.

Theo handed me my coffee and served me a scone. I sighed with a tiny bit of pleasure when I realized it was still warm. "Thank you."

"Very good, miss," Theo said, then left the room.

Taking a sip of his coffee, Bennett watched me with interest. I got the impression, as I often did, that he could read my mind.

Of all the people at Marshfield Manor, I felt the closest kinship to Bennett. Although he had initially been reluctant to accept me in Abe's role, Bennett and I had eventually forged a bond. Tied by history and possibly by blood, we now interacted not just as employer and employee, but more like uncle and niece. After so long, after so much heartbreak, I actually believed I belonged here. Bennett seemed to think so, too.

I'd waited long enough to share the morning's bad news. "I have something to tell you."

"From the look on your face, I think I should be worried."

I placed the scone plate down on the low table. Taking a deep breath, I closed my eyes for a brief moment. "You know the Civil War group that rented out the south grounds?"

Bennett nodded.

"A man died there last night. Possibly this morning," I said. "He was . . . murdered."

Coffee cup halfway up to his lips, Bennett stiffened. Blinking several times, he returned the cup and saucer to the table and leaned back. I watched him. While my tendency was to rush into a reaction, Bennett's responses were usually more measured. He took his time to process information before speaking. I could learn a lot from him.

"I see," he finally said. "The police are investigating, I take it?"

"They're there now."

Bennett's eyes took on a faraway look and he seemed to focus on a spot just over my head. When he lowered his gaze to meet mine, he asked, "Who was killed?"

I explained everything that had happened the day before, including the Taser incident with Tamara and Rani, and the subsequent scuffle between Kincade and Davey Embers. When I told Bennett what Kincade had said about Jack having killed Kincade's brother, Bennett flinched.

"What happened between them?" I asked. "Jack didn't actually kill anyone, did he?" My voice rose and I tried, without success, to slow my words down. "It must have been an accident, right?"

Bennett didn't answer.

"You know what happened, I can see it in your eyes," I said.

He returned his attention to the spot over my head.

I forged on. "Whatever it was had to have been a big deal. Everyone seems to know about it but me. Tell me. Please?"

Again Bennett took a long time before speaking. "Are you and Jack romantically involved?"

The question took me by surprise. "Not exactly. I mean, no. Every time we set a date to go out, something gets in the way."

He nodded absently, as though he'd anticipated my answer. "I don't know Jack's brother, Davey, very well," he began, "although I understand the boy has problems." He didn't elaborate. "Jack, however, is a good soul. I never believed the rumors."

My heart thudded against my chest as I echoed, "Rumors?"

Bennett leaned forward, picked up his coffee, and took a thoughtful sip. I could see a decision playing across his features. His eyes again took on that distant look and the clock on the mantel ticked about twelve times before Bennett finally spoke again. "I think," he said, "it would be best for you . . . for both of you . . . if you talked to Jack about this directly. This is not my story to tell and . . ." Bennett's eyes tightened. "I may not get the facts straight. Yes," he said, focusing on me again, "this is important. Jack needs to tell you himself."

My mouth was so dry I couldn't speak. Although I had to admit I didn't know Jack all that well yet, I agreed with Bennett on one count: Jack was a good soul, a compassionate person. There was no way he could have killed anyone. Not on purpose, at least. It must have been a tragic accident. I swallowed with difficulty, wanting to beg Bennett to please tell me the whole story right now—this minute. But from the expression on his face, I knew my pleading would be futile.

Bennett worked up a smile, clearly eager to change the subject. "How's the roof?"

"Better now, thanks to you."

I'd come home one day about a month ago to find workers on my roof, repairing the leaks and adding bright new gutters and downspouts. As much as I'd needed the repair, I couldn't afford the expense. I'd tried to stop the workers, convinced they'd begun work on my home in error. That's when I discovered that I had a benefactor in Bennett. I'd called him immediately. "This isn't your responsibility," I'd said.

Even though our conversation had been over the phone, I'd heard the smile in his voice. "This is a small thing, Gracie. Besides, I always loved the old Careaux house. Let me help out while I can. I'm not getting any younger, you know."

Staring at me now, he continued, "Your house needs a lot more work. You know, it could be a real showplace."

I knew where this conversation was going and I wasn't prepared to deal with it yet. I smiled, easing back into discussion of the recent murder. "The detectives have a consultant with them this time. A woman named Tank. She's supposed to help bring the department into the twenty-first century."

"Just like your job is to bring Marshfield Manor into the twenty-first century."

"Something like that," I admitted. "In any case, she seems very capable and I'm sure the police department is grateful for your generosity."

"Another small way to help," he said. To my dismay, he immediately returned to the subject I most wanted to avoid. "Have you given any further thought to my offer?"

I bit my lip to buy time. "I'm not ready," I finally said. "My roommates . . ."

"They could stay there for as long as they need to," Bennett said, "no one will try to force them out before they're ready."

My predecessor, Abe, had lived in a cottage on Marshfield property the entire time he'd worked as curator/director. One of the perks of the job. The house—which I'd seen from a distance but had never visited—was a sweet, two-story home with an adjacent garage converted from its prior life as a stable. Surrounded by mature trees far off the visitor access roads, it promised privacy, quiet, and stability. Best of all, being part of Marshfield grounds, it boasted round-the-clock maintenance and security. I'd be a fool to turn down Bennett's offer to live there rent-free. But the house I lived in now was my own, and had been my mother's before me. I wasn't ready to leave it. Nor was I ready to leave Bruce and Scott.

Bennett wanted to renovate my dilapidated Victorian with a vision of opening it to visitors during Emberstowne's annual summer house tours. And once Bruce and Scott decided to leave, Bennett pictured turning it into a mini-museum featuring the history of Emberstowne. I knew in my heart he wouldn't force my roommates out, but these changes—however excited Bennett was by them—felt wrong to me. He'd told me about walking past the old house as a child, when the gardens were well-tended and the flowers were in bloom. He said that his father, Warren, had often talked about what a magnificent structure it was.

It wasn't until much later—until I started working here—that Bennett discovered the reason the house stayed so pristine. Warren had taken care of its maintenance, at least while my grandmother was still alive. Bennett's life and mine were intertwined in more ways than one.

But moving into Abe's cottage at this time would mean leaving the only "family" I had. The idea of coming home each night to an empty house—however well-tended—made me feel sad whenever I thought about it. "I can't."

When I read the disappointment on his face, I amended, "Not now. I can't leave now."

He nodded thoughtfully. "We'll talk again," he said.

I knew that when Bennett wanted something, he usually got it. Maybe we'd both inherited a stubbornness gene because, at this point at least, I wasn't about to back down.

Chapter 7

I STILL COULDN'T REACH FRANCES AT HOME, so I tried her cell. It went right to voicemail. I decided not to leave a message about the murder. Chances were, my acerbic assistant would hear about it on her own anyway. Of all the individuals I'd met in my life, no one could touch Frances when it came to being nosy. I'd say she wrote the book, but doing so would have taken time from snooping. The woman was fearless and tenacious. To her credit, however, she was also usually right.

I assumed Frances knew Jack Embers's story. Why wouldn't she? Frances always seemed most cheerful when she had a particularly lurid tale to share. Which is why I was surprised she hadn't forced Jack's history down my throat yet.

Right now however, I didn't have time to ponder. I needed help. I called one of the assistant curators, Lois, at home. I brought her up to date on the situation and she promised she'd be right in. "I'm sorry to bring you in on your day off," I said. "I'll make it up to you."

"It's okay," she said. "I wasn't doing much today anyway."

Just as I replaced the phone in its cradle, I heard the door to Frances's office open. From the sound of it, several people walked in before the door shut again. By the time Detective Rodriguez called, "Ms. Wheaton?" I was already coming around my desk to see who it was.

"In here," I said.

Rodriguez, Flynn, and Tank strode in, Tank taking in the office and its furnishings as she crossed the threshold between my room and Frances's. I understood the awe on Tank's face and wondered if she'd ever visited the mansion as a tourist. Judging from her expression, this was her first experience. Marshfield Manor housed wonderful collections of priceless treasures, and every room was a mini-museum decorated with care. A feast for the eyes. I'm sure she was having trouble absorbing it all.

I gestured them into the office and urged them to take seats. Tank and Rodriguez took the two red leather wing chairs across from me. I returned to my spot behind the desk. I had a small sofa against the north wall and Flynn started for it, apparently changing his mind when he realized how far that would take him from the heart of the conversation. Instead, he opted to stand next to my desk and fidget.

Rodriguez flipped open his notebook. "So here we are again."

Tank lifted an eyebrow but said nothing. She sat back in her wing chair, watching, her right ankle resting on her left knee, her fingers laced across her stomach.

"Do you have any idea who killed Kincade?" I asked.

Rodriguez's bloodshot eyes roved about the room before he answered me. "We have several suspects," he said, "but nothing conclusive enough to make an arrest. That's why we're here. I need to ask you about two of your employees, Jack Embers and David Embers."

"They're not employees," I said. "We keep Jack on retainer. He's our landscape consultant. Davey—er, David—is his brother. He's Jack's employee."

Rodriguez knew Jack's status from our last encounter. Had he forgotten, or was this just the department's way of being thorough? Tank sat up. "What do you know about bad blood between the Embers and Kincade families?"

"Nothing," I said. That was the truth. "Until yesterday—until the altercation out back—I hadn't heard anything."

"What do you know now?"

I held up my hands. "Still nothing. I swear." Suddenly I was glad Bennett *hadn't* shared the story with me. I felt an inexplicable need to protect Jack. Sharing a tale I'd heard secondhand wouldn't do anyone any good. "What's it all about? What happened between the families?"

Rodriguez opened his mouth to speak, but Tank interrupted. "When did you first meet Zachary Kincade?"

I knew my perplexity showed. "You know the answer to that. Yesterday, when those two women tried to Tase him."

"Just covering all bases, no need to get shook."

I wasn't "shook," but I was curious. "What about those two women, Rani and Tamara? Aren't you questioning them?"

Flynn had begun pacing. Now he stopped to listen to his partner's response.

Rodriguez curled his lips in distaste. "It isn't easy to stab someone to death. Takes a lot of strength. And guts. Stabbing is messy business. I don't see this as a woman's crime."

Tank cleared her throat and sat up. "We aren't discounting any theories yet," she said with a pointed look at Rodriguez. To me, she added, "In a fit of anger, adrenaline can take over and even 'women' "—another disparaging look at the older detective—"are capable of superhuman strength. My colleagues and I plan to interview both of these ladies in due course."

Flynn jumped in. "I can bring in the two Embers brothers while you're talking with the women. The sooner you let me have a crack at those gardeners the quicker we'll close this case."

"Not so fast," Tank said. "We need some information from the evidence technicians first. We can't go around accusing suspects until we have more facts."

"What time was Kincade killed?" I asked.

Tank answered, "The coroner put time of death between eleven last night and one this morning. But he warned it was just an estimate." She sniffed. "This town needs a full-time medical examiner instead of a funeral director who plays coroner on the side. I don't think this guy's been called upon to establish a time of death in a murder investigation in his whole life. I caught him checking a reference manual on how to determine it."

"And a more accurate time frame would help you when you're trying to establish alibis?"

Tank scooched forward in her seat. "From what we're hearing from all those costumed people, no one keeps track of time after dark. Establishing alibis in this situation will be almost impossible, but come on . . . they were all right there. Somebody must have seen something, right?"

I nodded.

"Turns out the first night of one of these encampments nobody gets any sleep," she went on. "There's an Irish Brigade that sings into the wee hours of the night. Drinking nonstop around the campfire is standard. People wander in and out. Nobody can say when Kincade was there or when he left. Nobody can say who was with him or who might have left the camp at the same time. Everyone is coming and going all day, all night. We got a big, fat zero." She held up her hand, making an *O* with her thumb and index finger for emphasis.

"We haven't interviewed everyone yet," Rodriguez reminded her.

"We will," she said. "Make no mistake there. We will interview every last one of those crazy playacting weirdos or my name isn't Tank."

In actuality, her name wasn't Tank, but this didn't seem a good time to mention that. The determination blazing in her eyes made me feel sorry for the innocent folks who'd come out to our grounds for a week of camping and re-enacting fun. I'm sure none of them had expected to be part of a murder investigation. And being the Civil War, they for sure hadn't expected a Tank.

Flynn came around to stand between Rodriguez's and Tank's chairs. "Your 'gardening consultants' have access to the estate twenty-four hours a day, don't they?" His dark eyes skittered over the wall behind me, as though working out a question in his mind. "Either or both Embers brothers could have returned to the property last night. Nobody would have stopped them."

That was true. But I again felt a peculiar compulsion to protect Jack. My gut bounced in panicked circles, warning me not to say anything that could be misconstrued. My brain reminded me that I'd only met Jack a few short months ago, and Davey less than that. Why should I protect either of them? The likelihood that either man was capable of murder, however, was too much to accept. My gut won.

"I really doubt either of them would come back. Most of our gardening staff leave when it gets dark."

"Aha!" Flynn practically jumped in the air. "So if we can prove they did come back, we have them dead to rights!"

"No," I said. "I didn't say it wasn't *possible* for Jack or Davey to come back for a valid reason, I just said it was unlikely."

"Would they have had to check in with anyone if they did return?" Tank asked.

"The guard at the front gate. We close our employee

entrances two hours after the residence closes to visitors. Anyone coming in or out must sign in with the guard."

Flynn held up both hands in a fait accompli gesture. "Then I say we check with the guard. They came back. I know they did."

He was getting carried away with his theory. "Don't you think that someone intent on murder would avoid checkpoints?" I said. "That would leave a trail. Prove they'd been here."

Flynn would not be dissuaded. "Next stop, the guard house."

"By the way," I asked, "have you questioned Pierpont? He mentioned the name of someone who found and covered the body."

"Pierpont. Is he that little general?"

"Yeah," I said. "He's in charge."

"He's been complaining up a storm about us ruining his encampment." Tank placed her hands on her knees and boosted herself upright. Rodriguez and Flynn also made ready to leave. "Like we care about playacting authenticity when a man has been murdered," she said

"You mean the Civil War people are staying? Even after this?"

"From what we gather, they've had this event planned for a year. None of them want to give up their week of no electricity, no running water, no cable TV." Rodriguez waved a hand in front of his nose. "It hasn't gotten all that hot yet and already a couple of them are getting pretty ripe."

Tank was shaking her head, a disgusted look on her face. "Don't they care that someone died?"

"A lot of them *are* shook up about the murder," Rodriguez said. "How could they not be? But these Civil War games represent routine for them. They want to get back to it as soon as possible so things feel normal again. I see this a lot." Rodriguez offered a shy smile. "Not with war games, mind you. Just regular people. After a tragedy, they do everything in their power to get back to the mundane of their real lives. Knowing that 'normal' is just ahead helps them get through the dark parts."

Tank raised one eyebrow during Rodriguez's speech. "Very insightful." She rolled her eyes and walked out. Flynn followed.

Rodriguez put his hands out and shrugged.

"She really does roll right over people, doesn't she?" I said.

He stared at the empty doorway, looking as though he wanted to say something more.

"Are you coming?" Tank shouted from the other room.

Rodriguez ran a finger inside his shirt collar. "Yeah," he answered, "be right there." To me he said, "We should have brought in those two Embers brothers by now instead of pussyfooting around this place making sure all our back ends are covered. But she"—he pointed toward the outer office—"says that when we rush, we risk making mistakes. You ask me, I don't think it's a mistake to bring in the main suspect—or in this case, suspects—for a little Q and A. I'd call that good police work." He shook his head solemnly. "But we gotta do what Miz Tank says."

Relieved for Jack's sake that he wasn't being hauled down for questioning, yet, I could do nothing more than nod.

"Have a good day, Ms. Wheaton. You hear anything that sounds interesting, you let me know. Okay?"

"You got it."

Five minutes after he left, Lois arrived. She and I went to work writing up a press release that referred to an "incident" on the grounds but kept details vague. "Where's Frances?" she asked after about a half hour.

"Can't get in touch with her," I said. "I tried her house and her cell. No luck."

"I think she goes out of town most weekends. I never see her around."

"Maybe she has a vacation place."

Lois gave me a skeptical look. "I doubt that, but if she does I hope she takes early retirement and moves far away. The sooner the better. You haven't been here all that long. All her gossip and rumormongering can really get to you."

Lois was wrong about that. I'd been around plenty long to let Frances get to me.

"She has an opinion about everything and everybody," Lois continued. "Always negative. She's toxic and nobody likes being around her. And maybe I'm being uncharitable, but it seems unfair that she knows so much about all of us and we know so little about her."

"She is talented at mining gossip from just about everybody."

"She is that," Lois agreed.

I wondered what Frances had been saying about me behind my back, but Lois didn't seem inclined to offer up any tidbits. Instead, she wrinkled her nose and apologized. "Sorry for my outburst. I just can't stand the woman."

I gave a noncommittal nod and suggested we get back to work.

Good thing, because within twenty minutes the phones started ringing. E-mails pinged in my inbox, bringing word from the front gate that the press was clamoring to get in. "Private property," I reminded the guard on the phone when he asked what reason he should give for denying their persistent requests. "The matter is being handled and the proper authorities are involved. We will share information when it becomes available, but we are not required to allow the press access to our grounds."

"Got it," he said.

On impulse, I stopped him before he hung up. "By the way . . ."

"Yeah?"

"Do you have a log handy of everyone who came in after hours?" It was silly of me to double-check, but Flynn's accusations burned my brain with curiosity. "Last night, I mean."

"Sure, Ms. Wheaton, I have my clipboard right here."

I heard paper shuffling in the background as he shifted the receiver, breathing with exertion. This was Joe, a chunky, middle-aged guy who'd taken the gate guard position after retiring from his job as a high school basketball coach. "Hang on one second . . . okay. Got it." I heard the receiver shift back. "Who you looking for?"

"Can you just run down the list and tell me everyone who came through? After closing, that is."

"That's a lot of names, Ms. Wheaton."

"Really?"

"Lots of folks from the hotel go out for dinner in town because the food's not as expensive out there. No offense."

Our hotel's restaurant was known for its superior standards, but also for its equally lofty prices. "No offense taken," I said. "How about this . . . can you go through and give me the names of anyone who came through who isn't a hotel guest?"

"Like people who work here?"

"Exactly."

"Okay," he said. He took a deep breath and mumbled to himself while I waited. I heard a page turn. Then another. This was taking too long. I fidgeted, worried he'd still be on the phone with me when the detectives arrived. How to explain my sudden interest in our gate logs? After an interminable length of time he said, "I don't show any staffers coming through here last night. Can I ask who you were looking for? Maybe that would make it easier."

"Oh," I coughed up a lie, "just asking in general. Do we usually get many workers coming back late at night?"

"Only when they forgot to do something important. Mostly it's just hotel guests."

"Thanks, Joe," I said and hung up.

Pleased to know that Jack and Davey had not returned to the estate last night, I focused on the tasks at hand. Lois had paid close attention to my end of the conversation and fixed me with a skeptical eye. "You weren't really asking in general," she said, "were you?"

"Not really," I said. "The detectives are planning to interview all the Civil War campers, but they're setting their sights on staff members as well. I know the police will take copies of those logs, and I just want to be prepared and know what we're facing in case they drag any of our employees or consultants down for questioning."

That seemed to satisfy her.

At least someone was appeased. Until I knew the whole story behind Jack's involvement with Kincade, I didn't know whom I could trust. It didn't help that no matter how many times I tried to reach Jack—out of the range of Lois's eager ears—I came up empty. I left only one message on his cell phone and because it went immediately to voicemail each time I tried calling, I reasoned the device was turned off. That meant I wasn't racking up a ridiculous number of missed calls on his phone, thank goodness. In my message I asked him to get in touch when he had a chance. So far, no word.

Lois and I worked quietly, keeping the prying reporters at bay and juggling other tasks so that life would at least resemble normal when we returned to the office Monday morning. Normal. I thought about what Rodriguez had said and felt a twinge of guilt.

It was late afternoon when I thanked Lois for her time and decided I'd accomplished enough on my day off. I arrived home to find Bruce at the sink in the kitchen, his back to me. "What are you doing here?" I asked with a glance at the clock. "Isn't the shop open? Are you still dealing with a power outage?"

He half-turned, grinning from ear to ear and I was able to see what he was working on. "Yummies for our little

Bootsie," he said, holding up a can of cat food. Snapping the pull-top forward and then yanking it back, he said, "This kitty is hungry. I wonder how long it's been since she's had a decent meal." Next to him on the counter was a brand-new two-sided cat food dish. Bruce spooned about half the container's contents into one side. "This is the second can I've opened for her today. Oops, here she comes."

As though already accustomed to the sound of dinner being prepared, Bootsie leaped onto the countertop next to Bruce's arm. "Wait a second, sweetie," he said. "Almost done."

"You came home to feed the cat?" I asked.

"It's slow at the store today."

I waited.

"Okay, fine. Yes, I did. Poor little thing." He placed the dish on a small rug on the floor. That's when I noticed the bowl of water already there. Another brand-new bowl.

"Where did all this stuff come from?" I asked.

"Scott picked up a litter box. It's in the basement. Bootsie's already christened it, I might add. We found a few other things this morning when the pet shop opened. I just figured the little thing was lonely and I didn't know what time you'd be back."

I looked at the clock again. There was still plenty of daylight and I should probably start my door-to-door canvass of the neighborhood to see who the cat belonged to. I was so worn out from the day's adventure, however, that I dropped into the nearest chair instead. "It would be a shame to return her tonight after you guys bought all this great stuff. We should allow her at least one day's use from it all."

Bruce gave me a funny smile. "Yeah," he said. "You just relax and worry about all this tomorrow. By the way, what was the big emergency that had you running to work at five this morning?"

I told him.

Bruce's mouth fell open and he took a seat across from me. "You aren't kidding me, are you?"

I'd left out some of the details, but Bruce was quick to pounce. "The dead guy is the guy who got into a fight with your boyfriend yesterday, isn't it?"

"Jack isn't my boyfriend," I corrected. "And the 'dead guy' is named Kincade. He attacked Jack's brother, Davey."

"But only because he thought it was Jack."

I felt very tired all of a sudden. "Yeah."

"What does Jack say about all this?"

"I haven't been able to get a hold of him."

Bruce said, "Oh."

"What?"

"Nothing. Just seems like something he'd want to get straightened out quickly. Especially with you."

"Jack may not even know about the murder yet. We're keeping it out of the news."

"True, but then why isn't he returning your calls?"

I had no answer.

"Be careful, Grace."

Chapter 8

I WOKE SUNDAY MORNING WITH THREE IMPORTANT things on my mind: Call Jack—again—and hope to finally reach him this time; call Frances—again—and let her know everything that had happened at Marshfield and ask her to come in early Monday; and finally, find out who little Bootsie really belonged to.

The cat had crawled into bed with me again, curled up against my chest just under my chin, where I felt her purr until we both fell asleep. I'd rubbed behind her ears for a while. She seemed to enjoy the attention, and with each stroke I'd felt my own tension begin to ease.

She was so small, just a kitten, and I couldn't believe how soft her fur was. Having only had dogs growing up, I didn't realize that cats craved personal touch, too. I'd always assumed that felines were standoffish and aloof. Little Bootsie here was mighty cuddly. I already knew I'd miss her when she was finally reunited with her real family.

Unfortunately, I also awoke Sunday with something

else in my head. The cold was back, full force. I spent ten minutes in the bathroom blowing my nose.

"How can this be?" I asked Bruce and Scott when I came down to the kitchen. I was carrying Bootsie and shaking my head, still wearing my pajamas. "I had dis terrible code yesterday and then it went away. Now id is back."

My two roommates looked at each other and then at me with matching sad expressions.

"What's the matter?" I asked.

Scott pointed to the bundle in my arms. "I think you're allergic."

I looked down to find Bootsie staring up at me, wide-eyed. The answer was so obvious I felt like smacking myself in the head. It made sense—I was symptom-free everywhere but at home. "Oh," I said, dejected. "I had no idea I'd be allergic to cats."

"How are your eyes?" Bruce asked. "Itchy? Hot? Watery?"

"A little watery."

"Some people get full-blown symptoms. Their eyes get all swollen and red and they can't even see out of them. At least your symptoms are mild."

"Mild?" I said. "I've been blowing my nose since I woke up."

"I know," Bruce said, "we heard you."

Bootsie raised her head and let out a pathetic yowl. I pulled her a little tighter to my chest. "This isn't fair."

Scott chuckled. "I've seen it happen before."

I waited.

"Cats seem to have a sixth sense about who's allergic. Those are the folks they target. You've been adopted, Grace. I don't think you have much choice now but to keep her."

"You forget that this kitten was litter box trained. She already belongs to someone."

"I don't believe that," Scott said. "Cats have an instinct about litter boxes. She's just very smart."

I couldn't let my guard down. Couldn't let myself even consider keeping her. "Pets are important parts of the family," I said. "I'm sure whoever lost her is out of their mind with worry."

WITH THE KITTEN TUCKED INTO A SMALL cardboard box—flaps partially open for air—and feeling like a kid in a Norman Rockwell painting, I visited a dozen houses up my street and was now working my way back down the other side. Nobody was missing Bootsie, who, for the record, was behaving exceptionally well. She didn't seem to like being outdoors, though she apparently didn't mind being carried around in a brown box. The moment I'd stepped out the back door her ears had flattened against the back of her head. The first time a car went by, I felt her tremble through the cardboard. I wondered how long she'd been out on her own.

I'd left my purse at home, but carried my cell phone in my pocket in the hopes that Jack would return the second message I'd left him this morning. I wasn't so worried about Frances. Knowing she had a tendency to disappear for the weekend made it unlikely that I'd hear back from her until tonight at the earliest. But Jack should have called by now. I deserved that much. At least I thought I did.

Pushing aside my worries about Marshfield, Jack, and the murder of Zachary Kincade for the moment, I'd set out on my quest. House after house, I received plenty of compliments on how cute Bootsie was, but no clue as to where she'd come from. And no leads on whose cat might have had kittens in the past few months.

The homes on Granville were set about thirty feet back from the street, most featuring low, white fences protecting pristine lawns and gardens. A showplace neighborhood, except for the single eyesore—mine. Although my house boasted a turret and gables, and had been outfitted with classic gingerbread molding along its peaks and windows, it needed more repair than I could afford. Bennett's contributions to replace the roof had made an enormous improvement, but there was much more to be done. The last thing I wanted to do was run to him with my hand out, looking for help with every expense. That was not my style.

So far all my neighbors had been home—this early on a Sunday, most families were preparing to head out to church. But not one of them was missing a cat. I did get quite a few positive comments about my new roof, if you count "It's about time," as a compliment. Between sneezes and the occasional nose-blowing, I wound up fielding more questions than I'd expected.

"Another murder at Marshfield, huh?" Fenton Borlik asked from behind his screen door. Despite the fact that we'd done our best to keep the matter quiet until we had more information, the story had leaked but good. Borlik was the fifth person on the block to try to pry information from me. His wife shushed him and pointed to their two towheaded kids, who had run up to see what was going on. Fenton, I knew, was a vice president at one of the big conglomerates in the corporate corridor about forty-five minutes east. Quite a commute every day but many folks did it. Living in touristy Emberstowne had its perks. "You know, we moved here because we thought this was a safe town." Fenton stepped out onto his porch, making the wood floor squeak. The screen slammed behind him. "What happened out there?"

Hadn't he noticed the bundle trying to squirm out of the box? "Actually, I'm here to ask if you lost your pet."

The two kids had certainly noticed. One boy, one girl, both under age seven, they stared at the cat in my arms with instant love in their eyes. "A kitty," the girl said. "Daddy, is the lady giving the kitty away? Can we have it? I always wanted a kitty."

Fenton gave me a warning look. "Sorry, kids, this is Ms. Wheaton's cat. She just came by to show us."

Even though they were young, they adopted twin looks of skepticism that would have been at home on middle-aged faces. "I think you just don't want us to have a cat, Dad," the boy said. "Mom told us that you don't like cats."

Eager to get away before Fenton pressed me more about the murder, especially since this house was not a likely candidate for my mission, I thanked them all and started back down their walkway. I reached in to scratch behind Bootsie's ears and she purred again. "How could anyone not be missing you?"

At the next house, Mrs. Eastmore screamed, "No cat!" the moment she saw what I had in my hands. Without so much as a "Hello," she slammed the door in my face.

"Have a nice day," I said to the emptiness.

Starting home, I had to admit I wasn't exactly disappointed that no one had claimed the little black-and-white bundle. I pulled her out for the last leg of the trip, cradling her in my arms and gripping the empty box in my spare hand. Bootsie seemed to enjoy her perch up high. Her two front paws draped over the crook of my elbow and as I walked, her head tilted and twisted to watch birds and squirrels darting from tree to tree.

Bruce and Scott would have left for the wine shop by now so I was surprised to see an unfamiliar car in my driveway when I returned. A beat-up silver Corolla. "Hello?" I called. No one at the front door, so I headed around back. "Hello?"

From the weed-covered depths of my backyard, I heard a man's voice, "Hey, where have you been?"

He came around the side of my detached garage, dirt cupped in his hands. At least that's what it looked like. As he drew closer, the logical portion of my brain noticed that it wasn't just dirt, but a root of some sort. Amazed that I could notice any details at all while my breath was missing in action, I did the only thing that made sense. I said, "Jack?"

"Hey, Grace," he said with a crooked smile. "What's up?"

His unexpected appearance and his cavalier manner rendered me instantly cranky. What an idiot I'd been. I'd been certain that the only reason he hadn't gotten in touch was because he'd been dragged down to the police station and charged with murder because any other reason wouldn't have been good enough. Flabbergasted, I said the very first thing that popped into my mind. "You haven't returned my calls."

"Yeah." He stared at the root in his hands. "I didn't feel like talking."

My crankiness factor rose exponentially as my brain kicked in. "What was Kincade talking about when he said you killed his brother?" I demanded. "Did the police come talk to you about the murder yesterday? You do know about that, don't you? Where's Davey?"

"It's hard to know where to start."

I waited.

Jack turned the root over a couple of times, allowing little crumbles of dirt to fall. "I needed to get away for a while. To get my head straight. Before I talked to you."

Little sparkles of fury danced in front of my eyes, a sure sign I was about to say something I'd regret later. Rage bubbled up, and I pulled Bootsie closer to my chest, making the little kitten squirm.

"Sorry," I said to her, loosening my grip to allow some wiggle room, but not enough to allow her to jump out of my arms. To Jack, I said, "You could have at least let me know you weren't arrested."

He nodded. "You're right."

"What are you doing here?"

"I told you we needed to take a look at your daylilies." He held up the root. "This one's dead."

"We talked about that months ago. You needed to do this now?"

He shrugged and looked away.

Bootsie rested her chin in the crook of my elbow, one little paw draped over my arm. I tossed the box so that it landed near my back door and used my free fingers to stroke the cat's fur. The movement calmed me enough to force me to even my breathing. Jack's sudden appearance here was a slap in the face. I'd been worried for him, for heavens' sake. Worried when all it was, was that he just "hadn't felt like talking." What kind of a fool was I?

"Grace," he said. From that one word I detected caution, nervousness, and reluctance.

"I need to get the cat inside," I said as the kitten settled more deeply into my arms. "She might squirm away."

"Yeah, I can see that," he said, deadpan. Then, "I'm sorry I haven't called you back."

I said nothing.

"It's been a bad weekend. A lot of . . . stuff . . . got dredged up again. Stuff I thought I'd put behind me."

My heart rammed inside my chest, even as I tried to argue it down. The fear of the unknown twisted inside me, and at the same time I wondered why I was getting so worked up. Whatever "stuff" Jack was hiding had happened years ago. Clearly, it didn't concern me. I swallowed and tried to force a measure of calm. Or fake it, at least. "Did the police talk with you and Davey?" I asked. "How is your brother?"

His face reddened. "Listen," he said, "there's something you need to know. About me. I . . ." He stopped.

I closed my eyes ever so briefly. This was a make-or-break moment. Although my ego was still smarting from his admission that he'd been purposely ignoring my calls, I couldn't find it in my heart to shut him down without at least hearing what he had to say. Annoyed as I was with him, Jack had become a friend. Friends cut each other slack when they needed it. I couldn't turn my back now, not without giving him a chance to explain.

The smart move might very well be to turn my back, but I couldn't do it. The need to know was too great.

I wasn't sure whether it was loyalty or curiosity that made me answer, "Fair enough. Let's talk."

He let out a breath, then lifted his chin toward my back door. "Can I come in?"

Instead of quieting, my heart pounded harder. Faster. Fear for him. Fear for me. Although he and I hadn't ever even had a first date, I'd assumed we would get there eventually. Maybe it was time to challenge that assumption. Better I face whatever it was straight on, no matter what the consequences. After all, Jack and I worked together. At the very least, we needed to continue to do so. We couldn't do our jobs effectively if we were afraid to talk to one another. The last thing I wanted was another obstacle to communication in my life.

"Sure," I said, "we have to get past this, whatever it is."

"I'm not sure we can."

I swallowed around the fear that suddenly closed my throat.

As we stepped into the house, I pulled little Bootsie's face close to mine. "What are we in for?" I asked her.

She sneezed. So did I.

Chapter 9

INSIDE, JACK EXCUSED HIMSELF LONG ENOUGH to wash up. Bootsie, exhausted from all the house-to-house visiting, settled herself into the corner of one of the parlor's wing chairs. I sat across from her, watching her eyes blink at regular intervals, then ever more slowly until Jack came in and picked her up. "So who is this?"

"A stray," I said. "Bootsie. At least, that's her name until I find out who she belongs to. Found her Friday. Do you know anyone who's missing a cat?"

He cradled her in his arms and stroked under her chin. Even I could hear the purring. "Nope. She looks pretty young. I bet she's just recently weaned from her mother."

"Poor little thing."

He turned her to face him. "She's trouble."

"What?"

"Look at her. This one's a troublemaker. I'd bet on it."

Wasn't that exactly what Frances had told me about Jack?

He settled her back onto his lap and turned to me. "No luck finding her owners?"

"She seems to have appeared out of nowhere."

"Someone might have dropped her off to fend for herself."

Appalled, I said, "That's terrible."

"Plenty of people don't get their cats spayed or neutered, and the next thing you know they have a litter of kittens they don't know what to do with. Happens all the time."

Bootsie's eyes started to close again. At least somebody here was relaxed.

"Do you want anything to drink?" Fussing like a hostess helped me buy time. As much as I wanted to just come out and ask, "So did you kill Zachary Kincade's brother?" I couldn't make myself do it. As I searched for a good segue, I stood up, babbling, "We have Pepsi, lemonade, and, uh, wine, if you want it . . . I know it's kind of early, but . . ."

Jack had been gazing down at the cat in his arms. Now he looked up and gave me a sad smile. He had a defined jawline and a handsome face, marred only by the white line of his scar. Usually his eyes were bright and alert, but it looked like he hadn't slept in days.

"Grace," he began. "You're uncomfortable. I am, too."

No use denying it. I sat. "Just tell me," I said. "Tell me everything."

My house was old and it made noise almost all the time. But right now the room was perfectly still and I heard nothing but the sound of my own breathing. Bootsie had stopped purring the moment she fell asleep, and Jack stared down at her, continuing to stroke her fur.

"Thirteen years ago," he began in a soft voice, still not looking up, "Zachary's younger brother, Lyle Kincade, was murdered in his home. There was a big police investigation. I was questioned." His shoulders moved up and down. If his expression wasn't so morose, I'd have thought he laughed. "More times than I can count."

"They thought *you* did it?"

Jack looked up. "I was suspect number one."

"Why?"

"Because the guy deserved it," Jack said, his eyes hard. "And everybody knew I thought so."

Scenarios tumbled before my eyes. No one deserved to be murdered. Not even the lowest of the low. Confused, I couldn't prioritize the questions pounding in my brain, so I started with, "Were you arrested?"

"I was never charged. Not enough evidence against me. I had an alibi." He shrugged as though it was nothing. "But if I ever find out who really killed Lyle, I'll shake the guy's hand."

This was a side of Jack I'd never seen. I didn't know what to make of it. There had to be more—much more—to this story. "What was wrong with him? What did he do?"

"Thirteen years ago," Jack said again, getting a faraway look in his eyes as though he was watching a story play out before him, "my sister, Calla, was sixteen years old."

Jack had never mentioned much about his family before. Until I'd met Davey, whom Jack referred to as "one of my brothers," I hadn't even known he had siblings. I did the math. Calla would be younger than Jack by a few years. I waited, holding my breath.

"She's married now, with two little kids of her own."

I let out a *whoosh* of air. "Oh, thank heavens."

He blinked. "What do you mean?"

"Your sister," I said. "I was sure you were about to tell me that she died thirteen years ago."

"She's alive." His eyes tightened and I swore the scar pulsed. Very softly, he said, "But let me tell you, it was close."

I leaned forward.

"Lyle Kincade was Calla's boyfriend for a while. I don't remember how long exactly because I was away at school. Lyle was twenty-one and too old to be dating a teenager, if you want my opinion. Calla didn't. She didn't want to hear anything about her new boyfriend. But it was classic abuse—he drove a wedge between Calla and the family. Started limiting where she could go, how much time she could spend at home, how much time with her friends. Calla was in high school, for crying out loud. She didn't need that kind of manipulation. Nobody does." He took a deep breath. "This all sounds like normal stuff, doesn't it? Like an overprotective family not allowing their daughter to make her own mistakes." He stared at the ceiling as though searching for the right words. "This was bigger than that. The guy was around her *constantly*. He kept calling, kept showing up at the house even when he wasn't expected. We talked Calla into breaking things off with him. That's when the trouble escalated."

Jack's expression said he didn't want to explain, but I knew that if he didn't tell me everything now, he never would, so I prompted him. "Escalated?"

"Remember that old movie, *Mr. Wrong*, where Bill Pullman breaks his finger to prove how much he cares?" He waited for me to nod. "Like that, but when it happens in real life, it isn't funny."

I wasn't sure that *Mr. Wrong* qualified as funny either.

"Lyle would show up in the middle of the night, on school nights even, and sing to her outside the house, begging her to marry him. Half the time he was drunk. It scared us more when he showed up sober. We eventually got an order of protection . . . which he complied with. For a while."

I waited.

"But then the gifts started to show up outside Calla's window. Her room was on the second floor," Jack said. "This was no small effort. He started with normal date stuff, like stuffed bears and costume jewelry. Calla loved it. Thought it proved how much he cared and was oh-so-eager to take him back. But we managed to talk her out of it." His eyes tightened again. "Then came the DVDs. Movies that all followed a theme: serial killers stalking teenage girls. He must have run out of cash then, because he started leaving pictures."

"Pictures?"

"Of Calla, clearly taken when she was unaware. He splattered them with red paint, and drew lines across her neck. He scribbled notes warning her it was time to leave her family and grow up." Jack's mouth set in a grim line.

"Didn't that violate the order of protection?"

"Only if we could provide evidence that it was Kincade who left them. No one ever saw him around our house. We couldn't press charges until we could prove he was behind it."

"Fingerprints?"

"Nope. The man was careful. He skirted the law and made our lives a living hell. Finally, my mom and dad decided to do an intervention. They called me home from college and we sat Calla down and talked with her, told her how we felt." Jack cleared his throat. "Reminded her how much we loved her."

"She ignored you?"

The corner of Jack's mouth curled into a smile. "No. She listened. Turned out she was scared out of her mind and relieved by the family's support. She'd been afraid we might condemn her for making such a bad choice."

"That's not the end of the story, is it?"

"Lyle," Jack said, making eye contact again, "wouldn't go away. Calla couldn't go to school on her own without having to worry about him waiting for her, always trying to get her to come back. The restraining orders didn't do much good. Nothing did. Even when my dad and Keith and I decided to have a 'talk' with him. You know, man-to-man."

Three men to man, he meant. From the ferocity sparking Jack's eyes as he talked, I got the feeling they intended some serious intimidation. "Who's Keith?"

"Older brother," Jack said with a look that told me he

was surprised I didn't know that. "We didn't take Davey with us. He wanted to come too, but he was only a kid—maybe fourteen, fifteen years old at the time. And my dad was a cop. We thought with him along we could talk some sense into the idiot and let him know that plenty of other cops would be watching out for him."

"Your dad was an Emberstowne cop?"

He nodded.

I wanted to ask how come this tidbit of information hadn't come up before. "If he was on the force, then why was it so hard to get Kincade arrested when he violated the order of protection?"

"He lived up north in a different town. Had an alibi for every infraction we charged him with. His family was well-off and I think his dad had friends in that town's police department. Nobody would do anything to stop him."

"That's wrong."

"That's small-town politics."

Bootsie opened her eyes long enough to stretch and re-position herself with a little *whuff* of contentment. We both watched her as I waited for Jack to continue.

"Go on," I said.

"Not much more to tell," Jack said. "He kept bothering Calla, and we made it clear he needed to back off."

"You threatened him?"

Jack sat up so quickly Bootsie leapt off his lap. "She's my sister. What do you think?"

I held my hands up. "I'm not passing judgment. I'm just trying to understand."

"We got into a scuffle." Jack traced his finger along his scar. "That's where I got this."

I raised my eyebrows.

"I admit I threw the first punch. But then we both got into it, and Keith didn't want to see his little brother get pummeled, so he jumped in," he explained. "My dad tried to break it up and ended up hurting his back. Pretty bad, in fact. Laid him up for over a month. The cops came and we were escorted away. I can still see the smirk on Lyle's face when he told us we were lucky he didn't press charges."

"When was Lyle murdered?"

"About a week later." Settling back in the chair, Jack went on. "I didn't know anything about it until the police showed up at my apartment at school. They took me in, read me my rights, and questioned me for hours."

"They didn't charge you?"

"They wanted to. Heck, they wanted to charge me, my dad, and Keith. But Dad was laid up with his back injury. Keith had been at work the whole time, and although I hadn't left my apartment all that weekend—I was studying for finals—it was just lucky I'd ordered a pizza and that the delivery guy remembered that I'd tipped him." He stared away again. "As alibis go, it was pretty weak, but it was enough to keep me from being charged with murder."

"What happened then?"

"Nothing," he said. "They never caught who did it. But everyone in Emberstowne believes I'm guilty."

"That can't be true."

He laughed, but it wasn't a happy sound. "You asked me a long time ago why Marshfield Manor is my only real client." He sat up. "I'll tell you why. Because Bennett Marshfield was the only soul who would take a chance on me after all that. The stress from the murder threw me off my game. I flunked the few finals I managed to take, and skipped out on others. I couldn't stand the scrutiny, the pressure. I dropped out of school my last semester." His mouth twisted downward. "I was pre-law. Had my career all planned out. Heck, I had my entire life planned out."

I sucked in a sharp breath of realization. "What was her name?"

He didn't move, but his eyes flashed. "Becke," he said. "She couldn't handle it either. Being engaged to a murderer was not part of her life plan. Can't say that I blame her."

"But you're not a murderer."

"Tell the world that."

"There's got to be—"

"There isn't," he snapped. "I looked into everything. I was desperate to prove myself. For Becke's sake." His voice hardened. "And now"—he stretched out his arms southward, toward Marshfield—"I plant flowers for rich people."

His bitterness rattled me. I didn't know how to react. As usual I said the first thing that popped into my mind. "But I thought you loved what you do."

His gaze softened. "I've learned to."

"I'm sorry," I said.

"Not your fault. Not mine, either." He fidgeted and looked toward the door, as though now that the story was out he couldn't wait to get away from me.

"How is Davey?"

"Broken nose." Jack got up. "The police questioned him last night, but he was sedated after surgery and I was his alibi. Too bad he slept so much. He could have been mine. Your friend Rodriguez and that woman he's working with pulled me down to the station for questioning."

"What happened?"

"They think I did it, no doubt about that. But there's not enough to hold me yet. They stressed 'yet.' And they warned me not to leave the area." Pacing the room, he kept talking, almost to himself. "I hate this. I hate what it's done—and doing—to my life and to Davey's. He used to be such a happy-go-lucky kid. He used to look up to me. Even he believes I killed Kincade." Jack stared at me. "*Lyle* Kincade, that is. Ever since that murder, Davey has been different. He pulled away from me. From the family. Like he lost his way in the world, too. It was hard on my folks, hard on all of us." His voice drifted off. "Lyle Kincade ruined my family once. Now that his brother's been murdered, too, it's starting all over again."

Chapter 10

I WISHED I COULD COME UP WITH SOMETHING profound to say, something to ease the tension, to bring back the Jack I knew. But the truth was, the Jack I thought I'd known and the real Jack were different people. The telling of the story created a new distance between us rather than generate any sense of intimacy. A divide had formed, widening by the second. Jack saw himself as an outsider, that much was clear. It explained a lot. And although I wanted to reach out and help him, I knew there were no words to do so. Not now at least.

Changing the subject, I tilted my head toward the door. "What made you come dig up my daylily roots today?"

Jack gave me a look that was at once wary and amused. "I got your messages . . . you probably guessed that. I wanted to call you back, but every time I picked up the phone, I froze. I didn't know how to explain. To be perfectly honest, I didn't want to. I wanted to pretend nothing had happened and just walk away from it all."

"But?"

"That wasn't fair to you. I borrowed Davey's car and came up with an excuse to be here. I knew that once I saw you in person I'd have the guts to start talking."

"I've been furious with you."

For the first time he smiled. "I got that impression."

"I was worried, okay?"

The doorbell rang, preventing him from commenting. Instead, he pointed. "You better get that and I'd better be going."

"So soon?"

"Yeah," he said. "Davey's alone. I worry about him. By the way, he'll be back at work tomorrow."

"You think that's wise?"

"It will be good for him."

Jack accompanied me to the front door. As I swung it open, I gasped. "What are you doing here?"

Behind me I heard Jack make a noise of disgust. "On second thought," he said, "maybe I should stay long enough to help you take out the trash."

Ronny Tooney stood about five steps back from my front door, as though eager to prove he wasn't a threat. Clutching a dark gray fisherman's cap in both hands, he smiled sheepishly. "Good afternoon, Miss Wheaton," he said after a nervous glance at Jack. "I hope I'm not bothering you all. I just heard about what happened down at the manor and I thought you might want a little help."

"I'll take care of this," Jack said as he pushed past me.

I grabbed his arm. "Jack."

He stopped long enough to meet my eyes.

"Not a good idea," I said. "Not today."

"But this guy . . ."

"I'll take care of it. You go home."

He listened to me, but before he left, he shot an angry glare at Tooney. "Take some friendly advice and back off."

I wasn't afraid of Tooney, but I wasn't about to let him into my house, either. I didn't want to risk Bootsie running out, however, so I stepped onto the porch the moment Jack got into Davey's clunker and started it up. "So, what do you want?" I asked.

Tooney watched until Jack pulled out and the car turned the far corner before asking, "Are you seeing him?"

I pasted on a chilly smile. "That's none of your business."

Tooney shrugged. "You think he did it?"

"Mr. Tooney . . ."

"You can call me Ronny."

"No thanks." There were times, like this one, when I wished I had the talent of delivering zinger put-downs. I'd met Ronny Tooney almost immediately after Abe had been killed, when Tooney had attempted to insinuate himself into the investigation. Since then, the man had never let up. In his early fifties, carrying a fair amount of middle-aged spread, and with a prominent mole right above the bridge of his nose, he was hard to miss. He'd recently completed a course in private investigation and was eager to build up his clientele. Unfortunately for Tooney, all of Emberstowne saw him coming and ran the other way. "The police are handling the investigation," I said. "If they need your help they know where to find you." Did they ever.

Bootsie appeared behind the storm door patting the glass with her front paws.

"New roommate?" Tooney asked. "How's the boys' wine shop doing?"

The fact that this man knew so much about me was disconcerting. Harmless? Probably. But annoying as all get-out. "I found her," I said. "Couple days ago."

"Is that why you were walking door-to-door this morning?"

I stared at him. "Don't you have anything better to do than to pay attention to my comings and goings?"

Tapping the glass in front of Bootsie with his knuckle, his voice went up a notch or two. "Hey, cutie," he said, smiling, "you're a sweetie pie, aren't you?" Righting himself, he turned his attention to me. "I'm serious about my business and I know you've got troubles down at Marshfield. Again. I helped you out last time," he said, "remember? I think you owe me."

"The last time you 'helped' almost got me killed."

"That part wasn't because of me."

I didn't want to get into an argument with him. "I have a lot to do," I said. "Including feeding the cat."

"So you're keeping her?"

"Until I find out who she belongs to," I said, mentally slapping myself in the head the moment the words slipped out of my mouth. I hoped he wouldn't pick up on them.

Too late. "Hey," he said, enthusiasm blooming, "I can do that for you. I take pride in my work, no matter how small the job. I'll find out where she came from."

"No, really. I'm—"

"And I'll poke around a bit in town. I'm sure there's scuttlebutt about the murder at the manor. I'll keep you posted."

"No . . . no . . ."

He placed his hat atop his head, tipped it, and bounded off my porch before I could stop him. "Thank you, Grace!" he shouted over his shoulder.

"Great," I said to myself. "Just great."

JUST AS I SETTLED MYSELF WITH A SANDWICH and a glass of lemonade, my cell phone rang. It had been only about twenty minutes since Ronny Tooney left. I had a feeling it was him calling. I was wrong. And it took me a moment to place the breathless voice.

"Ms. Wheaton?"

"Yes?"

"I'm sorry to bother you on your day off . . ."

Light dawned—Rob Pierpont.

". . . but something has come up."

Gripping the phone tightly, I asked, "Is anyone hurt?"

"It's more than that . . ." I heard him swallow.

"More than anyone getting hurt?" I envisioned another dead body, a second murder among the Civil War re-enactors. "Did you call the police?"

"No, no, it's not like that. It's a problem we're having." I could almost see him bouncing with impatience.

"Can't it wait until tomorrow?"

"You know how I am about avoiding anything farby. The fact that I'm speaking on a telephone should lend some weight to my words."

"All right, Mr. Pierpont. Please go on."

"It's about the police. They're still here and they're stopping and questioning every single person in our camp. The officers refuse to allow anyone to participate in drills until they've been questioned. But we have plans. A schedule. This is throwing everything off. Worst of all, they won't let us handle weapons. Our *own* weapons."

"You have to remember, Mr. Pierpont, they have a murder to investigate."

"Yes, yes, and we've given them plenty of room. In fact, we moved two sections of tents just so that we'd be out of their way. Were they happy that we'd been so accommodating? No. They were angry because they hadn't had a chance to *process* those tents yet. What in the world needed to be processed? We didn't move Zachary's tent. We left that one alone."

Had Pierpont not watched a single crime-based television show in his life? You never moved anything without approval. "What made you decide to move tents?"

"To be frank, it wasn't my idea. Jim Florian took care of that. He suggested we separate ourselves from the activity going on with the police. That way we could resume our schedule. But it's not working."

"I can't stop the police from doing their job," I said. Nor would I want to.

He sighed. "It's not just the police, though. It's other guests. People staying at the hotel. The murder is pulling gapers out of the woodwork. Strangers are getting into everything. Upsetting our plans. I think they're contaminating the crime scene, too. Dozens, maybe even close to a hundred guests have driven their automobiles up into our encampment area. Motorized vehicles! Do they not understand that their very presence ruins the illusion? They say they want to see what we're doing, but it's clear they just want to poke their noses into where the murder happened."

"Security isn't keeping them away?"

"Does security care if twenty-first-century vehicles are cluttering up our sight lines? No. Nor do they care about maintaining the illusion of the 1800s. All they worry about is making sure no one walks past their precious yellow tape—and yet people are tramping through there all the time. Gawkers, all of them. We asked them nicely to park their cars where ours are parked—well out of sight. But no! They claim that's too far to walk."

I sighed. With our security department stretched thin between assisting the local police and maintaining control over the Marshfield property, there was not much I could do. The southern grounds were currently off-limits to guests. But people were like ants. They crawled in to get what they wanted and at this point there were just too many of them to control.

"I'm sorry to hear you're having difficulty," I began, "but I'm not sure what can be done at this point . . ."

"I know it's your day off, and especially after yesterday's tragedy, I truly hate to involve you, but I have a request . . ."

"What do you need?"

"First and most important, I need order. The police are running amok here. As soon as we get one of our drills set up, they come along and ruin it."

The man sounded near tears, but I had little patience for

his complaints. I wondered how he could be so focused on his war games and miss the big picture.

"Ms. Wheaton, it's unbearable. Can you come out here, please?"

"Mr. Pierpont, there's really not much I can do . . ."

"Yes, yes, there is. If you talk to the police in person and you tell them to leave us alone, they have to listen. Just like those two women. You were marvelous handling them. So marvelous." His flattery made my teeth hurt, but Pierpont obviously couldn't see my grimace over the phone. "Can't you do that again for us. Please?"

"Speaking of the women—they didn't ever come back, did they?"

Pierpont's voice went very low. "I didn't see them, no, but a handful of other soldiers mentioned seeing a couple of out-of-costume individuals skulking around that night. It was late, they were wearing dark clothing, and my colleagues couldn't ascertain whether they were male or female."

"You reported that to the police, didn't you?"

"Of course," he huffed. "And I reported something else, as well."

I perked up. "What was that?"

"Can't you just come down here? Please," he repeated, "I'm not comfortable being on the phone like this. Really . . . something needs to be done about—" Raising his voice, he shouted to someone else, "You! Get out of there. That's not yours!" To me again, he said, "I'm at my wits' end. There are just too many issues to handle and I can't do it on my own."

One thing I wished I could change about myself is the fact that I wear down far too easily. That insufferable politeness, yet again. A determined individual relentlessly hammering at me always eroded my resolve. Unfortunately, far too many people in my life seemed to be in on this knowledge. I needed to work on that.

I sighed. "Okay, fine." Glancing at the clock, I added, "Give me a half hour."

"Thank you, oh, thank you."

"Great," I said when he hung up. Bootsie joined me in the kitchen as I slapped my phone shut. "So much for relaxing on my day off."

Chapter 11

PIERPONT MET ME AT THE NORTHERN BOUND-
ary of the re-enactors' camp atop a small hill that over-
looked the meadow below. When he and Abe had
established guidelines for this event, they had chosen this
spot with care. The enormous flatland populated by tents
and re-enactors was surrounded on all sides by slightly
higher ground—an effective buffer against high winds.
Had this been the middle of summer, the location would
have been far too hot, but right now—though warm—it
was ideal. The participants in the low-lying ground couldn't
see outside their encampment, nor could idle passersby see
in. I supposed that's why Pierpont felt overrun by nosy
tourists. Guests' cars parked at the top of the embankment
would be impossible to miss.

Pierpont waved a greeting as I parked and made my way
up the rise. He was again in uniform but had unbuttoned
the collar of his navy wool coat. The morning chill had
dissipated and from the pink in his cheeks to the sweat
dripping along the side of his face, I could tell the uphill

walk had taxed him. "Thanks for coming," he said between breaths. "I thought this would be the easiest place to meet."

"I'm impressed," I said. Below us, the tents stretched out in neat rows, forming the transient community where costumed participants socialized, worked, and played. For the first time I grasped the scale of this exercise. "How many participants do you have here?"

"Over three thousand came out for this," he said with pride.

I nodded. With so many people walking, running, talking, and cooking, there was no corner without movement. In the meadow's far reaches, past the last line of tents, men marched in formation, carrying what looked like tree branches instead of rifles.

I would have felt transported into the 1800s except for the presence of the touristy folks gathered along the outskirts pointing in, and the police who were easy to pick out, even from here. Emberstowne had brought in a task force to help investigate and officers from several other departments were interacting with the participants. "There's tremendous police presence here," I said. I almost added, "this time," but caught myself before the words tumbled out. "How long do they anticipate staying?"

Three vertical lines formed between Pierpont's bushy brows. "I can't believe they haven't moved off-site yet. We're so far behind on our setup." He flung a hand toward the parked squads behind and below us. "At least they've managed to keep their cars out of sight, but they insist on conducting their questioning in our midst. I can't tell you how much this has thrown our schedule off." He led me down the hill into the camp itself. "It's spoiling all our plans."

I stopped short. "You do realize a man has been killed here," I said, disdain slipping into my voice. "What do you expect?"

"I know, I know." He waved his hands in the air and

indicated that we should resume walking. "I apologize for sounding flippant, but I can't stand to see plans ruined."

Our footsteps made soft noises in the wild grass as we descended the hill and continued our trek. "I'm not trying to diminish your concerns," I said, "but murder is a pretty big deal."

He nodded. "I'm doing everything in my power to help, but I'm sure you understand what it's like to be responsible for a large group." Gesturing out over the crowd, he said, "Most of these folks use their vacation time to be here. They've been looking forward to this for months. Although some are pushing harder than others, they're all waiting for me to make it right. They're depending on me."

I understood where he was coming from, but countered, "Didn't you tell me this was just a practice week before the big Gettysburg get-together?"

He stopped. "Get-together?" he repeated, fixing me with a glare. "This is much more than a get-together. Do you have any idea how much work it is to achieve authenticity? I've been doing this for over forty years and I still feel the need to improve each and every time I participate."

"Bad choice of words, sorry." Changing the subject, I asked, "What exactly did you need from me? It looks as though everything is being handled as well as it can be." I noticed him about to interrupt so I quickly added, "That is, of course, except for the gawkers. I'll talk with security about that. As far as having the police in your camp, however, I don't think there's much that can be done."

"Can't you talk with them? Ask them to set up their interrogation away from the heart of the action?"

"Don't you believe a murder investigation warrants a little inconvenience?"

"With over three thousand people this is one of the largest gatherings of the year. If any of our participants saw or heard anything suspicious, don't you think they would rush to report it?" His voice rose as he emphasized his point.

"Of course they would. Zachary was our friend. And yet this task force is determined to question each and every person on-site. Do you have any idea how long that will take? The cops claim they're starting with a 'quick canvass' of everyone, but that's only their first round. They intend a second and third round. More if necessary. There's no end in sight. People here are angry with me because of it. They're yelling at me almost constantly."

"I'm sorry to hear that."

We'd made it all the way down and started wending our way through the tents. I didn't know if he had a destination in mind or if we were just wandering as we talked. I caught the aroma of corn bread and sizzling meat. Heavenly. My stomach growled.

He turned and raised an eyebrow. "Somebody's hungry."

"No, not at all," I lied.

The grass in the lowlands had been trampled flat by the comings and goings of the many re-enactors. We stayed along the northern perimeter, but I found myself gaping. Just about every tent boasted its own personal campfire with a black cauldron bubbling above dancing flames. It was close to dinnertime. The women tending to meals wore dark muslin dresses. Others, in patterned gowns with wide hoop skirts, wandered about the camp, hems skimming the dirt as they walked. Hundreds of kids were left to run like wild things. For the life of me, I couldn't tell which parents any of them belonged to.

It frightened me to think that these children were unattended.

"I hate to point out the obvious, Mr. Pierpont," I said, keeping my voice low, "but has it occurred to you that there's a murderer in your midst? That you could wake up in the morning with a musket pointed at your head—all in the name of fun? With a killer on the loose, why wouldn't everyone want to hightail it out of here as quickly as they could?"

"Like I said before, you just don't understand Civil War re-enactments."

"Then enlighten me."

"Keep walking. Keep watching. You'll begin to understand."

"To be perfectly frank, I'm surprised you invited me in."

"Might as well. We've gone completely farby anyway." He waved a hand toward a nearby police officer and frowned. "These encampments are best when everyone takes things seriously. That's when we forget all about the twenty-first century and pretend we're out there, fighting for what we believe in. We work and live together here, whether we wear the blue or the gray."

"And you're here for fun."

"More than fun, Ms. Wheaton. It's a way of life we choose to embrace. A simpler time. We have the opportunity to share what we've learned with others through our Living History. We're happy to do so, even though it occasionally makes us feel like animals in a zoo. But the truth is, I really do need your help. Have you ever been in the military?"

I shook my head.

"Well, let me tell you, it's like nothing else. There's a camaraderie, a closeness, and a commonality of purpose that's sacred. Even though at least half of our colleagues have never actually served in the real military, they feel the same way I do. We trust each other. We rely on each other. No one leaves until the last tent is broken down. And even then most of us would rather stay than return to our dreary, dismal twenty-first-century lives."

He allowed his gaze to rove the tents, the people, and the trees in the distance, then drew a deep breath of air as he slapped at his chest. "This is the life, Ms. Wheaton. Here. Right now. I know that people view us as a bunch of playacting fanatics but these weeks we spend together are what make the rest of the year tolerable."

I didn't quite know what to say to that.

He continued. "Mr. Kincade has been killed. That's a fact no one disputes. But my point holds: If one of our members saw something, don't you believe they would share that with the authorities? That would be the honorable thing to do."

I acknowledged his argument. "What about that man you mentioned yesterday? Florian or something."

"Jim?" Pierpont laughed. "Jim's the nicest guy in the world. He would never . . ." Abruptly, he stopped himself, turning to stare out over the top of the tents. I watched a thought work across his features. Shaking his head, he said very quietly, "No, no matter what, Jim's not a killer."

"I'm not saying he is. I was just using him as an example. You said he found the body . . ." I let the thought hang and hoped he would run with it. Pierpont's reaction had given me pause. He'd started out with a knee-jerk, "no way" when I'd mentioned Florian, but then stopped. Why? What was behind the change? I wanted to know but Pierpont switched the subject back to his impassioned request.

"Please talk with the police on our behalf. I'm not asking them to stop their investigation, just to take the activity a little bit off-site. Let us have our privacy. We're not going anywhere. And you promised us a quiet week on your grounds. That's what we paid for."

"I have no control over the police . . ."

"All I ask is that you try."

I could do that much. "Fine."

"Thank you! I knew you'd understand."

"There's no guarantee they'll listen to me even if I do talk with them." I cringed, thinking of Rodriguez's comment about my interfering again. "But before I do, I want to know what you were referring to on the phone. You said that you'd reported something else. What was it?"

"I think I found a clue." Pierpont's eyes twinkled conspiratorially. "The police told me not to share this with any of the other re-enactors, but I'm sure they'd approve of my letting you know."

Near the center of the gathering we passed several very large tents with flaps open on all sides. Two little boys ambled out from behind one of these open tents, laughing and clearly enjoying rock candy sticks. Pierpont noticed me watching them. "We even keep our treats authentic," he said.

"Do their mothers make these?"

"Maybe, but those are from the candy store at the sutlers' area."

"The what?"

He pointed to where the kids had emerged. "Think of it like a Civil War mall," he said. "You need something, it's there. Uniforms, food, supplies. Blacksmiths, gunsmiths, you name it. One time my rifle wouldn't fire—on the first day of camp. I took it to the gunsmith and had it back in an hour. Good as new."

"Convenient."

"Part of what makes it real."

Taking deep breaths of the savory air and hearing the horses' distant whinnies, I began to appreciate Pierpont's point. Escaping civilization for a little while—to forget about e-mail and gas prices, to create one's own entertainment instead of just plopping in front of the TV—was an enticing prospect. I would miss my blow-dryer and curling iron, but the fresh-faced, bun-wearing women here seemed to be doing just fine without such gadgets.

A half step farther, however, I sucked in a breath of surprise. Two women strutted by decked out in shades of fuchsia, red, and pink. They both had curled hair and wore plenty of makeup. Strolling and laughing, they winked at every man they passed as they made their way toward the sutlers' area. "Who are they?" I asked in a hushed voice.

Pierpont shrugged. "Soiled doves," he said. "Wives of re-enactors who like to pretend they're working girls, if you know what I mean. It's just another role. Accurate, though unnecessary if you ask me."

"Back to the clue you mentioned," I prompted. "What exactly did you find?"

"Friday night, I went out for a walk by myself. Away from the camp."

"At the time of the murder?"

He gave me a weary glance. "No, Ms. Interrogator. They said Zachary was killed between eleven and one. This was much earlier. In fact, it was just after the storm cleared. I'd say closer to eight."

"Go on."

"As much as I enjoy the storytelling and socializing around the fire, it had been a hectic day and I needed some time to settle my nerves. I rejoined the group later that evening when the camp had quieted down." He winked. "It gets so much nicer when the young mothers put their small children to bed for the night."

He must have seen the look on my face because he hastened to add, "Don't get me wrong, it's not like I hate kids. At these gatherings, however, I simply prefer the company of the old-timers. We can be rude and crude and not chastised for our behavior. The real veterans of the group stay up late to drink and sing and talk about the old days."

This was getting me nowhere. "You were saying you found something?"

"Do you realize how close the estate fence is to our campsite?"

I thought about it. "A half mile south? Maybe a little more? That isn't a problem, is it? There isn't much traffic on those access roads and you should be protected by the higher ground."

"It's fine, fine. No, that's not it. We don't hear a thing. But Friday night I decided to take a long walk and I intended to avoid the paved roads and any fences because they serve as reminders that I'm not in the nineteenth century."

"Farby," I said.

"Exactly!" Pleased that I'd picked up some of the lingo, he continued. "But I'd misjudged the distance and walked too far. Before I knew it, I was at the south fence. Worse, I'd lost my bearings because of the cloud cover. I had to follow the fence until I found the road. At that point I was able to make my way back."

"What does this have to do with Mr. Kincade's murder?"

"Did you know that there's a gate back there?"

"We have a lot of gates."

"This one is at the junction of the road and the south fence. It doesn't look like it's used very often. The gate is rusted, as is the heavy chain. But the padlock is rather new."

I still wasn't getting it. "So?"

"The padlock was open," he said. "The chains were still in place and anyone driving past—like a guard or something—would assume it was secure. But when I was up close, I could tell that the lock was open."

"Why do you think that makes a difference?"

"Because after all this happened, I decided the police ought to know what I'd found. I took them out there to show them the open lock, and guess what?"

I couldn't guess.

"All secure again. Like someone with a key had opened it ahead of time for the killer, and then come back and locked it once the deed was done. With no one the wiser." He went up on the balls of his feet—supremely proud of himself. "Interesting, wouldn't you say?"

"You're suggesting this murder was premeditated? That it wasn't one of your members who got carried away in a drunken fury?"

Pierpont looked genuinely surprised by my question. "Come now, Ms. Wheaton. I think we both recognize that this was a targeted attack. I can assure you Zachary Kincade had no trouble accumulating enemies. You saw the truth of that yourself. Within fifteen minutes Friday you witnessed two altercations. I've seen many more."

"Any with Jim Florian?"

Pierpont gave me a shrewd look. "Believe me when I tell you that Jim is one of the most tolerant guys I've ever met."

"Is he Union or Confederate?"

"Union, like me, why?"

And like Zachary. There went that theory. "I thought maybe if he was Confederate he would have held a grudge against Mr. Kincade."

Pierpont laughed. "I've said it before and I'll say it again. Don't go jumping to conclusions until you truly understand re-enacting. At night when the drills are done and the fire crackles, we all join in the center to sing songs, share stories, tell jokes." He pointed toward the giant sutler area. "That central area serves both sides. We're only enemies on the battlefield, and even then everything is choreographed." With a wistful look in his eyes, he smiled. "This is one of the most welcoming, generous groups I've ever encountered. I'm proud to be their leader and I know no one in my division or in any of the regiments here who could have done such a thing."

"I highly doubt those two women came back that night to kill him."

"Oh no? They wanted to hurt him," he reminded me, "as did your gardener."

"No. That time Kincade attacked."

"Regardless, the bad blood between them would be evident to a child. Who else could it have been?" Pierpont raised his hands to the sky. "Both the women and that gardener had reason to hate him. Whoever killed Zachary got his or her revenge. I'm sure there's no danger to those of us here at the re-enactment." He gave a self-satisfied bow. "For what it's worth, my money is on that gardener."

Chapter 12

※

I WAS AT MY DESK MONDAY MORNING WHEN I heard the door to the outer office swing open. As it shut, Frances marched in, interrupting me from reviewing the prior week's time sheets.

"*Two* murders on the manor grounds since you started working here," she said, wiggling her head. "You know, this used to be a safe place to work."

She was wearing a white polyester shell with purple irises blossoming up from its hem. Her neck waddled and her eyes danced in anticipation, clearly eager for me to rise to the bait. Was I tempted? Absolutely.

"Good morning, Frances. How was your weekend?"

"Nowhere near as eventful as yours, I'm sure."

That was true enough. Niceties complete, I got right to business. "The re-enactors' 'Living History' was supposed to begin today, but they've delayed it because of the police investigation. We may need to ask security to pitch in and help with crowd control once the event opens."

She held up a finger. "First things first. How come they haven't arrested anyone?"

"I don't know, Frances," I said. "Why don't you call up the detectives and find out what's taking them so long?"

She grimaced. "I told you that Jack Embers was no good."

I bit back a retort and decided to change the subject. "Bennett called me early this morning about that auction he attended last week. He bought something he's quite excited about and said to expect delivery today or tomorrow."

"What is it?"

"He wouldn't tell me. Just that this acquisition was perfect timing."

"Hmph," Frances said, "if Abe were here, the Mister would have told *him*."

I kept my cool. "I'm sure you're right. But as you're always so eager to point out, I'm not Abe."

That shut her up. "I'll be in my office," she said and spun, ready to march away again.

Although I wasn't the only person Frances irked, I was the only one required to work with her on a regular basis. Shortly after Abe's murder, she had put forth considerable effort to get me discharged. For a while there I thought Bennett would take her word over mine. Fortunately, however, though a bit battered and bruised, I'd hung on. Unfortunately, so had she.

Joy of joys. I was stuck with Frances until she chose to retire, which, from the looks of things, wouldn't be anytime soon.

"Just a moment, Frances."

She turned and I hesitated. I didn't want to bicker with this woman. Nor did I want to become the tyrannical boss who always insisted on "my way or the highway." Frances had grown accustomed to working with Abe, a gentle fellow who had let her run the place because she could. She knew every employee, every procedure, and where every dust bunny was hiding. What she lacked in people skills she more than made up for in efficiency. Although I never got the impression she expected to be promoted into Abe's position, I did get the impression she resented me.

It would take a great deal of effort to turn our relationship around but every little bit might help. Over the weekend I'd come up with a radical idea, which I decided to broach.

"Frances, when you and I were discussing this re-enactor event, you mentioned that your parents had participated in something like this a long time ago."

She inched back toward my desk. " 'Long time ago?' " she parroted. "What are you saying? That I'm old?"

"Certainly not," I snapped. Mentally counting to five before I spoke, I tried again. "I've been thinking . . ." I pointed to one of the two wing chairs opposite my desk. "Have a seat."

Warily, she lowered herself into the chair on the left, perched on the edge as though preparing to leap if I made any sudden move. "You can't dock me for not being available over the weekend," she said. "Time off is my time. If I don't answer my cell phone, that's my business."

"Frances," I said, veering away from volatility, "you and I both know that you possess a particular talent for detail."

Her eyebrows were perfect little tadpoles. I wondered how long it took her to pencil them in so precisely each morning—they couldn't possibly grow that way naturally. Right now, the two were drawn together so tightly that it looked like they were trying to kiss. "What do you mean?"

I told her about Tank, adding that I believed the female detective brought a stronger skill set to the investigation this time. I didn't add my impression that she added a stronger personality, too. "But they still have an enormous task ahead of them."

"And you want to 'help' them? Is that it?"

I ignored her sarcasm. "Look at the size of our police

department. Even if you add Tank and the assistance from the task force, it's not nearly enough. There are over three thousand people at that encampment who might have heard or seen something they don't even realize is significant. Zachary Kincade was not a nice man. Whoever killed him either waited for him to separate himself from the group, or lured him away. My gut tells me he wouldn't have trusted those two women if they showed up, so I highly doubt they were involved."

Frances sniffed. "And of course you assume our landscape consultants are innocent too, right?"

I ignored the jab at Jack, and plunged on, "You have a unique talent . . ."

A tiny smile played at her lips. "For gossip."

"Basically, yes."

She pulled her chair closer and leaned forward. "You want me to go down to that encampment to snoop."

"That's the general idea."

For the first time in a long time, I saw a genuine smile break across her face. Her eyes sparkled with interest for a brief moment, then dimmed and narrowed. "What if what I find out isn't what you want to hear?"

"All I'm looking for is the truth."

She watched me without blinking. "That handsome gardener might have gotten away with murder once already. Do you really want to know the truth or are you just sending me in there because you're hoping to find a way to pin the crime on someone else?"

Anger mounted a hot path up my chest. "If you can't be objective, Frances, tell me now and you can just stay here in the office and reorganize the file cabinets instead."

"The files don't need reorganizing."

We stared at each other. "Fine," I said, "forget it."

"You don't want your Mr. Embers to be guilty so you've talked yourself into believing he's not. If you knew the whole story . . ."

"I do know the whole story."

She sat back, eyeing me suspiciously. "Who told you?"

"You don't need to know."

She chewed the inside of her cheek for a moment. I was about to dismiss her when she asked, "Are you going to make me wear one of those hoop skirt dresses?"

It took me a minute to shift gears. "Not at all," I said. "The Living History is open to the public during certain hours of the day and that means there will be plenty of visitors in street clothes."

Her face fell. "Oh."

"You *want* to wear one?"

"Civil War re-enactments are pretty big around these parts. Have been since I was little. My parents used to take us, but I never got to wear the really fancy clothes. I guess I don't really need one." She looked up at me. "But . . . if I had one of those hoop skirts I could meander around even when it's closed to the public. I could fit in better if I looked like one of them."

Well, knock me over with a feather. Nodding, and thinking about that central "mall" Pierpont had pointed out on my visit to the camp, I encouraged her, "There's a group of shops in the center of the camp—sutlers, I think they're called—if you like, you can go there first and pick out a dress."

"This gets reimbursed because I'm doing this on company time, right?"

"You promise to be objective?"

A shrewd smile. "As objective as possible for me. That good enough?"

"I suppose it'll have to be."

MARSHFIELD MANOR BOASTED 150 ROOMS IN its colorful, tri-fold brochures, but I suspected that whoever had come up with that number had miscounted. Hidden rooms, secret rooms . . . I would bet there were at least a few dozen the brochure writer didn't know about. One of these days if things ever calmed down and we stopped having murders on property, I thought I might actually attempt counting them for myself.

In addition to my office, several other administrative areas occupied the third floor of the mansion's west wing. Bennett's private living space—a suite of rooms expansive enough for a large family to live comfortably—sat directly above. Both floors in this wing were off-limits to visitors. In my comings and goings, I could easily avoid the public rooms if I so chose, but I preferred routes that took me through the mansion's busier spaces.

I walked east from my office down the long corridor, emerging in the Gathering Hall. While the administrative areas smelled of industrial carpeting, fresh paint, and copy machines, the rest of the mansion smelled like history. Whenever I wandered through the main rooms of the house—like this one—all newness dissolved. Musty cushions, old lace, and traces of cigar smoke graced every corner. I imagined patient ghosts peeking out, waiting to share their stories. I loved every inch of the place.

When the Marshfield family had first built this home, they'd entertained hundreds of guests every year. This room was meant for exactly that—coming together late in the evening for card-playing, songs, and stories. The Gathering Hall had been repapered recently as part of our plan to restore and renovate the manor. Based on small pieces of wall coverings we'd found behind switch plates, and working from old photographs, a French company specializing in custom wallpaper had been able to re-create the original design. Another company—this time a local one—had restored four coordinating sofas and chairs.

I smiled as I took it all in. Despite the new additions, the scent and sense of times gone by managed to remain.

Continuing through the Gathering Hall, I skirted around

the visitor barricades and thought about everything that had gone on. While the police conducted their investigation on the south grounds, I still had an estate to run. There was plenty of work for me every minute of every day, from cataloguing new acquisitions, to overseeing scheduled maintenance, to trying to be clairvoyant by anticipating problems before they arose. I'd certainly fallen down on the job on that score. Of course, predicting murder hardly fell under my job description.

One of the most important aspects of my job, however, was taking care of its people. Bennett viewed his employees as family and I needed to prove to him that I could protect those he valued most. With that in mind, I decided to head outdoors to check on Davey. Even though not technically an employee of the manor, he was currently working for us. And a broken nose was no small deal.

I made my way to the very center of the home, past the wide, winding staircase to the east wing. Still too early in the morning for visitors, the staff was busy preparing for their eventual onslaught. No one saw me slip through the first door to my right into the back stairway. Red-walled and dark, with only scant light from narrow windows to keep the area passable during the day, the stairway wound around an elevator shaft, a black metal caged monstrosity that ran between the basement and the fourth floor.

I exited at the first floor and made my way to the glass-walled Birdcage Room where we served a sampling of the good life to guests in the form of afternoon tea. Waitresses and other staff members were busy placing fresh flowers on each of the tables, preparing for the busy day ahead.

Pushing through the outer doors of the Birdcage, I breathed in the clean morning air. Today would certainly warm up nicely—I could feel it, smell the mugginess in the air—and the hint of sun on my face this early portended a gorgeous day ahead.

I found Davey working on the tall evergreen hedges that

formed our garden maze. The young man wore a huge white bandage across his nose, with lines of white medical tape stretching out from side to side and up and down. His beard was gone—shaved, I assumed, by the doctor who'd reset Davey's nose—and his chin and upper lip were strangely pale in comparison to the rest of his face. When he spotted me, he stopped clipping the greenery and placed his giant pair of pruning shears on the ground.

"You need something, Ms. Wheaton?" he asked.

"I heard you were coming in today. Shouldn't you be home?" I said, "I mean, if you sweat out here—and you will—your bandage will come loose."

He shrugged. "I've got extra."

I waited for him to continue. He didn't. "How are you doing?" I asked.

Without looking at me he shrugged again. "Been better."

"Is there anything you need, or something I can do for you? I'm so sorry you were hurt. Don't you think you should take a few days off . . ."

"Ms. Wheaton . . ."

"Call me Grace."

"Can't. You're my boss. Jack always says we have to be formal with our clients." Turning away from me, he ran his hand along the neatly trimmed line of greenery that served as the northernmost wall of the maze. "I don't want any days off. What am I going to do? Sit home and stare? I do that too much already."

I let that go without comment. "The maze looks great."

He finally turned to me. "You think so? I don't see much difference."

"It's looking much better." I waited a beat, and even though I already knew the answer, I wanted to keep the conversation going. "So how long have you been working for Jack?"

He ducked his head, and picked up the giant shears. "He

told you I'm the family screwup, didn't he? That's why you're out here, right? To check to make sure I'm not messing up on the job?"

"Not at all. I was worried about you."

He gave me a sideways glance. "How come? You don't even know me."

Was he always this difficult? "You're right. I don't. So tell me about yourself."

My question seemed to amuse him. "Let's see . . . didn't go to college, can't keep a job. Mom died thinking she raised a loser son."

"Davey," I said sharply, "don't talk like that."

"But it's true. You know that children's story where everything the king touches turns to gold?"

I knew where this was going.

"Everything I touch turns to . . ." he pointed down toward the base of the shrubs, at the manure fertilizer, "that."

"Look at this maze of shrubbery," I said. "It's gorgeous. You're doing an awesome job."

For the first time, he smiled. It was a crooked little grin that reminded me of Jack's. These Embers boys were a handsome bunch all right. "Just wait," he said, "it won't take long. One of these days I'll do something to get Jack angry and he'll toss me back to my dad's place. And I'll watch TV and play video games until somebody decides I need another chance again. But I'll probably just screw that one up, too."

"That's a pretty fatalistic attitude."

Another shrug. His favorite means of communication, apparently. Though he was twenty-seven years old, Davey came across like a kid in junior high—one who hadn't yet learned how to converse with adults, nor make his own way in the world. I started to understand why Jack spent so much time with him. He needed help.

"I think you're doing great," I said. "This maze has never looked better."

"You're just saying that," he said with a frown. "I mean, it's not like I created it or anything. All I'm doing is maintaining the thing. You're just saying that to be nice."

I opened my mouth to protest, but the truth was I *had* been just saying that to make him feel better. Although the maze had gotten a tiny bit overgrown recently, Davey's trimming had brought it back to its regular pristine self. No better, no worse.

"If you need anything," I said, unable to find a reason to keep talking, "you be sure to let me know."

He nodded and turned back to his trimming. I could have sworn I heard him mutter under his breath, "Yeah, well, how about a new life?"

Chapter 13

AS I WALKED BACK, MY CELL PHONE RANG. IT was Jack. "Hey," he said when I answered, "how are you holding up?"

"Me? I'm worried about you."

"You've got enough on your plate," he said, "I shouldn't have burdened you yesterday."

"I'm glad you did. I really needed to know the truth."

"Thanks."

"For what?" I asked.

"For saying that. About my story being the truth. It means a lot that you believe me."

"Of course I do." I waited a second then added, "Tooney's at it again."

Jack groaned. "What now?"

I told him about the would-be detective's offer to find Bootsie's real owners. "The guy is incessant. He thinks that if he finds Bootsie's family, I'll hire him to work for Marshfield. Not a chance."

"How do you feel about that?"

"Hiring him for Marshfield?"

"About giving up your cat."

I was about to protest that she wasn't my cat, but my reaction to Jack's question took me by surprise. I didn't want Tooney to find the kitten's owners. Despite the fact that my nose ran and I constantly sneezed around the little critter, I hated the idea of giving her up. "Uh . . ."

"Thought so," Jack said. "Fire the guy. You've done your due diligence looking for her owners. I'm sure she's a stray. And now she's yours. Enjoy her."

"I don't know . . ."

"And to celebrate your new pet parenthood, how about you and I go out to dinner tomorrow night?"

"Nice segue," I said, as my stomach flip-flopped.

He laughed. "I try."

"I'd like that," I said.

"I'll pick you up at seven. How's that? We can go to Hugo's."

"How about I meet you there? It's close enough for me to walk."

He hesitated. "I'd prefer to pick you up, if you don't mind. We can then walk to Hugo's if you like. It's supposed to be a nice night and it might be good to have time to talk without a crowd around us."

"Sounds great. See you then."

TANK WAS WAITING FOR ME IN FRANCES'S OF-fice when I returned. "Perfect timing," I said. "I was planning to call you." Tank stood to shake my hand.

Frances beamed. "I thought so," she said. "That's why I made the call."

"Well . . . thank you." There were times I was so taken aback by Frances that I didn't know whether to be impressed by her efficiency or frightened by how well she could predict my moves. What if I'd stayed outside longer?

Or had decided to make one of my frequent visits to the Marshfield Hotel? Tank would have been brought here for nothing. But Frances accurately anticipated my every move, sometimes before I did.

"My pleasure," she said as Tank and I made our way into my office.

"She's a tough cookie, that one," Tank said after I closed the door.

Frances would hate being unable to eavesdrop, but the precaution was necessary. "That she is."

I took my seat at my desk and Tank settled herself across from me. We made a little small talk with me asking about her impressions of Emberstowne and her sharing a little bit about her family life back in Michigan. Pleasantries complete, she leaned forward. "What can I do for you, Ms. Wheaton?"

"How's the investigation coming?"

Her eyes narrowed and her nose wrinkled in a feminine expression that was totally out of place with the package I had come to know as Tank. "Truth?" she asked. "Not well. Our esteemed coroner asserts Kincade was stabbed to death. No surprise there. But he also believes Kincade was drunk as a skunk at the time." She made a face. "Problem is your coroner here is not a trained toxicologist. Getting an accurate blood alcohol level reading post mortem isn't as easy as they make it look on TV. But even without an exact reading we can assume Kincade was probably feeling no pain."

"Too drunk to defend himself?"

"That would explain the lack of defense wounds." She went on, "The task force has interviewed almost half of those crazy costumed people, but nobody saw anything. And I gotta tell you, I believe them."

"Nobody saw anything?" I repeated despondently.

"I don't think it was one of them, to be honest," she said. "They're all so . . . into their roles. And the ones I talked to seemed to like Kincade."

"Really? I met him for about ten minutes and couldn't stand the guy."

"Maybe he was a happy drunk. Who knows? Anyway, he was about to be promoted."

"To what?"

"Grand poo-bah . . . head honcho . . ." She tried to smile. "Just kidding. He was about to be crowned the new general. The group was going to vote on it and he looked like the heir apparent."

"You mean he would displace Pierpont?"

She waved a hand. "Don't go looking for motive there. Pierpont had already decided to step down of his own accord. Gave his notice a while ago. The guy who found the body—Jim Florian—was supposed to take Pierpont's spot, but over the past couple months, Kincade generated a groundswell of support. He looked like a shoo-in."

"So maybe Jim Florian got jealous and decided to eliminate the competition?"

She made a so-so motion with her head. "We haven't discounted that possibility."

"I really appreciate you being frank with me."

"Why not? We know you didn't do it. And from what I hear, you like being involved. I get that. I figure that if we're transparent with you, maybe you'll be transparent with us." She eased forward on the chair, making direct eye contact. "Now, before we go any further, I want to talk about the *first* Kincade murder. Lyle Kincade. Thirteen years ago."

"Um, sure . . ." I said warily. "You do know I didn't live here at that time?"

"Yeah, well neither did I," she said, smacking her lips, "but I also know you're tight with that Embers fellow. I'm sure he's given you his side of the story. That case was never closed, of course, but we have reason to look into it again now. I hope your intimacy with Jack Embers won't cloud your judgment or impair our investigation."

"You presume too much," I said frostily. "Jack and I are friends. That's all."

She squinted. "For now, maybe. But I warn you: Be careful around him."

"I don't believe Jack had anything to do with either murder."

"Of course." Her world-weary gaze communicated just how naïve she thought I was. "But what about the brother?"

"Davey? He couldn't have been more than fourteen or fifteen when Lyle Kincade was killed. There's no way."

"Maybe Jack Embers killed Lyle and little brother Davey killed Zachary."

"And maybe not. From what I understand, Lyle was a jerk."

"Doesn't mean he deserved to be murdered."

"I'm not saying it does. But jerks make enemies. Anybody could have killed him. These two cases don't *have* to be related. It could just be a terrible coincidence that these two families collided again."

"Maybe so," she said, as unconvinced as ever, "but I don't like coincidences and I intend to find out the truth. Did Pierpont tell about that unlocked back gate on the property? The one that was suddenly locked again when we checked it?"

I nodded.

"According to your head of security, there are only three keys for that back lock. You have one, security has another"—she pointed at me for emphasis—"and your landscape consultant has the third. Supposedly for ease of access with heavy-duty machinery. So he won't disturb guests by coming in via public roads."

"That's correct."

"I have no doubt that was the key's original intended use. You have to admit, however, the evidence is mounting." She glanced out the wall of windows to her right. "You talked with that younger Embers kid yet?"

"Today, as a matter of fact."

She shook her head. "Damaged goods."

I didn't ask what she meant by that. I knew. I also didn't offer up the fact that Jack felt responsible for his brother's troubles. To do so would only make Jack look guiltier. My gut told me to protect him. At least for now.

"What I wanted to talk with you about . . ." I said, changing the subject, "I don't want to impede your progress, but do you think you can interview the rest of the re-enactors *away* from the campsite? It doesn't have to be far. We can offer you one of the nearby buildings on property to use for as long as you like. The actual Living History event starts tomorrow. They have drills and shooting contests scheduled. They're preparing for a big battle re-enactment on Saturday. Mr. Pierpont and his people are hoping they can have their guns back for practice."

She heaved a deep sigh. "People want their lives back faster and faster all the time. They want normal so they can feel safe again. Don't they understand? They still *have* their lives. But one of their friends does not." Grasping the armrests, she pushed herself to her feet. "Your secretary . . ." she said tilting her head toward Frances's office.

"Assistant," I corrected.

"Whatever. She told me about your suggestion for her to go in undercover."

"It may be a waste of time, but you never know. Frances is planning to visit the encampment this afternoon to buy the supplies she needs and then she'll start snooping tomorrow. She's the queen of gossip. If anyone can get the goods on people, she can."

"Smart move."

"Thanks."

"Next time you hatch a plan like that, however, it would be better to hear it from you first." She pointed her index finger at me like a gun. "Like I said, transparency goes both ways."

Chapter 14

WHEN FRANCES WALKED IN THE NEXT MORN-
ing, I barely recognized her. "Look at you," I exclaimed as
she navigated through the doorway with her hoop skirt.
Bumping, twisting, and complaining the whole time, she
finally made it all the way into the office out of breath.
"You look beautiful."

Gripping the cream-and-chocolate-brown-patterned
fabric with both fists, she glanced up at me in surprise, her
face flushing dark pink all the way down her neck into the
lace collar. "Thank you," she said. "This was the only one I
could find in my size that didn't make me look like a house."

I circled the air with my index finger indicating she
should turn around. She frowned, but obliged me with a
reluctant pirouette.

"Wow," I said. "Absolutely lovely." I came closer and
reached for the fabric. "May I?"

She shrugged. "You paid for it."

"Such quality." And it was. The fabric was heavier than
I'd expected, crafted from natural fabrics. "It might get

warm out there in this. This is obviously a dress gown. Did
you get yourself an everyday outfit, too?"

She nodded and pulled her hem up for me to see. "Look
at that stitching. Hand-sewn, all of it."

"These dresses must be expensive."

A wary look flashed in her eyes. "You told me it was
okay to buy it."

"Yes, of course it is. I'm just impressed by the handi-
work, that's all."

"I talked with that Pierpont fellow when I was down
there," she said. "He told me that for the opening ceremonies they want everyone in their ball gowns. So that's why
I'm wearing this so early. After the morning events, we're
all supposed to change into more comfortable period clothing. But it isn't required."

"Where will you get changed?"

"Mr. Pierpont said that a group of women share a very
large tent and they'll be happy to let me pop in now and
then when I need to. It shouldn't be any big deal. It's not
like I need a place to sleep or anything."

"A group of women sharing a tent?" I asked, suddenly
suspicious. Maybe Pierpont had a sense of humor after all.
"Did this group have a name?"

"A bird group," she said. "Pigeons or something?"

"Was it doves?" I asked.

"I think that was it."

I laughed out loud. "Soiled doves?"

Frances turned red again as comprehension dawned.
"Oh no . . ."

"Don't worry, they aren't really working girls. They're
wives of soldiers. This is their way to have a little fun. Female bonding."

Frances sniffed. "Just so they know I don't intend to
participate in any . . . questionable activity."

"This is all just pretend, Frances, I'm sure you'll be fine.
By the way, does Pierpont know the real reason you're par-

ticipating? I know your cover story is that this is an activity you've always wanted to try, but given the timing, I suppose it doesn't take much to put two and two together."

"Mr. Pierpont said he thought it was a marvelous idea," she said, rolling the word off her tongue accompanied by wide hand gestures. "That's exactly how he said it, too. I think that man may be a little light in the loafers." Then, perhaps remembering my two best friends, she added, "Not that there's anything wrong with that."

Rather than dwell on her gaffe, I decided to lighten the moment. "If there's one thing I can probably guarantee," I said, "it's that Pierpont isn't wearing loafers. They would be far by."

Frances and I decided that since the Living History was open for a portion of each day there would be no problem if I came to visit during those hours.

Frances appraised the office with a skeptical eye. "Are you sure you're going to be able to handle everything by yourself while I'm gone? You know I'm not allowed any technology down there. I can't even carry a cell phone."

My knee-jerk reaction was to say everything would be fine without her, but the moment I opened my mouth it occurred to me that such a response could be construed as diminishing Frances's importance.

"That's why I need to come down there to check in with you from time to time," I said. "You keep the place running so smoothly, I know I'll have plenty of questions."

That had clearly been the right answer. With a little chuff of pride and a squaring of her shoulders, she nodded acknowledgment. "Well, you know where to find me," she said. And with that she smoothed her skirt and maneuvered her way back out the door.

THERE WAS, INDEED, PLENTY TO KEEP ME busy throughout the day. Without Frances to run interference I found myself swamped in minutiae. The woman might be a trial on a personal level, but boy, was she good at her job. I'd been taught that no one was indispensable, but to my mind, Frances came pretty darn close. If only we could work on that attitude problem.

I thought about her several times during the day, wondering how she was faring at the encampment and eager to hear if she'd picked up any information worth sharing with Rodriguez and Tank. Fidgety Flynn, the hothead detective of the bunch, seemed to be out of the loop this time around. Thank heavens for small favors. Quick to accuse and reluctant to back down, he injected a volatile element I was happy to avoid.

The outer door to Frances's office opened and I stood up to greet whoever my visitor might be. By the time I walked around the desk, however, Bennett had already made his way through the anteroom and into my office. As septuagenarians went, Bennett was a strikingly handsome man. Blessed with good genes and the smarts to hire trainers who put him through the paces of a healthy regimen, Bennett could probably take on a man twenty years his junior and win.

"Good afternoon, Gracie. And how is our manor today?"

I gestured toward the wing chairs opposite my desk and took my seat behind it. "Not bad, all things considering," I said. I told him about Frances's undercover expedition.

His eyes widened. "Oh ho! Brilliant! That woman can coax gossip out of gargoyles. I swear she knows more about me than I do about myself."

"She is tenacious."

"That's a kind way to put it."

"When did she start working here?" I asked. "I mean, unless she suffered some major personality shift over the years, I wonder how she originally landed the job."

"To be honest, I can't remember. I'll have to think about that. I'm sure she knew someone who knew someone. Back in those days we didn't have much of a command structure in place. If you showed up and were willing to work, you were in."

Pretty much what I'd assumed.

"How is the cat?" he asked.

That startled me speechless for a half a second. "How do you know about the cat?"

He pointed toward Frances's office.

"And how does she know?" I asked, ever so slightly exasperated. I sighed. Should have anticipated this. "Bootsie is great. Unfortunately, I seem to be allergic."

His eyes brightened. "You are? How bad?"

"Sniffling, sneezing. My eyes sometimes feel a little puffy in the morning. Nothing I can't handle."

He considered this. "I have two cats."

"I know." Bennett's pets stayed up in his living space and most of us on staff rarely saw them.

"What you may not know is that I'm allergic, too. Slightly."

I leaned forward. "Seriously?"

"Mm-hmm," he said with a knowing look. "Something else you and I have in common, eh? I wonder what else we'll discover over time."

He'd just echoed my very thoughts.

"I don't know about you," he continued, "but I don't cotton to the idea of taking pills every day of my life just because I happen to have pets."

"Exactly!"

Leaning forward, he asked, "Are you keeping the little rascal?"

"Until I find her real owners," I said, "although our friend Ronny Tooney may beat me to it." I explained the man's eager involvement in Bootsie's future.

"Just in case you decide to keep her, let me offer you a home remedy," he said. "It works for me, I'm sure it will for you, too."

As he explained how he upped his daily intake of water, made certain to wash his hands every time he handled the cats, and cultivated a mind-over-matter attitude, I thought about how much I cared about this man. How much I wanted to please him. Though it was true that he was often out of touch where the real world was concerned, I'd come to understand that here—within Marshfield's walls—was the only world he'd ever known. As lively as a child, but with a lifetime's worth of wisdom behind those bright eyes, he was kind, generous, and eager to pull me into the Marshfield fold.

I wanted that, too.

A little voice whispered: *Enough to give up your house, your roommates, your independence?*

"Try it," Bennett was saying. "It will take time. A few weeks at least, but don't give up. I believe your body will eventually adjust—although you probably will have to blow your nose every morning."

"I hope you're right about all that. She's such a cutie."

The conversation turned to the new arrival—this time not an animal, but the item Bennett had recently purchased at auction. "You're going to love it," he said, his eyes sparkling.

My interest had been piqued from the moment he'd first mentioned it. Now I was practically ready to burst. "What is it?"

"Nope. Not yet. You'll have to wait."

I remembered Frances's pronouncement that if Abe had been here, he'd have been fully informed. Why keep it from me, then? I tried to force Frances's admonishments out of my mind while maintaining a cheerful air. But I had to ask, "Why the big secret?"

"Well," he drew out the word, "this is special. Any other time, I would have told you right off the bat."

"Really?"

"Why wouldn't I?" he asked rhetorically. "But this time I want to see your face when it comes in. It's due to arrive tomorrow. I'll let you know when it gets here and we'll check it out together."

Curiosity had me in its tantalizing grip. "Not even a hint?"

"Sorry, Gracie," he said with a grin, "you'll just have to wait."

Chapter 15

LATER THAT AFTERNOON WHEN I KNEW THE
Living History would be open to the public, I called down
to maintenance to request a ride to the site. Except for the
manor's shuttles, vans transporting staff members to and
fro, and of course, Bennett's cars, we tried our best to keep
motor vehicles out of our guests' sight. The idea was to
encourage visitors to experience the manor as its first
guests had experienced it, back in the day when horses and
buggies were the only real means of transportation. I supposed in many ways we at Marshfield weren't all that dis-
similar from the Civil War groupies. We wanted people to
let go of the real world for a little while—to be transported
from the craziness of the twenty-first century. To play
pretend.

When one of Marshfield's white minivans pulled up at
the back door, I was surprised to find Davey at the wheel.
The enormous bandage had been replaced by a much
smaller, flesh-colored strip across the center of his nose.
"How did you get roped into this job?" I asked as I climbed

into the passenger seat and rolled down the window. Too beautiful a day to keep the weather out.

He shrugged. "Guess the rest of the gardening staff doesn't want me around."

"I don't believe that for a minute," I said. He put the van into drive and I asked, "No other passengers?"

He gave a short, mirthless laugh. "No." A young man of few words, he shook his head as he pulled out. We cleared the ornamental iron gate that separated the manor house from the rest of its expansive grounds. He had his right hand draped over the wheel, his left elbow perched on the open window. "You don't have to do that, you know," he said.

"Do what?"

"Always try to cheer me up. I'm not blind or just feeling sorry for myself. I know that I'm doing a decent job on whatever projects Jack assigns, but the guys I'm working with?" He extended his fingers in emphasis, the heel of his hand guiding the car as he explained, "They're convinced I killed that Civil War dude. You can see it in their faces and they all try to steer clear of me." Keeping his eyes on the road, he gripped the wheel again, hard. "Can't really blame them, I guess. I'm bad news."

I didn't know what to say to that.

"Jack talked to the head of maintenance so maybe I could get some other training. Maybe learn a new skill or something. The guy in charge was cool about it." Still not looking at me, he added, "I can't keep a job myself. If it wasn't for Jack . . . 'Course, look at the job the guy gave me. No contact with visitors, hardly any contact with staff." His mouth twisted downward and he gave another unhappy laugh. "Let's keep everybody safe from the lunatic."

I started to argue, but that would just be me trying to cheer him up again. Instead I took a different approach. "How is it," I asked, "living with Jack?"

For the first time he turned to look at me. "Why? You thinking about moving in with him?"

"No. No. I was just making conversation."

He'd returned his attention to the road but glanced at me again. "You're blushing. You like him, don't you?"

"Does it matter?"

"If you wanted to move in with Jack, I'd find somewhere else to live."

"I'm not looking to move in with Jack," I said, exasperated. "We haven't even gone out on a date yet."

"Yeah, I know. Sorry. I shouldn't tease you." The hint of a smile curved his lips. "To answer your question, living with Jack is all right, I guess. He's clean. He cooks, too. That's cool."

So far, this was more than Davey had ever said to me at one time. I had a feeling he wasn't finished.

"Jack's a good brother. He sure cuts me a lot of slack. I don't know if I'd be that nice to somebody like me. I'm trouble. But he still always looks out for me. Sometimes too much, and it bugs me. But I can't really blame him for that. I've sure given him plenty of reason to worry."

We were silent for a long moment as the van eased up a small rise in the road and passed beneath a canopy of tall maples, giving us a brief respite from the sun.

"I need to find my way," he said quietly. "It's tough."

We were silent again. "I hear you," I said finally. "I'm still finding *my* way."

"You?" He turned to me in disbelief. "You're the boss here."

"So?"

"They wouldn't have hired you for your job if you didn't know what you were doing."

Davey must not have heard the circumstances behind my promotion. "I've got news for you," I said, "a lot of people don't know what they're doing. Some of us just hide it better than others. But I've learned a lot about myself these past few months." Taking a deep breath of the crisp air, I added, "Something about this place brings out the best in me."

"You've got everybody fooled then. You come across like Wonder Woman."

"Yeah, right." I had no idea why I felt comfortable opening up to Davey, but I plunged on. "The truth is, I'm just struggling to be the person everybody thinks I already am." I gave a low laugh, though this was anything but funny. It was truth as bare-bones as it could be. "I often feel as though I'm living two lives. One is the façade that everyone sees, and the other is trying desperately to make that façade come true." I sighed. "That probably doesn't make any sense."

Still facing forward, he gave a brief nod. "Makes more sense than you know. I feel like that, too." A moment later he added, "Jack's probably the best person on the planet. He's good, you know? Genuine."

"He doesn't face the same struggles?"

"Jack went through a lot when . . ." Davey took a breath. "He went through a lot last time. I can't even imagine . . ." He let the thought trail off just as we reached the encampment. I wanted to hear more, but Davey's expression darkened. "He turned his life around though; wish I could do the same."

"You were so young when everything happened. Last time, I mean."

Davey's eyes clouded. "Not young enough."

I wondered what he meant by that but before I could press him, Davey had put the van in park and shut it off. "I'm going in there, too," he said by way of explanation. "I want to see what it's all about. Sounds kind of interesting."

The killer always returns to the scene of the crime. The thought popped in, unbidden. "Oh, sure," I replied blandly, taken aback by his pronouncement. I didn't know how to broach the next delicate question. If he thought his co-workers suspected him, he was in for far more scrutiny from the re-enactors who had all heard about the skirmish the day of Zachary's death. "But aren't you afraid . . ."

"That people will have a problem with me strolling around?"

"Yeah."

He dug a baseball cap out from his back pocket and snugged it over his head. "I can't wear sunglasses for a couple of days yet—doctor's orders—but I think I'll be fine. None of these folks have actually ever met me. I'd be surprised if anyone even gives me a second look." He rubbed his clean-shaven face. "Especially now. Nobody really ever does. I kinda blend, you know?"

The only person who had seen Davey close-up was Pierpont, and that was when Davey still had his beard. With that gone, and the addition of the hat, he should be safe.

"Anyway," Davey continued, "I think this Civil War thing sounds like fun."

Fun. Although I'd known the young man only a short time, I sensed he rarely found life "fun." "It does," I agreed.

As we descended the hill to enter the re-enactors' camp, Davey stopped and looked around. "Way cool," he said, stepping into the crowd.

"Have a good time."

He started away, then called for me to hold up. "Here you go," he said, handing me the keys to the van.

"But . . ."

"I'll find my own way back. I left a note with the maintenance guy. Told him thanks but no thanks on this job. I'll give my notice to Jack later today. I guess that means I'm telling you now, huh?"

Stunned, I said, "But Davey, you were doing so well."

"No," he said, "you just wanted to believe I was. Thanks for your support, Grace. I really do appreciate it."

"Yeah, of course," I said, but he'd already turned away, setting off for the far end where the Confederate tents were set up.

Chapter 16

❦

I ENTERED THE LIVING HISTORY STUNNED BY
Davey's abrupt resignation. There was more going on than
he let on, of that I was sure. I sighed. With him no longer
employed at the manor, I might never find out what it was.

There were so many visitors—easily distinguishable
from the re-enactors by virtue of their contemporary
clothing—that it looked more like a giant block party than
a soldiers' camp. Surrounded by tourists in capris and
sports jerseys consulting BlackBerrys, Civil War women
carried pots and baskets, their skirts generating little puffs
of dust as the material skimmed the ground. Even though
the re-enactors had only been here since Friday, patches of
grass had already been worn down to bare dirt. The participants concentrated on their tasks, but seemed happy—
eager, even—to take the time to answer questions whenever
a T-shirt-clad tourist stopped them to talk. The sutlers in the
very center of camp were doing a brisk business. No wonder the re-enactors, for all their disparagement of "farby,"
chose to open their camp to the public from time to time.

I had no difficulty finding Rob Pierpont. Standing at the northeast corner of the camp with his arms folded and an intense expression on his face, he looked exactly the way I would have expected a high-ranking officer to look. His buttons and decorations contrasted brightly against the dark blue of his jacket. Although the temperature was only in the seventies, he had to be sweltering under all that wool. Plus, he wore a hat and boots. Angled as he was toward the gathering, he didn't see me approach.

Pierpont wasn't a tall man. But what he lacked in stature he made up for in his bearing. Nodding and murmuring greetings to passersby as they said hello, he stood with his feet shoulder-width apart, his gaze darting from spot to spot to spot, surveying everything with keen interest. He reminded me of a chubby, bearded meerkat. In uniform.

"Mr. Pierpont," I said.

He turned, smiling when he saw me. "Good afternoon, Ms. Wheaton. What brings you here today?"

"I'm sorry to bother you. Are you allowed to talk with me? Or is that . . . farby?"

"Of course I can talk with you. That's part of what Living History is all about. We strive to educate nonmembers. Who knows, we might even entice you to join us in future outings."

"You never know," I said. *Not a chance,* I thought. "I spoke with the police about your concerns."

"And?"

"It's up to them now. I offered them a location to use off-site, but I don't know how convincing I was."

"Thank you for your efforts, Ms. Wheaton," he said. "I truly appreciate it."

"By the way," I continued, "do you remember Davey, the young man Zachary Kincade attacked?"

"He and I were never introduced, if that's what you mean, but I do recall the incident." Pierpont fixed me with a quizzical stare. "Why?"

Despite Davey's attempts to wander incognito there was still a chance, however slight, Pierpont might recognize him. The last thing we needed was for this Union general to sound an alarm.

"He's here," I said.

Pierpont's eyebrows jumped. "I don't understand. Shouldn't the police have forbidden that? After all, he is a suspect." The little man shook his head. "I'm not sure I'm comfortable with him wandering around."

"Davey was under sedation at the time of the murder," I said smoothly, pushing away any of my own suspicions as I tried to allay Pierpont's fears. "He's got an airtight alibi. And remember, it was Zachary who attacked Davey, not the other way around. Davey probably hadn't even met the man before the altercation."

Concern tightened Pierpont's features. "What in the world is he doing here, then?"

"He claims to be interested in your re-enactment. He says it looks like 'fun.'"

For the second time in as many minutes, I could tell I'd surprised Pierpont. "Do you believe him?"

I gave a very Davey-like shrug. "I guess I do."

"Hmm . . ." Pierpont was silent for a long moment. "Maybe I'll have a talk with him and assess for myself." He began scanning the crowd. "He could be anywhere, but I should be able to recognize him." Turning to me again, he said, "Do you really think he's interested in joining? He's not just here to do some intelligence-gathering to exonerate his brother?"

"Who am I to know?" I said. "But his motives seemed genuine. By the way, his beard has been shaved."

"Pity. I hope he's willing to grow it back. We like beards." He stroked his own and said, "I'll see what I can find out from the young man. If he's truly attracted to re-enacting, then I'll coach him. Mentor him if he needs it. But if he has a hidden agenda, I'll have no choice but to have him removed."

A troop of soldiers, most of them in ragtag outfits, marched by.

"Drills," Pierpont explained as they passed. "The crowds really enjoy them."

"By the way, I'm here to talk with Frances. Have you seen her?"

"Your assistant? No, not for some time. I didn't even realize she was still here."

"I hope she is," I said, taking my leave.

"She may prefer to leave the premises by sundown," he said. "The doves can get pretty intimidating."

"Thanks for the warning. She and I will be heading back shortly."

He nodded acknowledgment and turned back to watch more troops march by.

I made a wide circuit of the area, reasoning that I'd have better luck spotting Frances from the outside looking in. Out here on the perimeter what grass remained was coarse and dry, tickling my ankles as I picked my way around. I'd been smart enough not to wear heels today, but the flats I'd chosen were not made of solid material. Designed for airiness, they had little decorative holes up and down both sides. Holes just perfect for prickly weeds and burrs to scratch my feet.

Circling counterclockwise, I'd gotten about halfway through the Union side and almost to the sutlers' tents when I spied her—still in her ball gown—talking with a tall gentleman in a Union officers' uniform. They faced each other on either side of a cold campfire complete with cauldron, just waiting for someone to start a fire. From here, the man looked to be in his late forties, with mutton-chops and a thick mustache. I started toward her, reluctant to interrupt, but when she saw me she waved me to join them.

"This is Ms. Wheaton," she said to the man as I took a spot next to her. "She's the one I told you about."

Inwardly, I groaned. What tales could she possibly be telling?

I extended my hand, but instead of shaking it, the man grasped my fingers in his gloved ones and made a courtly little bow. "A pleasure."

I reassessed. Late thirties or early forties. All that facial hair aged him.

Before I could ask, Frances provided the answer. "This is Jim Florian. He and I were having a lovely conversation just now about how important it is to keep things as authentic as possible."

"Jim Florian," I repeated. "I know your name. You're . . ."

Frances delivered a sharp kick to my ankle.

I'd been about to say that he'd been the one to find Zachary Kincade's body, but I took the hint. "You're . . ." I stretched to find an appropriate finish to my sentence. Frances apparently had no faith in me and kicked again, this time harder. I sucked in the pain so he wouldn't see me wince. "You're . . . second in command here, aren't you?"

"That's right," he said, smiling. "From what I understand, that's a position you and I share."

I inched away from Frances. She inched with me.

"Yes, I suppose that's one way of looking at it." Reluctant to say anything that might further incapacitate me, I smiled blandly at Frances. She smiled back.

We both smiled at Jim. He smiled back.

This wasn't getting me anywhere. "Well," I said, bringing my hands together in an "all done here" gesture, "we might want to start heading back, Frances. That is, if you're ready."

"So soon?"

She'd been here all day. It was nearly five o'clock and I had a dinner date tonight with Jack. "You're planning to return tomorrow, aren't you?" I asked.

The smile still plastered on her face, she narrowed her eyes and cocked one eyebrow. Quite a feat. I doubted I could duplicate it. "But I'm having such a nice conversation with Captain Florian here," she said.

"Colonel," he corrected.

"*Colonel* Florian," Frances amended smoothly, "will probably be promoted at the end of the week. He'll take over for General Pierpont, who is stepping down. I guess the job gets to be too much after so many years. Is that it?" she asked him.

"Pierpont has been the top man for more than ten years. It takes a lot of effort, even off the field, to organize this many people, to notify everyone when we're meeting. To set up the location . . . you get the picture."

"But I'm sure there's prestige in holding that position," I said.

He waved his hand dismissively. "Oh yeah. Big time. When you're in charge here, you're the man."

Frances jumped in. "And you're the next in line, right?"

Jim Florian's expression fell. "I wish I could feel better about it. I've been gunning to take the job for a while, and I thought I had it, but Zachary Kincade—the guy who got killed—started to talk about taking over. To be honest, he wasn't cut out for the job, but that didn't stop him from trying to muscle me out."

Was Florian actually giving us his motive for killing Kincade?

Frances fixed me with a look that said, "See why we needed to stay?" She asked Florian, "And it looked like he was going to win, didn't it?"

Florian nodded.

"Were you disappointed?" I asked.

"Oh sure. I've been re-enacting since I was a kid. My dad died before he could rise to the rank of general, so I've always wanted to do it, you know, in his honor. It would have meant a lot to him to see his son as the top man."

Before I could come up with a way to keep him talking, Florian offered up another tidbit. "But then"—he jerked a thumb toward the hill behind which Kincade was murdered—"that happened. I felt real bad about that." He pointed to himself. "I found the body, you know."

"Did you?" I asked innocently.

Frances continued to smile encouragingly. "That had to be devastating," she said.

"Tell me about it. I mean, I've seen death before, but not like this." He looked away, shaking his head. "And I've never *benefited* from somebody dying. This is just terrible. I feel guilty, you know? The troops really wanted Zachary to be the new general. He's not as hard-core as Pierpont, and I think in this day and age people still want to immerse themselves but they crave their creature comforts as well. Zachary understood that and I guess that's why everyone supported him." He worked his tongue in his cheek. "I've always been more of a progressive myself. I like to keep the event as authentic as possible. I can get obsessive about it, actually. Almost as much as Pierpont. And it bugged me that Zachary planned to change everything. To loosen our standards. That's why I didn't think he was a good choice for the job. But things change, I guess."

I wanted to ask him to write all that down and sign it. I'd be happy to deliver a copy to Tank on my way home.

"The mood has shifted in the ranks," he said. "I've been trying to ignore it, but it's been slowly changing every year. Gives me food for thought. Maybe when I take over I'll consider implementing some of Zachary's updated ideas. I won't like it, but it's better to be commanding happy re-enactors than to command no one at all."

We talked a little more and although I needed to get back to the manor to pick up my car and race home for my date tonight, I stayed rooted to the spot. The only thing that prevented me from accepting Florian's guilt, however, was his soft-spoken, earnest admission that he'd benefited from Kincade's death. Guilt propelled him to spill his guts, but to me it felt more like survivor guilt than killer guilt.

A kid ran up to him. "Dad, Mom needs you back at the tent."

Florian nodded to both of us, tipped his hat and said, "Duty calls."

Frances and I thanked him and started the climb up the small hill toward the van. We walked at a slower pace than I would have liked, but I appreciated how hard it was for her to move in that giant gown. "Well, wasn't that something?" she said the moment we were out of everyone's earshot.

"I'd say so. I didn't realize how big of a deal this re-enacting is."

"A lot of the folks I talked with were ready to put Zachary Kincade in charge." She huffed as we crested the hill. "Some reluctantly—and I found that odd, but they were the old-timers and less willing to talk than the younger participants. These young people—and by that I mean those under forty—want authenticity, but within limits. Some of the rules in place here now are pretty strict. Even though their tents are off-limits to visitors, everything in them has to be approved despite the fact that no one will see any of it. These people are even required to keep their coolers in their cars."

"That's a problem?"

"You bet it is. Say your kid wants a cold drink, or it's time to prepare dinner, you have to trek all the way here"—she pointed—"to get your supplies, only to have to trek back again like a pack mule. A lot of them try to hide their twenty-first-century equipment where the progressives won't see."

"What happens if they get caught?"

"They're fined. It's not a lot, and the money all goes toward regiment expenses, but I can see how that would take the fun out of things, can't you?"

We were walking down the other side of the hill now. "The van's just ahead," I said. "You doing okay?"

Her breath was coming in short gasps. "Just fine."

"So I take it you think Florian is our man."

"You don't?"

I kept my strides short so as not to outpace my assistant. "He handed us his motive on a silver platter. The murderer would never have done that, not unless he was incredibly wily and trying to throw us off the scent by coming across like a nice guy who could never do such a horrendous thing. He doesn't strike me as smart enough for that."

Frances was silent. When I turned to look at her, she was staring right at me. "Know what Florian does for a living?" she asked.

"No idea."

"He's a rocket scientist."

I stopped walking. She did, too.

"Yes, ma'am," she said, "a bona fide rocket scientist. Top man of his division at NASA. And a private inventor on the side. Has about thirty patents to his name."

I stayed silent.

"Beside this Civil War hobby, he has one other," she added. "Chess player. Championship level." She waited a beat before continuing, "Still think he's not all that sharp?"

I stared back the way we'd come even though I could no longer see the encampment. "Well, what do you know about that."

Chapter 17

"I DON'T KNOW," BRUCE SAID THAT EVENING, "after all the times your plans with this guy have fizzled and with his connections to these murders, are you sure you still want to go out with him?"

I'd left the door to my bathroom open and Bruce stood in the doorway holding Bootsie as he watched me twist my blonde hair around the hot curling iron. I didn't need to defend my decision. "What are you doing home so early?" I asked.

"Business is slow tonight and I'm completely wiped. Scott told me he'd handle things and sent me home. Don't change the subject." He gave me a critical look. "What are you planning to wear?"

"Black cotton skirt, pink top, silver flats."

He made a so-so gesture with his head. Bruce was the more fashion-conscious of the two men. Scott's interests gravitated more toward paperwork and sales figures. More than once, Bruce and I had to talk him out of wearing the same shirt-and-pants combination three times the same week. "But it's so much easier that way," he'd said. "Besides, no one even notices what I've got on."

Bruce had said, "I notice," and had taken it upon himself to try to help his partner develop a personal style. So far Scott had made a little progress, accumulating a handful of new shirts and several pairs of pants. I wouldn't term Bruce's efforts a rousing success. Not yet at least. But he did have an eye for style and color. I valued his input.

"I thought you *liked* Jack," I said.

"The pink and silver are fine. But a skirt? Could give him the wrong impression."

I started to balk, but he interrupted.

"Sweetie, you've been waiting to go out with this guy for months, right? He's constantly disappointing you."

"It hasn't been his fault."

"Don't defend him. He's a big boy and responsible for his own actions. I admit, I liked the guy, too, when we first met him. But now . . . the jury's out. I think you need to dress it down a little. Don't come across so eager."

"I'm not *eager*," I said. "And besides, I wear skirts to work all the time."

He narrowed his eyes as though picturing me in the outfit I'd described. "This is different. He's going to be looking for clues. Show him this is no big deal for you. Wear jeans."

"You're overanalyzing."

Scratching Bootsie behind the ears, he wore a rueful smile. "Kitty and I are going to take a nap on the couch. Wake me up when you get in. I want to hear all about it."

"Don't get attached to her," I said as he walked away. "That Tooney guy promised to find her owners."

"Too late," he called as he walked down the stairs. When he reached the bottom, he shouted, "And don't *you* get attached to your gardener, either."

I stared at my reflection in the mirror and whispered, "Too late."

* * *

TO ENSURE THAT JACK'S ARRIVAL WOULDN'T wake snoozing Bruce, I decided to wait on the front porch. I stepped outside just a little before seven. My skirt fluttered in the breeze, twisting around my bare legs. I took a deep breath of the warm evening air thinking that Jack had been right. This was perfect weather for walking together. I wondered if he would walk all the way here from his house or if he planned to drive and leave his car. Jack lived about a mile or so on the other side of Hugo's. I probably should have asked.

I strolled over to the far side of my porch and looked up at the hole in the ceiling. At one point this spot had boasted a two-person swing but shortly after Bruce and Scott had come to live here, it had crashed when they had tried it out. The porch roof's beams—rotted from years of neglect—had given way, dropping them both to the floor. Lots of bumps and bruises but no serious injuries. Thank goodness.

I thought back to when I was just getting to know my roommates. Back when my mom was dying and when my sister avoided dealing with our mother's terminal illness yet managed to find time to flirt with my fiancé. Liza and Eric were out of my life now. At least until the next time Liza called in dire need of cash because she'd gotten into trouble again. *Sorry, sis,* I thought. *You're a married woman now. Let your husband bail you out.*

I shook myself to dispel the negativity. This was no way to start a first date. I pulled my cell phone out of my purse pocket and glanced at the time. I'd been outside for about ten minutes. Seven-oh-five.

The floorboards creaked as I made my way back across, passing the front door again. This house needed more work than I could keep up with. I thought about Bennett's offer to help me repair, clean, and spruce up the place. I knew that this was his attempt to bring me into the family fold.

But I wasn't ready to turn this house into a tourist stop, nor move into the curator's cottage on my own. That seemed like a step away from the independence I'd been trying so hard to cultivate. I'd lived alone and with roommates in apartments before, but being a homeowner was new and different. I needed to prove I could do it.

Although I often found myself overwhelmed and more than a little terrified, I had to admit to another emotion as well: exhilaration. I felt stronger than I ever had before. Surviving the tough times through the death of my mom and subsequent disappearance of my sister, I'd grown in ways I'd never imagined I could. I was still a people-pleaser by nature—and probably always would be—but down deep in my soul something had shifted. And I liked it.

This job as curator and director of Marshfield—though I wished I'd come into it another way—was the instrument for much of this change. I'd always felt uncomfortable with conflict and avoided sticking up for myself. But I'd discovered I had no trouble standing up for members of my staff. I viewed these situations less as confrontations and more as my responsibility to be an advocate for my people. Even better, I was learning to be an advocate for myself.

The wind brought a delicious gust of green-scented air. Caught up in my reverie, I'd almost forgotten I was leaning on a shabby porch rail staring out over a cracked driveway and a lawn overrun with weeds. Back to reality. I checked my cell phone clock again. Jack was late. More than just fashionably.

The urge to walk down to the street to see if he was coming was overwhelming, but I held myself back. That would undoubtedly make me look too eager. He had said seven, hadn't he? I was sure of it.

Jack was not one of those chronically late people, so this was surprising. He'd always arrived for meetings at the manor right on time if not a little bit early. Had he forgotten? Did I get the day wrong? Had something happened to him? I glanced at my cell phone again. I hadn't missed any calls or messages.

Why did Jack and I seem to be cursed every time we tried to go out together? That had to be it. Not his fault.

Bruce's voice singsonged in my head. *Defending him again?*

I decided to give Jack another few minutes and if he still didn't show, I'd call.

Sitting on the top step in a skirt wasn't exactly ladylike, but I figured that if I forced my body to relax, my mind might follow suit. I had my backside down on the uneven floorboards for about two minutes before I realized that this plan wasn't going to work. My body was quiet but my mind kept jumping around. I waited, adjusting myself to find a comfortable spot on the bumpy floor. *Yet another repair,* I thought.

Financially, it made sense for me to take Bennett up on his offer. But in my heart it just didn't feel right. I was finally making it on my own, finally making friends here. To live and work within the fancy gates of Marshfield Manor would be to isolate myself again. I'd had enough of that, thank you very much.

I wondered if that was what had caused me to fall so hard and so quickly for Eric. I'd been wrapped up in school, work, not to mention my career in New York. Always trying to keep ahead of my bills, barely making time for fun.

Eric had been the first guy to show interest in me after I'd decided that all work and no play was making Grace a dull girl. Hindsight allowed me to see just how emotionally vulnerable I'd been back then. Thank goodness he'd left me when he had, otherwise it might be me rather than Liza married to him right now.

I forced myself to smile at the thought. It didn't work. Their double deceit still hurt.

Why was I dwelling on this tonight? For the second time since I came outside, I pushed negativity away.

When the wind lifted the edge of my skirt again, I didn't even bother checking the time. I got to my feet dreading the idea of having to face Bruce and admit I'd been stood up.

So much for plans. So much for the gorgeous night.

A pickup truck *whooshed* up and screeched to a stop in front of me.

Jack reached over and opened his passenger window. "Grace," he said, "I'm so sorry." Before I could answer, he threw the vehicle into park and ran out around the front of it. Fighting back my irritation, I waited.

"I am so sorry," he said again.

I waved away his apology even as I took a step back. "It's okay. Maybe we just aren't supposed to go out together."

"No, no. Look at you. You dressed up. And I let you down."

I desperately wished I'd taken Bruce's advice and worn jeans. My reply came out snappish and defensive. "I always wear skirts."

"Let me make it up to you. I can't even begin to tell you everything that's gone wrong."

"I'm not really in the mood to go out anymore."

We were directly outside my front door, Jack edging closer as he spoke. I had peripheral view of one of the closest windows. The drapes moved, then moved again. Was Bruce spying on us? I hoped to heaven it was Bootsie instead.

"Grace, I don't blame you for being angry."

"I'm not angry."

"You're hurt, and that's worse."

"You want to know the truth? My ego is a little bruised, that's all. I'll get over it. I've gotten over bigger disappointments."

"They hauled Davey in for questioning," he said. "Interrogation. I had to go down there."

Like sugar in hot tea, my anger instantly dissolved. "He's in jail?" I knew Tank suspected him, but she'd given no indication that he was about to be arrested. What was all that blather she gave me about transparency?

"Not anymore," Jack said. "My dad went down there with him and I got there as fast as I could. We called our lawyer and he came down, too. The cops said they just needed to clear up a few open issues, but you know how they are. They'll tell you anything to get what they want."

"But what *could* Davey tell them? Wasn't he under sedation when the murder occurred? Did they forget he had a broken nose?"

"The cops consulted some quack doctor who said it was 'theoretically possible' for him to have killed Kincade. Yeah, well, just like it's theoretically possible for Bennett Marshfield to come in first in a marathon."

In his age group, Bennett had a fair shot. But I let that go. I was stunned by the news. "They think Davey killed Zachary Kincade?"

"That's how they see it."

"I'm so sorry."

"I swear, Grace, if it had been anything else, anything at all, I would have blown it off. But Davey needed me." He grimaced. "I heard he quit Marshfield, too."

"He did."

"I'm sorry you've been pulled into the middle of all this family stuff. This hasn't been fair to you."

A car meandered down the street and we both watched it navigate around the double-parked pickup. Jack eyed me warily. He looked ready to bolt and move the vehicle if necessary, but at the same time worried that if he did, I might scurry inside.

"I understand." And I did.

He heaved a deep sigh. "Thank you, Grace."

"How is he?" I asked. "Davey?"

He looked away. "They should have taken me instead."

"What?"

"Davey can't handle this."

"But you said he's out of jail."

"You don't understand." He turned to face me again. "Davey isn't . . . completely stable." He must have read alarm in my expression because he hastened to add, "I don't mean he's dangerous or capable of violence. He's just not strong. Ever since the last time this happened he's had . . . problems."

I'd told Tank that Davey was much too young to have killed Lyle Kincade but now I wondered. Teenagers killed people all the time, and I didn't know Davey all that well. The young man did appear conflicted and depressed. Could he be haunted by guilt? "I'm sorry," I said again. "We can make this another time. Maybe you should go back and be with him."

"He's with Dad for now. It's okay."

I was no longer interested in our date this evening and I could tell Jack wasn't either, but the intensity in his eyes warned that canceling now would be the last straw in a series of backbreaking events.

"Please," he said, "can't we make at least one thing go right tonight?"

He was counting on me to turn this terrible day around. Maybe Frances was right. Maybe he was trouble. Emotions jockeyed for position, making my head ache, my heart twist, and my stomach tumble. I didn't know what to do.

He waited, silently encouraging me.

"Sure," I said.

WE LEFT JACK'S CAR IN MY DRIVEWAY AND walked the short distance to Hugo's. Our conversation centered on the lovely weather and the lovely homes, safe subjects that allowed us to restore equilibrium to the evening. Although I completely understood the reason for Jack's tardiness, it took several blocks of strolling along Embers-towne's tree-shaded streets to help me square emotion with logic. Jack seemed to sense that and except for him point-ing out an occasional plant he thought might be a good choice for my yard, he stayed quiet. The silence allowed us both to decompress.

The restaurant was relatively empty and I was glad. During the busy tourist season—which would peak in a couple of weeks—there was often a line out the door and a two-hour wait for a table. Jack and I were seated on the far left of the dining room at a table for four. I liked the slightly secluded location. Rather than sitting directly across from me, Jack chose the chair kitty-corner to my left.

The waitress recited the evening's specials then took our drink orders—a glass of merlot for me, a Heineken for him—before leaving us alone to study the leather-bound menus. I decided on the Cobb salad just as our drinks ar-rived. We placed our food orders—Jack chose the trout special—and the waitress was off again.

Jack raised his beer. "To finally having a real date?"

I clinked his bottle with the edge of my glass. "To real dates," I said, and sipped my wine. "Mmm . . . very good." I swirled the ruby liquid in my glass. "Hugo's buys their wines from my roommates. This is one of my favorites."

"That's nice of them."

"Good business, too. Keeps things local."

"How's the cat?"

"Great."

He took a long drink of his beer and held the sweating bottle between his hands as he surveyed the dining room. "Happening place tonight, huh?"

Not much to say to that, so I nodded. "I like it."

"That's good."

Quiet settled upon us again, but this time I was uncom-fortable. We didn't have an elephant in the room, we had a Tank. I decided to face it head-on.

"Did the detectives say anything else?" I asked. "I mean, when you were down there with Davey?"

Jack's jaw tightened. "Unfortunately that female detective woman is convinced my brother and I are guilty. No question about it. She has it in for us. Davey for this murder and me for the one thirteen years ago."

"There wasn't enough evidence to charge you then, what makes her think you're guilty now?"

The heat from his glare pushed me back. "You don't think she's going to let anything like facts get in her way, do you? Why do you think she got that 'Tank' nickname? She's going to run us both down flat unless we confess."

"Which you aren't going to do," I said.

The look in his eyes shifted. "If I could get Davey off the hook long enough to find the real killer, I'd consider it."

"You can't be serious."

He rubbed the side of his face. "Everything about this investigation is wrong. Just like last time."

Tank had referred to Davey as "damaged goods" and Jack had admitted that Davey was "unstable." Maybe there was more to this story than I'd been led to believe.

"There's no way Davey could have been involved with Lyle's murder, is there?"

Jack's face registered shock, then anger. "Why would you even say such a thing?"

Backpedaling quickly, I said, "I'm just trying to imagine what the police are thinking. You mentioned how Davey hasn't been the same since you were accused. Maybe there's more to the story."

"No way. Not a chance. He was fourteen, for crying out loud," Jack said. A moment later he continued, more calmly, "Davey was such a sweet kid up until then. The best of all of us. Outgoing and optimistic. Friends with everyone. But that all changed after I got accused." He stared up at the ceiling. "Our older brother, Keith, had just graduated college the year before. He was away a lot, but tried his best to help by doing 'big brother' stuff with Davey just to clear the air. But it didn't work. Davey pulled further away. It's obvious Davey believes I murdered Lyle. He's been haunted by that tragedy ever since."

I took a sip of my wine and after an extended silence, changed the subject. "Bennett wants me to move into Abe's old cottage," I said, and told him about the proposal.

Jack's expression softened. "How do you feel about that?"

"Honestly? Not too thrilled. I mean, the idea of living where everything is taken care of for me, and of having my current house restored to its original grandeur is tempting beyond belief." I thought about telling him more about the real reason Bennett wanted me nearby—about the possible blood ties my family might have with the Marshfields—but this was not the right moment. I hadn't told anyone beyond Bruce and Scott. Maybe I never would.

"What?" he asked. "You just drifted about a million miles away."

I smiled. "I was just thinking about Bruce and Scott." That wasn't a lie. "They're more than roommates. They're my friends. Really the only friends I've made since I moved back here."

Jack took my hand. "Not your only friends."

Tingling warmth raced up my arm through my chest, to my face where I felt myself blush. "Thank you," I said.

He didn't let go. His dark eyes had lost their angry intensity and had acquired a very different sort of passion. "I think about you," he said simply, "all the time."

I thought about him all the time, too. Unfortunately lately, that had less to do with matters of the heart and more to do with murders, old and new.

He let go. "I've enjoyed getting to know you, Grace. But I want to know you better. I understand this is a tough time—for both of us. But you moved back here to create a life for yourself and I've lived here forever. There's no rush. I'll wait for you." He gave a shy smile. "This kind of rough patch has the power to split people apart. So right there we're luckier than most. We can't split up because you and I aren't officially together yet."

I laughed. "Good point."

The mood had lightened considerably, thank goodness. I wanted to keep it that way.

"So . . . I'm sure you get this question a lot," I began.

His eyebrows came together as he waited for me to finish.

"But . . . your family name is Embers . . ."

"Last time I checked."

"Ha ha. And the town's name . . ."

He sighed. "Is Emberstowne. You're right, I do get that question a lot. Mostly from newbies. People who haven't lived here all their lives."

I held my hands up. "Can I help it my dad moved us away when I was young?"

He shrugged. "Not much to tell, really."

"I don't believe that for a minute."

He settled in, elbows on the table, leaning forward. "There's the town history and then there's the family history. Which do you want?"

"Both."

He nodded. "Town history is quick and easy. Henry and Martha Embers came here from England before the American Revolutionary War. With them they brought sisters, cousins, aunts, uncles, friends, and anyone else who was game for adventure. This group named the town, were pillars of the community, and formed a strong allegiance to their adopted land. Without the Embers's influence, this might just all be a pretty place in the country." Winking, he said, "That's the official version."

"And the real version?"

Wagging his head from side to side, he said, "It changes some depending on what branch of the family is telling it, but from what I've been told, Henry was the son of a wealthy member of the British aristocracy. But Henry was a ne'er-do-well . . ."

"Ne'er-do-well?" I repeated. "What generation are you?"

He held up a finger, grinning. "I'm telling it like it was told to me, remember? Henry flunked out of school, couldn't hold a job, and was in and out of jail for everything from public indecency to attempted murder."

"Nice guy."

"Yeah. Things got so bad that his father disowned him. Very bad times for Henry."

"Let me guess, that's when he came to America."

"You got it in one," Jack said. "Managed to talk his way into a job on a ship sailing west and eventually found himself in the Carolina territory."

"What about Martha?"

Jack took a drink of his beer. "The captain was bringing his own family to the new world," he said. "Martha was his sixteen-year-old daughter. She ran off with scalawag Henry the moment the ship docked."

"Scalawag?"

He shrugged. "Turns out old Henry just needed a change of venue, I guess. He and Martha set up a small dry goods store and named it Embers General. They were barely making ends meet when the Revolutionary War began. Henry joined up immediately, fought hard, and was commended by all his superiors. Returned here a real hero. No doubt he enjoyed thumbing his nose at his father by fighting their mother country. Either way, he and Martha flourished. After the war, word of Henry's valor got around and their little business took off, the town got named after him, and the rest, as they say, is history."

"Succinct."

He took another drink. "The truth is probably somewhere between the two."

"Where was their store?"

"Not far from your roommates' shop. There's a tiny plaque marking the building. I'll show you sometime."

"That would be great."

Another extended moment of silence but this time it was quiet and contented. With the way the evening had begun, I would never have predicted this.

He reached for my hand again, this time rubbing my knuckles with his thumb. "You can tell me I'm wrong, or foolish, or maybe even delusional, but today is a start, Grace. A baby step toward something I hope will grow between us. Think about it: If we're starting in the middle of all this turmoil, we have nowhere to go but up."

As he talked, the protective wall I'd tried to maintain began to crumble. Parts of my body that had lain dormant for too long began to awaken. Warmth rushed through every nerve ending and I pictured myself getting closer to Jack. A lot closer.

"I've enjoyed getting to know you, too," I said, giving his hand a little squeeze. "And I don't think you're wrong. I think today could be the beginning of something good."

Oh so reluctantly I fought my churning emotions and tamped down my physical reaction to the handsome man with the shiny dark eyes focused only on me. I cleared my throat. "As long as we take things slowly."

"That's exactly what I think," he said. "The best relationships are those built on solid foundations. I want you to know, Grace, I . . ."

At that moment the waitress arrived with our dinners, forcing us to release our entwined hands. Couldn't she have waited thirty more seconds?

As soon as she left again, I asked, "You were saying?"

He smiled at me. "Better left unsaid. For now at least."

I didn't push him. For the rest of the evening we found a lot of common ground and the time flew. I almost didn't notice the waitress whisking away our plates. I declined dessert, but Jack ordered chocolate chip cheesecake. "The best in town," he said, offering me a bite. "Homemade."

I leaned over to sample a taste from his fork, feeling a peculiar intimacy bubble up between us. Sitting back as I allowed the creamy treat to melt in my mouth, I pointed to his plate and said, "That is fabulous."

"See, you should have ordered some, too."

Nope. That one bite had been exactly perfect. "Next time."

He grinned up at me. "I like the sound of that."

Darkness enveloped us on the walk back to my house. Neither frightening nor ominous, it felt more like a cocoon we shared as we strolled. Our pace was much slower this direction, our path lit by the soft glow of streetlamps and of moonlight drifting down between the leaf-laden branches above. The world smelled green and full of promise.

About a block away from Hugo's, Jack grasped my hand, glancing at me sideways as he did so. We were close enough for me to see the inquisitive expression on his face and I smiled, squeezing his hand and bumping my shoulder against his arm in reply.

Our footfalls were soft on the old, uneven sidewalks. We barely spoke, and I was glad. With my heart beating like a trip-hammer and a little giggle swelling up in my throat, old unpredictable teenage urges took over, raging hormones and all. Take it slow, I told myself.

But I didn't want to.

I was on Jack's right and tried to surreptitiously study him in profile but every time I glanced his way, he turned and smiled. I was happy for the dark. At least he couldn't see me blush.

Our unhurried pace slowed even more as my house came into view. We arrived at my door much too soon. Where earlier I'd been willing to forgo tonight's plans, I was delighted now that Jack had pressed the issue. It had been the loveliest of evenings and all that was left was to say good night.

At the front door, Jack turned to face me. "I had a great time," he said, his hands running up my forearms and tugging me closer.

Frogs croaked in the distance and above us leaves *shush*ed in the breeze. "I did, too," I said. "I'm really glad we were able to put aside all the unpleasantness of the past few days."

"Although it's never really far from my mind, I think we needed this time away from it all. Both of us."

Close now, so close, I allowed that little giggle to pop up. "It's been a crazy few days, hasn't it? But I know things will settle back soon."

"I hope so. It's just that woman . . ." Jack looked away. "But we shouldn't be talking about her right now. We should be concentrating on other things." He pulled me closer still. "Because not even a Tank can squeeze between us right now, can she?"

"I won't let her," I said, tilting my face up toward his. "The last thing I need is to hear another conspiracy theory from her."

Jack leaned back. "Conspiracy theory?"

"Nothing," I insisted, wishing I hadn't mentioned it. I tried to dismiss the subject and restore the evening's mood. "Remember I told you she came to see me yesterday? She went on and on about that back gate."

Jack's arms around me loosened. "What are you talking about?"

"The back gate that was unlocked? Then mysteriously locked again?"

He frowned. "I hadn't heard anything about a gate. Are you talking about the access road near the Civil War encampment?"

"Exactly. The bolt was unlocked before the murder—

somebody noticed it and told the detectives. But when they went to look it was locked again."

"I have a key to that back gate."

I nodded, truly sorry I'd opened my mouth. "That's Tank's point. There are only three keys. Yours, mine, and Terrence's."

My heart dropped when Jack's arms did. He stepped away from me, rubbing his forehead. "This is bad."

"What is?" I asked. "What's bad?"

"That Tank woman asked me about my keys the day of the murder."

The reverberations in my heart pounded their way up to my temples. I didn't want to hear more, but I had to ask, "And?"

"I told her I'd lent them to Davey." He stared upward, hands on his head. "What have I done? I didn't think anything of it when she asked. I didn't know about the back gate being unlocked. I just answered the question." He walked to the far side of the porch, down to where the swing used to be. I wanted to follow him, but the deep angry sounds he made as he looked out over the far rail rendered me immobile. He banged the rail with his fist.

After a long moment of silence I tried to help. "But you said Davey was in no shape to go back that night."

Jack turned. "I'm not saying that he actually *used* them. He couldn't have. But I keep an extra set of my personal keys on that ring, and Davey had left his house key back at the manor. When I got him settled at home I figured I'd take off for a while to let him sleep. I didn't want him to be without keys—just in case." He rubbed his face. "How do you think this looks to the cops? The evidence is mounting against my little brother and—look at me—I'm contributing to the pile."

"I'm sorry."

Although he said, "Not your fault," his tone contradicted his words. He worked his jaw. "I better go."

"Go where?"

"To my dad's. I need to see Davey. Talk to you later, Grace."

He jogged to his car and I called, "Let me know how it goes," to his departing figure, but he drove off without even a wave good-bye.

Chapter 18

❦

FRANCES FOUND ME AT MY DESK THE NEXT morning staring out the windows. "They arrested the Embers kid?" she asked by way of greeting. She was wearing a different Civil War costume, a foggy gray shift that hung straight to the ground.

"No hoop today?" I countered, surprised she was in this early. I hadn't even heard the door open.

"I'll wear the gown again at the ball after the battle Saturday. For now it's going to be easier, not to mention cooler, to wear this." She fingered the fabric then looked at me expectantly.

"No, they didn't arrest him," I said. "They just pulled him in for more questioning. I'm surprised you already heard."

She lifted both shoulders as if to say, "What did you expect?" Settling herself into one of the wing chairs, she narrowed her eyes. "He didn't do it."

Her pronouncement surprised me. "I don't think so either."

We were quiet for a long moment.

"Davey is staying with their father, from what I under-stand," I said, "until all this blows over. *If* it blows over."

"Gordon."

"Excuse me?"

"Their dad is Gordon Embers. Used to be a big-shot cop here in town. You ask me . . ." She paused, as though gaug-ing my reaction.

I flipped my hand up. "Go ahead, say it."

Wiggling herself deeper into the seat, she went on, "I think the only reason your gardener, Jack, got off last time was because Daddy pulled strings. Now, I'm not saying Jack is guilty, but I do think they cut the investigation short because Jack is Gordon's son."

I started to shake my head.

She drew a finger along her cheek and up toward her right ear. "Know where he got that scar?"

"Wrong side," I said, "it's on the left."

With a Cheshire cat smile, she said, "He beat up the dead guy—the dead guy from thirteen years ago, I mean. Just a week later, that man was murdered in cold blood."

I knew Jack's side, but I let her continue.

"I know some folks up where Lyle Kincade lived," she said. "I didn't know the man personally, but there's no question he was crazy and dangerous. I don't blame the Embers family for getting their girl away from him, but the fact remains, Jack and Lyle got into a fight that sent them both to the hospital. Lyle slashed Jack with a broken bottle, and Jack kicked in Lyle's knee."

"I heard a little about that," I said carefully. "But I thought *three* of them went there. Jack's older brother and father, too."

"Gordon? Never. He wouldn't have jeopardized his ca-reer that way," she said. "I know the man. He's smart. He might have sent the boys to do some mischief, but he wouldn't have stepped foot inside Lyle's house unless it was with an arrest warrant in hand."

Same basic story Jack had told me, shaded slightly differently.

"So why don't you think it was the older brother who killed Lyle?"

"Couldn't be. I talked to some folks who worked with him back then. At the time of the murder, Keith was upstate working a construction site with his team. Impossible for him to have taken off and come back for that length of time without anyone noticing."

"Some folks," I repeated. "You know a lot of 'some folks.'"

"I make it my business to know."

"I think the Emberstowne Police Department should have hired you instead of that Tank woman."

Frances's mouth twitched. "It's their loss."

It sure was.

When she was ready to return to the Civil War encampment for round two of her gossip-harvesting, I wished her good luck. "You did great cornering Jim Florian yesterday," I said. "We got a lot of useful information."

"You weren't so bad yourself. Maybe you ought to pick out a dress from the sutlers and have a go out there, too."

"Thanks, but I'll leave the undercover work to you."

"Undercover," she repeated, shuddering.

"I thought you enjoyed this."

"I do . . . it's just . . ." She shook her head. "Never mind. I'll deal with it."

"Is there a problem?"

"Nothing I can't handle. I'll catch up with you later."

MID-MORNING WHEN THE OUTER DOOR TO Frances's office banged open I jammed a finger to hold my place on the massive spreadsheet that tracked the mansion's past twelve months' expenses for paper goods. I looked up to see who my visitor was, thinking again how much I needed to persuade this staff to go green. Bennett rushed in. "It's here," he said.

"What is?"

Joy suffused his features and he threw his hands up in the air. "The auction item, of course. What else?"

He wasn't carrying anything. "Where is it?"

"Come on, come on," he said, urging me to hurry.

I placed a Post-it note on the expense sheet and stood. I doubted whatever it was would disappear if I didn't show up in the next two minutes, but Bennett's enthusiasm was contagious. Taking on Abe's directorship in addition to being head curator wasn't working out exactly as I'd hoped. Rather than traveling the world to discover exciting relics and historically significant pieces to add to the Marshfield collection, rather than spending blissful hours cataloguing the hundreds of pieces we already had in storage, I mostly found myself poring over minutiae in order to keep the mansion running smoothly. I hadn't had a chance to flex my curator muscles in some time and an opportunity to experience something new—or old, as it were—would be a breath of fresh air. I grabbed my walkie-talkie and followed him. "Lead the way."

The manor was buzzing with tourists. They took no notice of us despite the fact we were walking against the normal flow of traffic. Most visitors wouldn't recognize the owner of the manor if they ran into him, and certainly no one would recognize me.

Bennett led the way with long strides. I kept up, trying to calculate where he was taking me. We took the central public stairway down to the main floor. I wondered, not for the first time, how much longer the carpet here would hold out. Stairways always took a beating and although the thick red runner wasn't yet showing wear, the color had faded ever so slightly where the sun beat through the windows. I had no idea how long this particular floor covering had been in place. Another task for me to add to my to-do list.

Bennett strode toward the front entry. The docents recognized "the Mister," of course, and rushed to open the giant doors for him, eagerly greeting him with a cheerful "Good morning, sir."

He nodded acknowledgment and thanked them but didn't slow his pace. I was long-legged enough to stay next to him, but I couldn't help but be impressed with the man's power. I hoped to have his strength and stamina when I reached that age.

The sun warmed our skin as we walked, a faint breeze carrying the sweet scent of flowers. I smiled, thinking that Jack would probably recognize the fragrance immediately and be able to name the plant that produced it.

Jack.

Remembering his abrupt departure last night, I bit my lip. This wasn't the time to dwell on disappointment, however. I resolved to keep upbeat for Bennett's sake.

Just outside and to the east were the manor's former stables. Off-limits to guests until we refurbished the area, this section had seen plenty of use in the early 1900s when the Marshfield family entertained guests. U-shaped like a mini castle around a courtyard, the two-story structure originally housed about fifty horses and to this day remained in good shape, structurally.

I had ideas for future changes. Plans to maximize this space and to ramp up the manor's income while we were at it. Not that Bennett needed the money.

At the gate to the courtyard, he stopped. "You ready?"

"As I'll ever be."

Eyes sparkling, he grasped the gate's handle and swung it open. "Then let's go."

I followed him past the thick stone walls of the passageway. Bennett stepped back to allow me to proceed first, and as I did, my breath caught. In the very center of the court-yard, sparkling in the sunlight, was a dazzling cream-colored antique car. So huge, it was almost as big as my first New York apartment. A convertible, with its top down. "Oh my," I said.

Bennett swept the air with both hands, shooing me closer. "It's a 1936 Packard Phaeton."

That meant nothing to me. "This looks like the kind of car you'd see in *The Great Gatsby*."

Bennett laughed. "You're a few years off. And I think he drove a Rolls."

I took a slow walk around the car, admiring the wide curved fenders, fat white walls, and stately silver grill. "You bought this at auction?"

"Outrageous, isn't she?" he said as he ran a hand up and along the front fender. "I've never before seen one in such pristine condition. Just over three hundred thousand miles." He must have caught my expression. "That's very low for a vehicle of this age," he said. "And this was a steal, if I do say so myself. I'm lucky. This was quite the whim. I couldn't believe how few people bid on it."

There were times I wondered if Bennett had any idea how the rest of the world lived, worked, and did their best to get by. In this economy I was surprised *anyone* had bid on it. "It's just wonderful," I said. I rested my hands atop the passenger door and peered in, then thought better of it. "Oops, sorry," I said as I yanked my hands back. "Fingerprints."

"Don't worry." Bennett's grin was as big as I'd ever seen it. "I thought you'd like to drive it."

"Me? No way. But I'd be thrilled if you'd take me for a ride someday."

"That's not what I had in mind."

Bennett didn't drive much anymore, so I clarified, "I

meant that Grant or one of your other drivers could take us."

"As you know, we don't allow staff cars up near the manor where they can be seen by guests."

"Right. It ruins the illusion." What did that have to do with him taking me for a drive?

Still grinning, he said, "But this car, even if parked out front, wouldn't look out of place at all."

"No," I agreed, "it would fit right in."

Bennett's cheeks flushed a pale shade of pink. "I thought you might like to have this car to travel back and forth between the cottage and work every day." As though he expected me to interrupt, he hurried to add, "There's plenty of space at Abe's cottage for the car you own, too, but I'd like to think you wouldn't need it anymore if you had . . . this one."

Speechless and dumbfounded, I alternated glances between Bennett and the car, trying to come up with an appropriate response. "Bennett," I began, "you're too kind."

"I'm not kind at all. This is a bribe. I want to be up-front about that. You can't imagine how much it would mean to me to have you move into the cottage. So much so, that if you like I'll sign a deed that makes it yours for life."

"But . . ."

"This feels right, Gracie. You belong here. And I'm determined to convince you to take advantage. Just think about how much easier it would be without having to worry about the roof falling in, or replacing broken pipes. Not to mention the short commute."

The happiness on his face had shifted to one of great concern and I could practically read his thoughts. He was worried he'd overdone it in trying to change my mind. He had. Completely. I stood there mute for what felt like a long time. I wanted to tell him no. To tell him definitively. But doing so would hurt Bennett. I couldn't do that. So I hedged.

"I told you I needed time to think about it, right?"

He nodded guardedly.

"I still need more. Can you give me just a little more time to think? Please?"

"Gracie, I know you feel as though I'm pressuring you, but the loss of Abe makes me appreciate the importance of family. I want you to always feel as though you're part of Marshfield Manor. A real part. How can you do that if you live so far away?"

I knew how lonely Bennett was. He'd cocooned himself in the mansion for so long he didn't know how to break out. His solution, instead, was to pull me in.

To buy time, I ran my hand along the car's sleek fender, but the truth was I had a very different life planned for myself. I didn't want to live on Marshfield property. Not now, maybe not ever. I loved my house despite the work involved to keep it in shape.

"I do understand," I said, but I couldn't disappoint Bennett at this moment. Not when he was staring at me with that hopeful expression on his face.

I felt my resolve waver, but giving in wasn't the right answer. "Just a little longer, Bennett. I still feel like that's Abe's cottage after all."

He didn't argue this time, but the look on his face about broke my heart.

My walkie-talkie buzzed and I answered. "There are some women to see you, Ms. Wheaton," one of the attendants at the visitors' desk said. "Shall I show them to your office?"

"I'm outside. I'll be there in a minute." Turning to Bennett, I said, "I have to go."

"Of course."

I gave the Packard a long look before I took off. "She is beautiful," I said. "Have you named her yet?"

Looking depressed, Bennett ran a hand along the driver's side door. "No."

"My grandmother's name was Sophie," I reminded him.

His expression brightened. "Sophie," he repeated, "yes. That's it."

"SOMEONE TO SEE ME?" I ASKED WHEN I GOT back inside.

The elderly docent behind the desk pointed to three women gathered behind velvet ropes along a far wall.

"Thanks," I said and started toward them. I hadn't taken five steps when I recognized one, then another. Rani and Tamara, the two women who'd come to Taser Zachary Kincade the day he'd been killed. What on earth were they doing here today?

I approached them with caution. "Welcome back to Marshfield," I said keeping my tone light and friendly. We had at least six security guards in this area, so I knew I would be safe. "What can I do for you?"

"Hello again, Ms. Wheaton," Rani said. This time, instead of all black, she was head-to-toe in buttercup yellow. Linen pants, silk shell, and matching jacket. On any other woman the effect might have been amusing, but this gal carried it off with style. Tamara wore a shapeless dress of pale blue and blue flats. Their companion, a stunning woman of about forty, had the purest, clearest skin I'd ever seen in a woman her age. She had wavy red hair that fell to her shoulders and eyes so tragically blue there left no doubt she'd been crying. Wearing silver sandals and a sage green form-fitting dress that accentuated a body most women would kill for, she gripped a deeper green sweater in one hand and a silver purse in the other.

"This is our friend Muffy," Rani said, pointing. "The one we told you about."

Muffy's cream-colored cheeks blushed bright red.

"Nice to meet you, Muffy," I said. "Is there something I can help you with?"

She stole a glance toward Rani. "No, I just . . ."

"Muffy might have a clue about who killed Zachary," Rani said.

Muffy sniffled. She pulled out a tissue and wiped her nose.

Suddenly aware that we'd attracted the attention of the staff behind the visitors' desk, I suggested we take this conversation elsewhere. "There's a small room off the library where I think we'd have more privacy," I said, and called Terrence Carr on my walkie-talkie, asking him to meet us there.

"I DON'T UNDERSTAND," I SAID WHEN WE were all gathered.

This room was only about one-third the size of the mansion's library but it housed almost as many volumes. Treasures crammed every corner, filling the space with the musty scent of a used bookstore. Coupled with a faint trace of pipe tobacco, it was as though a ghost returned here every evening to enjoy a book and a smoke. The adjacent library was two stories tall and large enough to entertain a hundred guests if the need arose, but this side room was much more intimate. Bennett's grandfather had purportedly kept this as his private room, off-limits to everyone but immediate family. If we did indeed have a pipe-smoking ghost, it would be Warren, Sr.

Four caramel-colored leather chairs circled a round coffee table near the tall stone fireplace but the five of us—including Terrence—remained standing.

"We're here to help you," Rani said. She placed a hand on Muffy's arm and spoke for her. "We told you about how Zachary jilted our friend here, right?" She turned to her and said, "I'm sorry, Muffy, but we had to explain."

Terrence interrupted. "Last time you were here, you mean? As in, when you attempted to assault Mr. Kincade?" His chin rose. "That being the same Mr. Kincade who was recently murdered?"

Muffy choked back a sob and held the green sweater up to hide her face.

Rani gave Terrence a dismissive glare. "Assault? Hardly. You exaggerate."

"You tried to Taser him," I said.

She waved a hand. "Whatever. What's important now is that the police stop hassling us. I mean, they obviously still consider us suspects in the murder. How silly is that?" she asked rhetorically. "Muffy has some information we'd like to share with you. Information we think could help the police catch the real killer instead of wasting their time investigating us."

"If it's such good information," Terrence said, "why not take it directly to the police?"

"Have you met that . . . that . . . Tank? All she wants is to toss us into a cell and walk away whistling. We tried to tell her about what a jerk Kincade was but that woman had no sympathy whatsoever for poor Muffy. Probably never had a man in her life so she can't understand what pigs they can be."

"She's happily married," I said. "Two kids. One grand-kid she's crazy about."

Rani gave a dainty shrug. "Whatever," she said again. "We just don't like her, do we, girls?"

Tamara shook her head vehemently. Muffy looked ready to die where she stood.

"Fine," I said, despite the anger I sensed building in Terrence. "What's so important?"

"Go ahead, Muffy," Rani prompted.

After much sniffling and false starts, Muffy began. She had a deep Southern drawl that pulled you in and made you want to do something to help. Her tears began to subside with the telling of the story. "Zachary talked about this hobby of his—this military playacting—all the time. Now, he always called it his Civil War games, but as you know around here we refer to that time as the War Against Northern Aggression. Zachary and I sometimes had words about that." She sniffled.

I nodded. "Go on."

"Zachary was always so worked up about his playacting. I was afraid he was more interested in this pretend stuff than he was in me." Her voice cracked. "I guess I was sure right about that, wasn't I?" she asked with a self-deprecating smile.

"Be strong, Muffy," Rani said.

She nodded, not looking strong at all. "Well, now, it had to be right like two or three weeks before he . . . died, Zachary told me that he was pretty sure he was goin' to be elected to be the top man of the group. He was a Union soldier, you know. I don't understand why he'd choose the north, but that was his business. Anyway, I think maybe he said he'd be the general. But that some people were against it."

I thought about how Jim Florian, now running unopposed, was expected to be elected to that position. "Did he say anything about the man he was running against?"

"I have to be honest about this part. When he got to talking about his war games, I lost interest and started thinking about wedding plans instead." She sniffled again, loudly. "I probably should have paid better attention. There wasn't even ever goin' to be a wedding, was there?"

I waited until she settled herself before asking, "Why do you think this is important now?"

"Because Zachary told me he was worried about one fella in particular. When he said that, I started listening more closely. He said he was worried because this man had it in for him."

I thought about Jim Florian again. "Did he say why?

Was this guy jealous that Zachary was going to be elected and he wasn't?"

"I don't know," Muffy said. "Just that Zachary said he was worried about one of the men coming after him, but he didn't say any name that I recall. What he said was, 'This guy's not going to be satisfied until I'm dead.'"

We talked a little longer with Terrence asking additional questions, but there was not much more information to be had. As we escorted them out, I turned to Rani. "I don't get it. Why did you make the effort to come out here when you hated Zachary Kincade so much?"

Her eyebrows arched. "We hated him, sure, but we never wanted him dead. In fact, we wish he was still alive."

"You do?" I asked.

Tamara bobbed her head. "He got off too easy. We wanted to Taser him." She gave a wicked smile. "For a couple of hours or so."

Chapter 19

FRANCES WAS IN HER OFFICE WHEN I GOT there. "You're back early," I said.

She fanned herself. "It's getting warm."

The day had been fairly mild. "I would have thought it would have been hotter under that heavy dress yesterday."

"It was."

Pointing out the obvious, I said, "But the temperature is lower today. And you're wearing a much lighter garment."

She fixed me with a look. "I know that."

Deciding to try a different tack, I lowered myself into one of her visitors' chairs. "What's wrong?"

She had been standing behind her desk, but now sat down hard, making the seat creak in protest. I'd be the first to admit I had trouble reading my assistant. Other than perpetually cranky, she didn't seem to have a wide range of emotions. To buy her time, however, I told her about our recent visitors and Muffy's "clue."

She listened with interest, her small eyes sparking when

I mentioned that Zachary believed one of his Civil War mates was out to get him.

"Hmph." Her brows came together. "That fits with what I've pieced together," she said. "Zachary Kincade was having an affair with one of the wives."

"Was making enemies his favorite hobby?"

Frances crinkled her nose. "Who knows? Some people are just like that."

I kept my mouth shut on that comment. "So you think the woman's husband is a suspect. Who is it, by the way?"

"Guy named Jeff. I met him. He's either drunk or sleeping it off all day every day. Nobody blames the wife for stepping out on the guy. Can you believe it?"

"So this is common knowledge?"

"Talk about circling the wagons," she said, leaning forward. "I highly doubt anyone thought to mention this illicit little tête-à-tête to the police." She lifted her shoulders when I exclaimed my disbelief. "The re-enactors don't believe Jeff could have done it. He's incoherent most of the time. Plus, the consensus is he doesn't really care."

"That's sad."

She shifted in her seat. "There's more."

"About Jeff and his wife?"

She wiggled again. Sniffed. "No."

I waited.

"You know how I'm sharing space with the soiled doves?" Frances's face darkened as she looked to me for acknowledgment. I nodded and she went on. "All those women have husbands participating in the re-enactment."

I had no idea where this was going.

"Their husbands get into the game and pretend they're . . . *hiring* their wives. They come by and flirt and make eyes. It's ridiculous."

"That has to make you a little uncomfortable."

"*Pfft!* Tell me about it. At least they have the common decency to consummate their little game elsewhere.

But . . . these people have worked and played together for years so they don't think twice about . . . well, about getting *into* their roles." Disdain dripped with every word.

"I'm sorry, Frances. Aren't there any other women who are willing to share a tent with you?"

"The soiled dove tent is the only all-female spot I've found. All the other women at camp share tents with their husbands. If I want to change clothes or even just get out of the sun for a few minutes without some man skulking inside, I have to stick it out with these soiled doves." Frances shot me with a piercing look.

"I'm sorry to hear that you're having issues."

"There's one more thing."

I couldn't decipher the look in her eyes. "Go on."

"One of the Confederate soldiers—a man named Hennessey—has been following me around."

"Ah," I said, "he's figured out what you're up to, I take it? Do you consider him a suspect?"

"No," she said slowly, "he's not even aware of my investigation." She blushed again more deeply this time. "He keeps following me around. Keeps trying to get me to visit his tent." She wagged her tadpoles. "You know . . ."

My jaw dropped. "He came on to you?"

"With gusto."

"I definitely do not want you uncomfortable out there. Would you prefer to give it up?"

Her eyes widened. "Don't you think I'm bringing you good information?"

"Great information. In fact, I plan to share this with the police."

"Then why are you trying to take me off the job?"

My head spun. What convoluted logic led her to that conclusion? "I don't want you off the job. I just assumed—"

She squared her shoulders. "I can handle myself, thank you very much."

"Okay then," I said, perplexed but not willing to argue, "just let me know if you need anything."

She made an unladylike noise. "Saltpeter, maybe."

I couldn't help it. I laughed out loud. To my surprise, Frances chuckled, too.

I STOPPED BY AMETHYST CELLARS ON MY WAY home. The cozy tasting room was practically humming with cheerful customers. Scott was behind the bar pouring samples while Bruce chatted up the clientele. They looked far too busy for me to bother them, so I caught Scott's eye and waved hello, indicating that I'd see them later at home.

To my surprise, he looked alarmed and quickly beckoned me forward. Excusing himself from a couple of thirty-somethings sampling a red, he spoke quietly. "Just a heads-up," he said, "that Tooney guy was here looking for you a little while ago."

"He didn't know I was at work?"

Scott laughed quietly. "I'm sure he did, but you and I both know how welcome he is at Marshfield."

"True enough. What did he want?"

"He said to tell you he might be stopping by tonight. Around seven."

I groaned. "Remind me not to answer the door."

Scott's expression tightened. "He says he found Bootsie's owners."

My heart dropped. "Oh."

"Yeah," Scott said, "that's pretty much the reaction I expected."

TOONEY SHOWED UP AS PROMISED JUST AS the parlor clock chimed the hour. Wearing an open trench coat over a dress shirt and pants, he removed his hat the moment I opened the door. "Good evening, Ms. Wheaton." Glancing at the bundle of fur in my arms, he added, "I see you got my message."

He was alone. "I thought you'd be bringing the owners with you," I said.

"May I come in?"

Reluctantly I pushed open the screen door and stepped aside, leading him into the parlor to talk. This was his first time inside my home and he made no effort to disguise his curiosity, his gaze taking in the high ceilings, threadbare furniture, and photos I'd arranged on the mantel. He pointed to one of them. "Family?"

I ignored the question. "What proof do you have that Bootsie belongs to these other people?" I asked. "I don't intend to give her up until I'm sure."

Tooney was not a particularly attractive man. Fiftyish, bloated, and pale, his appearance, coupled with his scheming personality, made for one unpleasant package. But his face transformed whenever he smiled, which he did now, clearly proud of himself. "I'm sure they're the cat's owners," he said, "but I understand your concern." He pulled a small digital camera from his coat pocket and wrapped the strap around his wrist. "That's why I'm here tonight. I'll take a few shots of your little charge there and see if this is Mittens after all."

"Mittens?"

"That's her name," he said, nodding toward the kitten, "because of her white paws. There's even a reward out for her return."

I took a step back, clutching Bootsie so tightly she squirmed. My nose began to run again, and I loosened one hand long enough to pull a tissue from my jeans pocket and blow. "How do you know they won't claim this is their cat when it really isn't? Don't I get to see pictures of the cat they lost to compare for myself?"

Tooney watched as I shoved the tissue back into my pocket. "I thought you'd be happy to be rid of her."

"It's one thing to give her back to the family that lost her," I said, fighting my runny nose. "But I have to be sure. And anyway, how did this 'Mittens' get out? Weren't they watching her? How old is the cat they're missing? This one is just a kitten."

He shot me a sad smile. "Mittens has only had one vet appointment so far. She was too young to be spayed and she got out when the kids' grandmother opened the door to accept a package delivery. That was about a week ago. The family figures Mittens was too young to know her way home."

"Are they nice kids? Responsible, I mean?"

"Yeah," Tooney said, "the youngest one is nine. They're heartbroken that Mittens disappeared."

I swallowed my disappointment. "Where do they live?"

He tilted his head. "Westville."

"That's awfully far."

Tooney held up the camera. "That's why I want to snap a few shots before we arrange to hand her over."

I wasn't about to hand her over without more proof. I raised my point again. "What about pictures *they* took of Mittens? Don't I get to see those?"

He shrugged. "I don't know if they have any."

"Well, ask," I said to him. "If they have kids, I'm sure they have pictures of them with their cat. That's just the way people do things, you know." I caught myself muttering and stopped immediately. "They will have pictures," I said more confidently, "and I want to see them."

Raising an eyebrow, he focused and shot four pictures in a row. "Can you shift her so I can see more of the white?"

I complied and sneezed.

As he continued, he said, "I thought you wanted to find her family."

I shrugged.

"Especially with you being allergic and all. I thought this was what you wanted."

Feeling cross, I looked away. "Just doesn't seem right, that's all. How do we know they won't *say* this is their cat? I mean, if they only had her a week, they may look at your pictures and think it's Mittens. But maybe it isn't."

Tooney gave me a thoughtful stare before thanking me and starting for the door. "I'll be in touch," he said, "real soon."

I saw Tooney out, still holding Bootsie, wishing the PI wannabe had never gotten involved. As I shut the door after him, I snuggled my face into the kitten's fur. "Oh, Bootsie," I said. Then sneezed again.

Chapter 20

NOT HAVING FRANCES TO RUN INTERFER-
ence for me was becoming a problem. I was getting little
done during the day because phones rang off the hook,
the media kept demanding answers, and staffers needed
guidance when faced with unexpected decisions. I began
to think that my irritable assistant might deserve a raise.
I pushed that thought aside for the moment, because I
didn't have time to think about that now. I had work to
do.

The back of my brain nagged that I had more to worry
about than running the mansion. I had Bennett's plea for
me to move into Abe's cottage and Bootsie's future on my
mind. Not to mention the ongoing murder investigation.
Investigations. Plural. That was enough for one day. Heck,
that was enough for a year.

I found myself spending more time in Frances's office
than in my own. We kept most of our records in there, although I hated having to find anything. Frances had a very
personal method of organization, one that no one could fig-

ure out. I supposed she considered our dependence on her a form of job security.

Phone receiver crooked tight on my shoulder, I was talking with Lois about where to temporarily house Bennett's new 1936 Packard until its final spot was decided, when Tank and Rodriguez ambled into the office. They waved a greeting and sat down in the chairs across from me without my inviting them to do so.

"Let me call you back, Lois," I said quickly. "I've got company."

"Before you go, Grace, let me just share one little tidbit. Mr. Marshfield ordered a special keychain made."

"For the Packard? I don't understand."

"GLW. Your initials. Is he giving the car to you? Some kind of bonus?"

"No," I said trying to be truthful without actually spilling all the beans, "but he, uh, thinks it's a good idea for me to use it on-site."

"Gotcha," she said, buying it. "Makes sense."

When I hung up, I turned to the two detectives in front of me, trying to read their expressions. "How is the investigation coming?" I asked.

"We're getting closer to an arrest," Tank said. Rodriguez grimaced.

I addressed him. "You don't agree?"

He waved a hand dismissively. "We're here as a courtesy call."

I directed a questioning look at Tank then shifted back to Rodriguez. "What is it you need?"

Tank lifted her hand toward her partner. "Go ahead."

Rodriguez rubbed his neck, then ran a finger inside his collar, as though to loosen it. "Ms. Wheaton, we know you went out with Jack Embers the other night. On a date. Am I right?"

I sat up, startled. "Am I being investigated?"

He shook his head slowly. "Like I said, this is a courtesy. We just want to make you aware that Jack Embers is a person of interest."

"In Zachary Kincade's murder?"

The two exchanged a glance.

"You have evidence?" I asked, hearing my voice go up a few notches.

Another glance. "Nothing we care to share at this point," Rodriguez said.

"What does that mean?"

Tank again held her hand toward her colleague. "Detective Rodriguez was not part of the Emberstowne force thirteen years ago so no one holds him responsible for any mistakes that were made back then. Nor for any instances of bad judgment."

My temples throbbed and my vision narrowed. "Your point?"

"Gordon Embers was a high-ranking cop on the Emberstowne force. We think he pulled strings to get his son out of trouble."

"But . . . but . . ." I realized I was sputtering. "The murder happened in a different town. There's no way he could have pulled strings with them. Is there?" My question trailed off with such a pathetically hopeful lilt I could have bitten my tongue.

"As you're no doubt aware, Ms. Wheaton," Tank began, "Lyle Kincade was a contemptible individual. No one disputes that. His murder saddened no one beyond his immediate family. I think Emberstowne's finest banded together. They realized that Jack Embers wasn't a threat to society at large, so they managed to finagle him a get-out-of-jail-free card." She turned to Rodriguez, who looked like he'd like to be anywhere but with Tank, and added, "That is, until I got here."

I felt a sharp sinking in my stomach.

"Murder is murder," she said. "It's wrong. No matter who does it. No matter what the circumstances. Wouldn't you agree?"

I nodded dumbly.

They seemed to be waiting for my reaction. "Are you planning to arrest Jack?"

"We're waiting on some evidence," she said. "We may be able to tie him to both murders. We suspect the Embers brothers tag-teamed to kill Zachary Kincade. You know what they say about it getting easier each time."

I couldn't believe it and I said so. "Did you know," I said quickly, "that Zachary Kincade was having an affair with one of the re-enactors?"

Their expressions didn't change.

"She's married," I added, "and Zachary told his fiancée that he felt threatened by one of his colleagues. Don't you think that's significant?"

"Would this be the *jilted* fiancée?" Tank asked.

"Yes, but just because he left her at the altar doesn't suggest she's lying. What reason would she have for doing so?"

"What reason would she have for coming forward now?" she asked. "Except to clear her two girlfriends of any suspicion."

I was getting nowhere but had to keep trying. "The husband whose wife was having the affair is named Jeff. I didn't catch the wife's name. But my assistant, Frances, could get that for you at a moment's notice."

Rodriguez slid forward in his chair. "Ms. Wheaton, I hope we haven't made a mistake by sharing our suspicions with you. I convinced my partner here that you could be trusted. After working with you last time, I came to know you as a fine, upstanding citizen. I hope you'll keep this information to yourself. At least until we take action."

My mouth was dry. "When will that be?"

"Soon."

I ASKED LOIS TO HANDLE THE OFFICE FOR ME. I needed to act quickly—to do something—although I didn't know exactly what. As I moved, I planned. Frances needed to understand how imperative it was we come up with something to redirect the finger of guilt away from the Embers brothers.

Forgoing the company van, I raced to the basement, where I hurried through the tunnel that led to underground staff parking and my own car. It would be faster and no one would pay me any mind.

What strange need to protect Jack propelled me? I mean, if truth be told, after the debacle that was my oh-so-brief engagement to Eric, it could be argued that my character-judging abilities could stand some improvement. But I knew deep in my heart that Jack was not guilty of killing Lyle Kincade and I believed both he and Davey were innocent of killing Zachary. What a terrible mess all this was, and no one except Bennett, Frances, and I seemed willing to seek out the truth.

What a peculiar team we made.

The re-enactment was open to the public for another hour or so. I hurried down the small hill and eased my way in. Although the area was as crowded as ever, with tourists milling around and re-enactors going about their 1800-era lives, I spotted Frances right away. Holding her skirt so she wouldn't trip, she was hurrying across the center of camp from the Confederate to the Union side, shouting over her shoulder to a man following her at a quick clip. Wearing Confederate gray, he was at least sixty years old, hatless, with a trim gray beard and a gut that hung over his belt. At least, I assumed there was a belt under that bouncing mound. Still, he kept up with Frances and that was saying something.

As I drew closer I heard her shout, "How many times must I tell you, Mr. Hennessey, that I am not the least bit interested in helping you clean your weapon."

Not slowing his pace, he threw back his head and laughed. "But it's a very special weapon, Frannie honey.

The best you'll ever see. Come on, sweetheart. You and I are meant for one another. I had a dream last night and you were in it. Want to hear what happened?"

I cupped my hands around my mouth. "Frances!"

She turned immediately, her face brightening when she spotted me standing there. Well, wasn't that a first? She veered in my direction, taking time to glare at the man in her wake. "That's my boss," she said, pointing. "Now get away from me before she kicks your backside out of here."

He stopped long enough to grin and wave. "Nice to meet you, miss. See you later, Frannie," he called and blew her a kiss.

Coming up to stand next to me, she shuddered. "That man."

"Your suitor, I take it?"

She made a noise of disgust as she watched him leave. "He'd hit on a tree if he thought it would bear fruit." Turning to me, she asked, "What brings you down here?"

Now that I was here, I wasn't sure where to begin. "Have you heard anything more about this affair Zachary was having? Anything at all? About the husband? Do you think he could be the murderer?"

She studied me before she answered. "What happened?"

As much as I wanted to protect Jack and Davey, I'd promised the detectives I wouldn't talk about their visit. It killed me to say, "Nothing really, just that it's coming close to a week since the murder and I think the detectives are getting restless."

Scrutinizing me, Frances nodded. "The Embers boys are in big trouble, aren't they?"

Surprise must have shown on my face because she added, "No, I'm not psychic and I don't have a microphone in your office, but from the look on your face and from talking with Gordon"—she waved a hand toward the Confederate camp—"it's not hard to put two and two together."

"Gordon Embers? Jack's father? He's here?"

"He came to check on Davey. I guess the kid has been getting into this re-enactment more than anyone expected. The Confederate group didn't know Zachary Kincade all that well, and they don't have any idea about Davey's possible involvement, so he's been spending time there. From what I can tell, he's fitting in. *Tsk*."

"You don't approve?"

Her brows came together. "Just the opposite. It's the first time I've seen the boy happy since I've met him. But if the cops come and arrest him—even if he's innocent—it's going to ruin everything for him."

Compassion from Frances? That was a new side to my assistant I hadn't anticipated. "What about his dad?" I asked. "You said he's here?"

"I saw him a few minutes ago." She looked around, searching.

Mr. Hennessey spotted her and waved an exuberant hello. "Don't forget about me," he yelled.

Brushing the air violently as she might a killer fly, she repeated her noise of disgust and continued our conversation. "Gordon Embers is a strong-minded man," she said, "and he's fiercely protective of his sons."

I was about to say something, but she interrupted.

"There he is." She pointed, then called, "Gordon!"

He looked around before spotting Frances. I immediately saw the family resemblance. *So this is what Jack will look like in thirty years,* I thought. Carrying about forty extra pounds, Jack's father was extremely handsome with a full head of salt-and-pepper hair. He made his way over, a questioning look on his face.

"Gordon," Frances said when he joined us, "this is Grace Wheaton, the . . ." She stumbled over the words, ". . . the new curator. Since Abe died."

"Yes," he said, shaking my hand. He had a firm grip and alert, wary eyes. "I've heard your name a lot lately. I'm sorry if my boy Davey is causing you any trouble."

"Not at all," I said, "he's great."

He seemed surprised by my answer. "I came out here to convince him to come home. The last thing he needs is to be hanging around a place where people suspect him of murder." Gordon wagged his head. "Shame how scandals taint the innocent."

"Davey's going home with you, then?"

"Unfortunately not," he said, looking around. "He told me he wants to stick around a little longer. I guess one of the Union guys loaned him some equipment and a uniform and now he's hooked in this playacting."

I turned to Frances. "I thought you said Davey was on the Confederate side."

"From what I understand there's a lot of interaction between teams when they're not battling. They all converge in that sutlers' area and around the campfire at night."

"Ah, that's right," I said, remembering. "Pierpont mentioned that, too."

"Pierpont has been helping Davey learn more about the whole re-enacting business."

"Seriously?"

She nodded. "That man is relentless about signing new people up. He keeps telling me how much I'd enjoy being a part of the group on a permanent basis. The man is a fanatic."

"I got that impression," I said.

Gordon had been listening in. "Who is this guy you're talking about?"

I explained that Rob Pierpont was the top man on the Union side and that he was soon to be replaced by Jim Florian. I didn't mention anything about Zachary Kincade, nor about how he had been vying for the general's position.

"And you say he's been taking Davey under his wing?" he asked Frances.

She placed a hand on his arm. "Davey seems to be enjoying himself here," she said. "Maybe you should just let him be."

He yanked his arm away as though burned. "I want to meet this guy for myself," he said. "I don't want some weird costumed idiot talking Davey into doing something stupid."

"Charming man," I said when he left.

"Apples don't fall far from their trees," Frances said. "Gordon has always been a hothead." She traced a line along the side of her face, mimicking Jack's scar. "Remember the fight I told you about."

I was about to repeat my concern about Frances keeping an open mind, when Jim Florian ambled over. "What brings you down today?" he asked, tipping his hat.

Too much negativity in one day had worn me out. I didn't have the wherewithal to come up with an excuse that made sense. "Just visiting Frances."

Addressing my assistant, he said, "Sorry to hear old Hennessey has been bugging you. He's a character, that one." Chuckling, he added, "I hope that won't keep you from joining up. Pierpont says you're thinking about it."

From the set of her mouth, I could tell Frances was annoyed. "Not if I have to deal with the likes of him I won't."

"Maybe you have a husband who might be interested in re-enacting? If so, you should bring him down here. That would slow Hennessey down, I'm sure."

Frances scowled and changed the subject. "The election is Saturday isn't it? How does it feel to be taking over as the new general?"

Florian looked away. "I don't know," he said quietly. "I might not be taking over after all."

"What happened?" I asked.

Squinting into the distance, Florian said, "I told you how I like things to be authentic, you know, not farby. I think it takes away from the experience when you have re-enactors cooking on propane grills or walking around with a handful of Oreo cookies. Just not real, you know?"

I thought about how *none* of this was real, but kept my mouth shut.

"We talked before that times are changing and people want their little luxuries," he said with a sigh. "Pierpont and I instituted some stringent guidelines in the months leading up to this event. Rules were supposed to get even tighter for the Gettysburg battle. But that makes sense. Gettysburg is our main event." Florian gazed out over the group. "Some of the people are chafing at the new guidelines."

"The younger participants, I'll bet," I said.

"You'd be surprised. A lot of the old-timers are getting fed up, too." Turning to Frances, he grinned. "Your buddy Hennessey is one of them. He keeps a margarita blender in his tent. Geez, how much more farby can you get? Worst of all, he thinks he's being so clever hiding it from us. But we hear the motor running almost every night."

Frances wrinkled her nose. "He is *not* my buddy."

"Yeah, well, if he doesn't get rid of the blender, he's going to get fined." Florian seemed to forget we were there. "I really want the job, though," he said. "My dad would have been so proud."

"Who's running against you now?" I asked.

"I'm still unopposed, but that's not the point." He sighed, deeply. "I have some serious thinking to do."

"I wish you luck," I said. Frances echoed my sentiments.

"I'm going to need it."

Before I left, I asked him, "Do you know anything about an affair Zachary was having with one of the wives out here?"

Florian nodded. "I wondered if anyone would find out about that. Yeah, I know about Zachary and Mary Ellen. But I don't see Jeff as a suspect. He's drunk all the time.

We all wish Mary Ellen would dump the guy and come out to these events on her own. She's a nice lady. Really pretty and she's wasted with a loser like Jeff. Maybe she shouldn't have been fooling around, but if you met Jeff . . ."

"I've met Jeff," Frances said. "Seemed pretty lucid to me. Furious with Mary Ellen. Especially since she's taking Zachary's death pretty hard."

Florian shrugged.

"You expect us to believe that Jeff didn't hate Zachary?" I said. "That he didn't want him dead?"

Florian looked grim. "Maybe he did, maybe he didn't. And who knows what any of us are capable of?"

We talked a little longer. "I'd better be getting back," I said. To Frances, I added, "You're spending the rest of the day here, I take it?"

She wagged a finger in Florian's face. "You make sure that Hennessey stays away from me, you hear?"

Chapter 21

BACK AT THE MANOR, I DECIDED TO GRAB A little something to eat in the Birdcage Room. They were still serving afternoon tea, and I was famished. The two-story windowed room jutted out from the back of the mansion to the south. Our harpist was on a break, and the area was beginning to empty out. Since I wouldn't be taking up the space from a paying customer I sat close to the windows, and asked one of the waitresses to bring me a sandwich and some iced tea.

While I waited, staring out over the patio and the grounds beyond, I couldn't help think that something wasn't making sense. Zachary was apparently respected enough to be a shoo-in for the re-enactors' top job. Yet he was having an affair with a colleague's wife . . . while engaged to Muffy, a woman he'd jilted at the altar. This didn't sound like the behavior of a person who was esteemed enough to be voted into office.

Just as my food arrived on a dainty china plate, my cell phone rang. I silenced it as I checked the display. The last thing I wanted to do was disturb the serenity of this elegant room, so I headed outside to the patio to take the call. The number was local, but unfamiliar.

"Grace Wheaton," I said the moment I pushed through the glass door.

"This is Ron," he said.

"Who?"

"Ronny."

It took me a minute. "Tooney?"

"Yeah." He sighed. "Hey, good news."

"I'm a little busy right now," I said as I walked the patio's outer edge, thinking about my sandwich back inside. Keeping just inside the perimeter of the patio I tried to stay far enough away from meandering guests so as not to bother them.

"The people I took those pictures for?" he went on as though I hadn't spoken. "They're 99 percent sure the cat is their Mittens. They want to arrange a time to come pick her up."

"Wait a minute," I said, stopping in my tracks. "I haven't seen any proof. I'm not just handing her over on your say-so."

"Don't you trust me?" he asked. A second later, "Don't answer that."

"I'm not giving her up, you understand? Not unless you can prove it. And I haven't seen anything yet, let alone anything convincing. For all I know, you just want that reward and you're making all this up to take her from me."

There was silence on Tooney's end for a long moment. Then a low whistle. "Pushed a button, did I?"

"It wouldn't be the first time, Tooney."

I hung up and returned to my table inside. I sat and stared at my plate realizing I wasn't hungry after all.

JACK STOPPED BY MY OFFICE THAT AFTER-noon and took a seat at my desk, studying my expression. "What's wrong?" he asked.

As much as it killed me to keep silent about Tank and Rodriguez's revelation, I knew how Jack would react if I told him what the police had shared with me. He'd go storming down there in a fit of frustration and that would serve no purpose whatsoever.

I had to think hard before I took a step that could potentially hamper a police investigation. I knew, deep down, that Jack was innocent. He had to be. But I'd been led horribly astray by my heart before and no matter how hard I tried, I couldn't determine what the right answer was. Until I knew for certain what I should do, I decided to keep quiet.

Instead of sharing Rodriguez and Tank's suspicions, I told him about Tooney's phone call and Jack nodded sympathetically. Not for the first time, I cursed my rule-follower tendencies. But that didn't mean I couldn't try to lead Jack to his own conclusions.

"I met your dad today," I said.

He rolled his eyes. "Down at the re-enactment?" he asked. "I told him to stay home. I can handle Davey."

"He seemed upset that your brother is hanging out down there."

"Davey has a history—pardon the pun—of getting involved with a hobby, or a job, or even a girl, and then dropping it for no reason. He's been like that for a long time."

Jack didn't say the words, but I knew what he was thinking. That Davey hadn't been like this before Lyle Kincade's murder. "You never know," I said, "this time may be different."

"You don't know Davey."

"True . . ." I began. I thought about how Pierpont had taken Davey under his wing, and although the fanatical little general would hardly be my first choice for a role model, I'd seen stranger combinations. Maybe what Davey needed was an outsider to point him in a new direction. Maybe like his great ancestor, Henry Embers, Davey just needed a change of venue.

I was no psychologist, but from what I'd gathered, the older Embers brother, Keith; their dad, Gordon; and Jack had all tried to step in and "fix" Davey. A stranger just might offer enough distance to coax Davey out of his shell. "What harm is there in letting him participate? These re-enactors are moving out on Sunday anyway. Davey hardly has time to lose interest this go-round."

"Maybe."

"Have you talked with the police lately?"

"Why?"

"Just curious. They seem to be hanging around here a lot. I thought you might have some idea about that," I said.

"They've been hanging around here?"

"A bit."

"Talking about me?"

"Just a little."

"Why do you think they'd be looking for me?" Jack asked. "Did they say something about Davey? Something you're not telling me?"

"Not much more than they've said before," I hedged, "about Davey, that is."

The lines bracketing Jack's mouth deepened as he frowned. "Let's change the subject. I left you pretty abruptly the other night and I want to make it up to you. I was wondering if you'd like to go out again tonight. I thought we'd drive out to Westville for a change of pace."

Westville. Where the purported cat owners lived.

I hesitated.

"If you don't want to go, that's okay. Just say so."

"No, no. It's not that . . ." I didn't want to think about giving Bootsie up. I didn't want to think that the man seated across from me might soon be arrested for murder. I was failing miserably at my plan to keep my confidence yet somehow alert Jack to his predicament. Conflicting arguments battled within me. Brain versus heart with a little bit of gut thrown in. If I was so convinced of Jack's innocence—convinced enough to date the man, for crying out loud—then why wasn't I warning him about the cops' plans?

"You're very important to Davey," I said.

"Where did that come from?"

"You keep telling me that Davey was different when he was younger."

Jack looked about ready to jump out of his seat. "Yeah?" he said sharply.

This wasn't going well. "But I don't think the reason he has problems now is because he doesn't look up to you. Just the opposite, in fact."

"What are you saying? That because he thinks I killed Lyle, he wanted to be just like his older brother and so he went out and killed Zachary?"

"No!"

"I can't believe you think that about my brother."

"I don't. That's not what I'm saying at all."

Jack stood, threw up his hands, and started for the door. "Forget tonight. I'm not in the mood."

"Jack," I called to his back, "you're misunderstanding me. I don't think Davey killed anyone."

He held up a hand to let me know he'd heard. At the door he turned. "I'm sorry, Grace. I know you're trying to help. I know you don't believe Davey is guilty. But you're making judgments about people you don't know or understand. Until all this is resolved, I think we need our space."

And with that, he was gone.

I put my head back and closed my eyes. There had to be some way to fix this. I just wished I knew how.

WHEN I RETURNED HOME THAT EVENING, I found a manila envelope wedged under my back door with my name scrawled across in black marker. Though lightweight, it didn't bend easily, as though a piece of cardboard was wedged inside. Whoever placed it here apparently knew I generally came in the back way. No indication who had left it; I worried for a moment that it was one of my neighbors sending an anonymous note warning me to step up the house repairs, or else. I'd received a couple of those in the past, one with a handful of dead grubs the sender claimed had been harvested from my front lawn. Nice folks, these neighbors. I did my best to keep up, but fifteen new projects always seemed to pop up to take the place of the single one I completed.

If Bennett took control of this house, all that would change. That would make my neighbors happy for sure. I stared at the envelope in my hands. For all I knew, it would explode the moment I opened it. Annoyed now, and grumbling, I threw caution to the wind—why not? the day was ruined as it was—and ripped it open.

Four photos spilled out. Along with a note. "Here's your proof," Tooney wrote, "I'll be by Saturday to pick Mittens up."

I sat down on the concrete stoop to check out the pictures he'd enclosed. There was no denying this kitten's resemblance to Bootsie. In the first shot, two kids sat on a hardwood floor, dangling a fuzzy toy in front of little Mittens, who was in the process of jumping to reach it. In the next two pictures, the kids took turns holding the kitten. Her face was blurred and turned away from the camera, but her markings looked frighteningly familiar.

It was the final shot however, crisp, clear, and of the cat all by herself sitting on a window ledge staring out, that dropped my heart to the floor. Although I couldn't see her left side, and the picture was cut off just above the tip of the kitten's paws, it sure looked like the cat I'd come to love.

I turned back to the pictures of the kids. Both of them looked clean-cut and cheerful. The cat as happy as a cat can look. At least Bootsie would have a good home.

I heaved a sigh and went inside.

Chapter 22

TERRENCE CARR RAISED ME ON MY WALKIE-talkie early Friday morning. "Don't leave your office. I'll be there in five."

"Sure," I said, but when I tried to ask, "What's up?" he cut me off.

"I'll be right there," he repeated. "Don't go away."

Frances hadn't arrived yet, but I expected her at any moment. I wondered what sort of Civil War getup she'd be wearing today. As though in answer to my unspoken question, she trundled in less than thirty seconds later. When I got up to meet her in her office, I noticed she was dressed in lilac pants and a coordinating paisley top. Very twenty-first-century.

"You're not going back today?" I asked.

"If you order me down there, I don't have much choice," she said. "Is that what you want?"

"Mr. Hennessey getting to you?"

"I imagine there's a backlog of work mounting here. I didn't want it all to be waiting for me Monday morning."

"Lois has been helping."

She sniffed. "It isn't like I'm learning anything new anyway. When I left last night everything was normal. Too normal, if you ask me. These people don't even seem to remember that one of their friends was murdered."

Terrence opened the door, putting an end to the conversation. "Good morning," he said to both of us in a grave voice. Lips tight, he flicked his gaze from one of us to the other. "I may as well tell both of you."

We waited. Whatever it was, it wasn't good.

"They arrested Jack Embers last night," he said.

He held up his hands to quiet our exclamations. "I got a courtesy call this morning from Rodriguez," he said. "Gordon, Jack's father, went down there immediately to try to arrange for bail. With any luck, Jack should be released fairly soon."

"He couldn't have done it," I said. "He couldn't have."

"One of the re-enactors claims he saw him the night of the murder. Says he could tell Jack didn't belong but thought he was just a new recruit. Didn't think twice about it until he found out Jack was one of the suspects. Reported it to the cops immediately."

I couldn't help myself. "Do you believe he's guilty?"

"Doesn't matter what I think, or what anybody thinks. What matters is what the evidence tells us."

I said, "I'm going down to that camp and find out for myself. What's the name of the person who reported Jack?"

Terrence didn't know.

Frances said, "I'm going with you."

"You will?" I asked. "Why?"

"You won't know what you're doing."

"But you keep telling me Jack is trouble. Why would you want to help me?"

"What I believe is my own business. Now, do you want my help or not?"

* * *

BECAUSE WE WERE INFILTRATING THE CAMP
during its non-public hours, Frances was in charge of visiting the sutlers' tent to buy me whatever supplies I needed
to fit in. Before we left the manor I visited the ladies' room
to rinse off my mascara, then waited in the office while
Frances got changed. I tried calling Jack on his cell phone
and I even tried him at his house. No luck. I left a message
on both phones, asking him to call me. Just as I hung up
after the second call, Frances emerged wearing her Civil
War work dress. "Ready?" she asked.

"Let's do this."

She and I drove down to the south grounds, parking
among the vehicles left there, some of which had accumu-
lated a faint coating of dust.

"Shoe size?" she asked. I told her. Tucking a credit card
into her pocket, she gave me an appraising glance. "I can
figure out the rest. Wait here. I won't be long."

"They take credit cards?"

"These sutlers may not sell you anything farby, but
when it comes to accepting payment, rules about authenticity go out the window."

Whatever she picked up I hoped it would be cool. The
sun beat down from a cloudless sky and even though it was
still only mid-morning, I could already feel the stuffy
weight of hot air settling around us thick as a blanket. I
didn't know what I planned to do here, nor what I thought
I might discover, but there just seemed no other course for
me to follow.

I'd have to remember Lois's willingness to take charge
of the office so often this week. She was truly performing
above and beyond her job description. I made a note to
keep that in mind come bonus time.

Even though the windows were open and a slight breeze

blew in, my car baked in the heat and I felt like a turkey waiting to be pulled from the oven. All I needed was to be trussed. I certainly hoped corsets weren't involved.

True to her word, Frances was back in record time. I watched her clear the rise in determined strides, mounds of fabric draped over one arm, a bag clutched in the other. I got out of the car to meet her, noticing one dress of pale blue and another patterned fabric that appeared to be a formal gown. "I got you two dresses," she said, confirming my assessment. "One day dress similar to mine, only yours is a lot smaller. The other we'll keep on hand just in case. There's a big shindig—a ball—planned for tomorrow evening. I know we probably won't be there, but the sutlers were running low on merchandise and I didn't want us to come up short."

The day dress was a pin-striped blue cotton, long sleeved, with a button-front bodice and a petite white collar. Frances had picked up an unbleached muslin apron to wear over it. "Thanks, I'll put this on," I said, scooching over the center console into the passenger seat and casting a wary look around.

"Nobody's near," Frances said. "I'll stand guard."

Changing into a floor-length dress is not usually difficult, but trying to do so in the front seat of a car made for some interesting contortions on my part. After much wiggling, grunting, and sweating, I finally pulled the skirt into place. "This bodice is tight!"

"That's the way they're made. Does it fit?"

I sucked in my gut. "Yes." I had a feeling she was waiting for me to say something more. "Good guess on the size, Frances."

She grunted.

I got out and gave the formal gown a quick perusal. The deep-green-and-cream-colored dress featured a lace bodice and peplum waistline over a wide, gathered skirt. "It's absolutely lovely," I said as I stored it in my backseat.

"We can get you a hoop later," she said as she handed me a petticoat to slip under the work skirt. "I couldn't carry everything at once. But a lot of women don't bother with them anyway."

"I'll be fine."

Eyeing me critically, she said, "Part your hair down the center."

I complied.

"Turn around," she said.

"Why?"

She made a little circle with her finger and I did as I was told. She pulled my hair back, keeping my ears covered, and clipped my hair into a loose bun. Whipping a snood out from one of her cavernous pockets, she finished the job by covering my new 'do.

"Well?" I asked when I turned back.

There was surprise on her face. "I don't believe anyone will recognize you."

"Let's hope you're right."

When we reached the camp, no one gave us a second glance. "What do we do now?" I asked in a low voice.

"Stop whispering, for one," she said. Keeping her eyes forward, she nodded a greeting to two women walking past even as she continued talking to me. "Act like you've done this your whole life."

"Easy for you to say. This top is so tight I can barely breathe."

"You're lucky I didn't get you a corset. And that nobody will be checking what you're wearing underneath. Ten dollars to a doughnut every single woman you see here has a chemise and stockings, with garters to hold them up."

"Ugh."

"Most important, keep a lookout for Hennessey." She huffed. "That man."

* * *

WE VISITED JEFF, THE CHEATED-UPON HUS-
band who happened to be semi-sober at the moment. He
was sitting on a log outside his tent when we stopped by.
Frances greeted him as she might an old friend. "And how
are you today?"

Skinny and gray-skinned with bad teeth, Jeff looked to
be about fifty. He stared up at us with bloodshot eyes. He
wore a dingy white undershirt and stained pants. Gripping
a tin mug of coffee, he shrugged. "Been better." Indicating
the tent behind him, he said, "Wife's giving me grief.
Again."

As though summoned, a woman emerged from the tent.
Presumably the wife, Mary Ellen. "Nice to see you again,"
Frances said.

Mary Ellen was far younger-looking than her husband.
Mid-forties, she was voluptuously proportioned, the seams
of her cornflower blue day dress near to bursting. Freckled,
with blonde hair pulled back into a snood, she greeted us
with a thin smile. "Don't give him anything he asks for,"
she said apropos of nothing. She nodded hello to me, obviously puzzled as to my identity, but too polite to ask. Frances didn't bother with introductions.

"Beautiful day," Frances said.

Mary Ellen shrugged. "If you say so."

Jeff glared at her. "Is that any way to treat our guests?"

"Pierpont is going to be happy," Frances said, staving
off what looked like the beginning of a war between the
states—excess and temperance, that is. "I've decided to
become a regular."

Mary Ellen murmured an appropriate response but the
look behind her eyes asked, "What do I care?" She forced
a smile and strove mightily for hospitality. "May I offer
you a refreshment?"

Frances answered for both of us. "No, thank you," she
said, "we're on our way to see Pierpont right now to tell
him I've even brought a new recruit."

"I'd hold off a bit if I was you," Jeff said. "Him and Florian were having a little battle of their own earlier and I just saw Florian heading to Pierpont's tent for another go."

My interest perked up.

"Oh? What now?" Frances asked coolly, but I caught the glint in her eyes.

"Who knows? Who cares?"

Frances waved dismissively. "Men," she said, laughing like a girl, "always arguing." Without wasting even the smallest of movements, she nodded to both Jeff and Mary Ellen. "We'll leave you two alone now. Good day."

We set off, me at a brisk pace. "Slow down," Frances said. "You don't want to call attention to yourself."

"But I want to know what's going on."

Frances shook her head, causing her neck to waddle. "In good time," she said.

It turned out Pierpont's tent, more impressive than most of the others, was only about fifty steps away. As we drew closer to it, we heard the unmistakable cadence of an argument in process. The voices were hushed, but the spite and anger came through quite clearly.

"If I would have known you were a traitor, I would never have stepped down," Pierpont said, his voice zinging with tension.

Florian's more modulated answer, "I'm not a traitor, Rob. You know that."

Their next words were lost to us.

Frances spoke close to my ear. "We need to get close enough to understand, without raising suspicion."

I was ahead of her. I peeked inside the tent next to Pierpont's. Uninhabited at the moment, it provided the perfect listening post. Whoever owned this one didn't have a problem with farby; there was a double-sized blow-up mattress on a raised platform, a folding table piled high with pre-packaged foods and liquor, and next to it a small generator, along with an electric fan, lamp, and blender. Familiar logos dominated the space. But the most important consideration was that no one was there. I ducked inside and whispered for Frances to join me.

She did, but not without a glare of disapproval. "What do you think you're doing?" she asked. We could stand up straight if we stood in the center of the tent but we both kept ourselves hunched over. Maybe we thought that by making ourselves smaller we'd be harder to spot if the tent's owner suddenly showed? Yeah, right.

"Shh . . ."

Pierpont: "The only decent thing you can do now is to withdraw from the election."

Florian: "I'm unopposed, Rob. Did you forget?"

Pierpont: "You can't take over. Not anymore. I'll just keep the position awhile longer. There's precedent set for this situation. Remember when Sutherland died and they asked me to stay on for a couple more years?"

"That was a long time ago. Things have changed, Rob. People don't like all your rules."

Pierpont's voice was thin with tension. "My rules are not new and I'm not going to let you ruin this for all of us. Remember, I can ruin you." Pierpont's voice dropped. Frances and I leaned closer and cupped our ears in order to hear what he said next. "I know you want this position, Jim. I know how much it means to you and what it would have meant to your father. But if you don't back out of the election, today, I won't hesitate to use what I know."

Florian was silent for several seconds. "You can't do that," he said very softly.

"Don't push me."

They were both quiet for so long I thought they might have walked away.

A moment later Pierpont asked, "Do we have a deal?"

Florian uttered an expletive, then agreed. "I really despise you, Rob. Everybody hates you, you know. You better watch your back before you end up like Zachary."

We heard the snap of tent flaps, letting us know that Florian had left. Frances and I stared at each other wide-eyed as Pierpont said something under his breath.

But we missed what it was because Hennessey stumbled into the tent at that moment, nearly jumping out of his breeches when he saw us hunched there. "Hey," he said, his expression morphing from anger to delight in the heartbeat it took for him to recognize Frances. "Changed your mind, have you?"

"Certainly not," Frances snapped, ignoring my frantic gesticulations to keep it down. There was no way I wanted Pierpont to recognize either of our voices right now.

"Sorry, didn't know this was your tent," I said quietly. I started to shove Frances out ahead of me, but Hennessey blocked the way.

"You're trespassing," he said, "and now you two are going to sit down and tell me why."

"But—"

"Sit."

There was nowhere to do so but on the bed. Frances and I remained standing.

"I'm not stupid enough to think you two came to visit me," he said. "What's really going on here? You trying to steal my stuff?"

Frances, forgetting to keep her voice low, said, "How dare you!"

"This is all just a big misunderstanding," I said quietly, trying to keep close enough to the truth to talk our way out of this without actually spilling too much. "We thought we heard someone talking about . . . us." I waved my hand in the opposite direction of Pierpont's tent. "We wanted to hear what was being said. And it's hard to eavesdrop where everybody can see you doing it. We just ducked in for a minute to listen. We didn't realize this was your tent. Now, if you'll let us go . . ."

He didn't budge. Instead, pointing to Frances, he said,

"I'm a good catch, Frannie. Ask anyone. You shouldn't be so quick to judge."

She stayed silent, but if looks could kill he'd be dead on the floor.

"I'll let you go on one condition," Hennessey said. He waited for us to respond. When we didn't, he continued. "You," he said, pointing to me, "tell me what you're really doing here. I don't believe your cockamamie story for one minute."

I slid a glance toward Frances. She shrugged.

"Frances and I are looking for information."

He waited.

"We thought that if we blended in we might pick up clues about who killed Zachary Kincade."

"Didn't they just arrest the guy who did it?" he asked. "Jack Embers?"

"We don't believe he's guilty."

"Who do you two think you are? Jessica Fletcher and Nancy Drew?"

I put my hands up. "I know, but . . ." I suddenly realized there was no time like the present for gathering information. "Someone from your camp reported seeing Mr. Embers here the night of the murder. Do you know who it was who reported him?"

"That would have been Florian."

"How come he never said anything to us?"

Hennessey shrugged.

I asked, "Don't you think it's possible another re-enactor might have killed Kincade?"

His eyes narrowed. "Who are you thinking of?"

"Oh, I don't know," I said, thinking, *Florian, who else?* The way my luck was running, Hennessey would turn out to be one of Florian's best buddies. Sharing my suspicions could put my head on the chopping block in a hurry. "I mean, I know how ridiculous that sounds because of how much everybody liked Kincade . . ."

He made a noise. "Are you kidding?"

"I thought he was next in line to win the general's position?"

Hennessey laughed. "Only because he was buying votes. The old-timers hate his guts and only some of the younger crowd—the ones who think these weeks are for partying and getting drunk instead of experiencing history—were willing to vote for him. He wanted the job bad enough to fill those youngsters' tents with liquor and line the older folks' pockets with cash. Made me sick to watch."

"You didn't do anything about it?" I asked.

"Do what? Everybody saw what was happening. Everybody knew he was going to win."

Frances asked, "Did you tell the police this?"

He shrugged. "Sure, I mentioned it. They didn't seem to care. Not much motive for murder there, you know?"

Unless you were his opponent, I thought. Hennessey must have read my mind. "Not Florian," he said, "not a chance."

"Why not?"

"The man may be a brainiac, but he has no passion." He looked at Frances and wiggled his eyebrows. "And honey, that's where he and I are worlds apart."

JUST OUT OF EARSHOT OF THE CIVIL WAR group, I put in a call to Ronny Tooney. Frances stood next to me listening in, but for the first time I didn't mind. "Grace," he said when he answered. "You got my package of photos?"

"I'm not calling about the cat."

"You're not? You're not backing out of handing her over, are you?"

"Tooney . . ."

"Ron."

"Tooney," I continued, "I might need your help."

I could practically hear his attention perk. "For what?" he asked.

"First of all, what are your rates?"

"Seriously? You want to hire me?"

"Your rates?"

He mumbled to himself and I heard paper moving in the background. "I get a hundred an hour plus expenses."

Marshfield Manor could easily afford that, but I said, "Too high."

"Okay, fifty an hour."

"Deal. This is what I need." I asked him to do some digging. "Specifically, a guy named Jim Florian. Got that?" I spelled it. "He seems to want to take over for his boss, a Robert Pierpont, but Pierpont isn't letting him."

"This Pierpont. Is that *P-i-e-r* like a dock by the lake, or *P-e-e-r*, like what I sometimes do into windows?"

"Tooney!"

"I'm just messing with you," he said with a chuckle.

"Well, don't mess this up, okay?" I said. "And it's *Pier* like a dock."

"Got it."

I explained a little bit about the structure of the re-enactors' group as I understood it, and mentioned the conversation Frances and I had overheard. "Sounds like a little blackmail going on here. See what you can find out."

"You got it. How soon do you need it?"

"Yesterday."

"You know that will probably mean I have to put the cat owners on hold for a couple more days."

"Really?" I said. "What a shame."

BACK AT THE OFFICE, I LOOKED UP AN ADDRESS then spent my drive home arguing with myself as to whether I should actually use it or not. Half my brain warned not to get involved because unsolicited interventions are almost universally unwelcome. But the other half, my more empathetic side, encouraged me to trust my gut.

So, when I reached the center of town, I didn't stop at Amethyst Cellars. Nor did I take the turn onto Granville, which would have seen me home. Instead, I drove past the shops and businesses and headed east about five more miles to the very outskirts of Emberstowne.

The house I was looking for was a cookie-cutter copy of its neighbors, a modest two-story, probably built in the 1970s, with tan-colored brick and pale green siding. Mature trees shaded the deep front lot, and I pulled onto the gravel driveway wondering if anyone was home. There was a vacant, lonely feel to the place despite the fact that the shrubs were trimmed, the lawn was lush, and colorful annuals danced in the breeze. As I pulled all the way up and put the car into park, I realized what gave me that impression. The roof was uneven, the siding streaked with dirt, and one of the corner downspouts had separated from the gutters.

I made my way up the front steps, noting the weak and wobbly iron railing and the grimy film on the storm door. Taking a deep breath, I told myself that my concern outweighed my dread. I rang the doorbell.

Almost immediately I heard heavy footfalls. The big wooden door swung open and Mr. Gordon Embers gave me a quick once-over. "What do you want?"

"Good evening, Mr. Embers. I'm Grace Wheaton," I said. "We met the other day down at the Civil War reenactment camp."

He squinted. I watched recognition dawn. "Oh sure. My son talks about you."

"He does?" I said, pleased to hear it. "Is Jack here?"

"No, I mean Davey talks about you. You seem to have impressed him. That doesn't happen too often."

"Actually," I said, "I was looking for Jack."

Abruptly, his demeanor changed. "So I heard. What do you want with him?"

"I'm a friend," I said. "I heard he was out and tried calling him on his cell, but I haven't had any luck. I thought maybe he was here with you. I'd like to talk with him."

"Don't know where he is. When he's upset he goes off by himself. Nothing any of us can do about it. Just the way he is."

This was not turning out the way I'd hoped. "Is Davey here?"

Suspicion clouded his eyes. "He didn't just walk out on the job without telling anyone again, did he?"

I held up both hands. "No, not at all. He gave notice to me directly, in fact. Can I come in and talk with him for just a few minutes?"

"I don't know . . ."

"Dad," Davey said from behind his father, "let her in."

Grudgingly, Gordon Embers stepped aside, widening the door to allow me to pass. The place smelled of old sweat and burning toast. I must have reacted because he said, "We were just making dinner."

"Sorry, I didn't mean to interrupt."

"It's okay, Grace," Davey said. "Grilled cheese reheats pretty well and I wasn't really hungry anyway. Dad was making me eat something."

From where I stood, I could see into a bright yellow kitchen. Very 1970s. They showed me into the living room, where a flattened brown shag carpet and a white flagstone fireplace were focal points. Davey invited me to sit on one of the two gold sofas that faced each other in front of the hearth. All they needed was a ceramic avocado-colored lamp in the corner . . . And, yep. There it was.

"I just wanted to see how you were doing, Davey," I said. "I know that sounds lame, but it really isn't. This has been a tough week for you and now with Jack's arrest . . ."

"Have you talked with him since he was released?"

"I was hoping you had."

Davey flicked a look over my shoulder before meeting my gaze. "Ever since the first time this happened, Jack's become a real loner."

Mr. Embers hovered behind me, as though he was afraid I would make a fast move and send his son scurrying for cover. I wanted to assure him I was no threat, but there was no tactful way to do so. I tried to ignore his presence, but it was tough.

Davey must have sensed it because he said, "Why don't you go eat while it's hot, Dad? I'll join you later. I want to talk with Grace for a little bit."

"Sure, of course," Mr. Embers said, and left us alone.

Davey waited until his dad was out of the room to whisper, "I think he thinks you're my girlfriend." Before I could say anything, he added playfully, "Just wait until he finds out it's Jack you're interested in, not me. That'll throw him."

"How's he handling the latest developments?" I asked.

Davey stared up at the ceiling, sinking deeper into the cushions of his couch. I knew he was in his late twenties, but right now he looked like a terrified ten-year-old. "It's starting all over again," he said. "It's like there's a curse on our family. At least as it relates to that other family."

"The Kincades."

"Yeah, them." He looked away. "I thought this was over thirteen years ago. I thought we'd put it all behind us. And now this."

"I'm so sorry," I said. "Jack will be cleared soon. He has to be."

He tilted his head. "Doesn't matter if he's innocent. Everybody in town believes he's guilty of killing those guys."

I thought it was interesting that he didn't use the names of the victims when he spoke of them. "I believe he's innocent. I'm convinced one of Zachary's Civil War reenactment buddies is guilty." I didn't want to confuse the issue or get anyone's hopes up with my theories about Florian, but I added, "And I'm sure the police will figure that out soon, too."

Davey looked unconvinced. "You have faith in these local cops?"

"I have to."

"They don't know what they're doing," he said. "Either that or they're all just corrupt."

"I'm not crazy about that woman, Tank, but she certainly doesn't strike me as dishonest. A little bit stuck on herself, maybe," I said, "but Rodriguez seems like an honorable guy."

Davey shrugged. "Honorable," he said derisively, "right." Suddenly his eyes brightened. "You want honor? I talked with those Civil War guys for a while the other day. They can tell you about honor. About duty. About staying true and doing what's right."

I didn't know where this was coming from, so I kept my mouth shut and listened.

"I'm going back down there tomorrow," he said. "It's the last day of this encampment and my last chance to hang out with people who really take pride in what they do, you know?"

"Your brother Jack takes pride . . ."

"Jack wants me to do everything his way. He thinks he understands me, but he has no idea. None." Davey's voice lowered, and he glanced toward the kitchen. "I've only hung out at this Civil War re-enacting camp for a couple days but I already feel like I've learned a lot. About history. About myself even."

"That's great," I said.

The light went out of his eyes. "Yeah, well, what about when they leave again? Then what? I'm back to where I was."

I bit my lip. "Davey," I said, "I don't want to come off like someone giving advice . . ."

He waited. "Go ahead, you might as well. Everybody else does."

"Why not use the enjoyment you found in Civil War re-enacting as a springboard? Maybe there's something you want to do that isn't . . ."

"Gardening?" he prompted.

"I don't know what other interests you have, but there's nothing stopping you from learning."

He seemed to consider it. "How did you get to be such an optimist? I guess you've never experienced a personal loss, huh?"

"Are you kidding?" I said. "I've just learned to fake it long enough to get through the tough times. By faking it I sometimes even fool myself." Hearing my words, I added, "Sounds pretty ridiculous, doesn't it?"

Davey shrugged. "I envy you. I wish I could feel positive about life. I've tried, but it just doesn't work. Not in this life, anyway."

"Have you ever talked with anyone? Professionally, I mean?"

"Like a psychologist?" He gave an unhappy laugh. "No. My mom tried to talk me into doing something like that, but I didn't want to."

"What about your dad?"

He fidgeted. "My dad backed me up. Said that it would go on my record as a mark against me."

"What record?"

He shrugged. "Any record. All records. Whatever." He shrugged again. "Lotta good it's done me to avoid the head doctors, though, huh? I'll be thirty in a couple of years and I've got nothing to show for my life. How much worse of a record can you get than that?"

I decided to change the subject. "When did you last talk with Jack?"

"He doesn't want to talk to me," Davey said, playing with a fingernail. "He thinks I think he's guilty. Of both murders."

"Do you?"

Eye contact. "No!"

"Have you told him that?"

"He should know." Davey went back to his fingernail. "And besides, Jack believes what he wants to believe. He knows people still suspect him of the first murder. He clumps me in there with everybody else. Even after all these years." The thought seemed to depress him. "And now it's starting all over again. How am I supposed to deal with that now?" he asked rhetorically. "I want to be like those Civil War re-enactors. I want to do something honorable. To make it right for everyone."

I waited for him to explain what he meant by that, but he went back to examining his fingernail.

"I don't know why I'm talking with you," he said quietly, "I just don't think I can do this anymore." He finally made eye contact again. "You know?"

"Do what, Davey?"

He glanced toward the kitchen, hunching over as though trying to make himself small. Again, I felt as though I were talking to a child rather than a grown man. "The only reason they arrested Jack this time is because they believe he's guilty from last time."

I nodded encouragingly.

"But if they *knew* he was innocent, then maybe they wouldn't . . ."

Acting on a hunch, I leaned forward. "The only way the police will ever know Jack is innocent is if they found out who really killed Lyle."

Davey's face tightened in pain. "I know," he said under his breath, "I know."

Mr. Embers strode into the room, lasering his gaze on me. "I thought you were here to cheer Davey up," he said, "not to open up old wounds. What are you really here for, anyway?"

I stood. "Davey and I were just discussing . . ."

"I know what you were discussing. And your visit is over. You want to talk to Jack, go ahead. Good luck. If last time was any indication, you won't see or hear from him until he's ready."

"Mr. Embers . . ."

"Time for you to go home," he said. With a nervous glance at his son, he added, "I think Davey should have his dinner now." He turned back to me. "And next time you feel like stopping by, Ms. Wheaton, call first. We may not be home."

He and I stared at each other across the family room. In my peripheral vision I noticed Davey avoiding looking at either of us. There was something unimaginably wrong with this family dynamic.

Behind Gordon's angry glare, I caught a flicker of something else. Fear. I wondered what possible threat I posed to him. I turned to the young man on the sofa, who studiously refused to make eye contact. "Take care of yourself, Davey," I said. "Have fun at the closing ceremonies tomorrow."

"Ceremony?" Gordon demanded. "What are you talking about?"

Davey rolled his eyes. "The Civil War group. Tomorrow's the last day."

"You're not going back there?"

Davey made eye contact with his father, a defiant look on his face. "Uh, yeah," he said in the tone usually reserved for *Duh!* "I am."

I couldn't get out of there fast enough. "Thank you for your time, Mr. Embers," I said. "Talk to you later, Davey."

I hadn't even made it to the sidewalk when I heard the door slam behind me.

Chapter 23

I CALLED TANK ON MY WAY HOME.

"Working a little late, are you?" she asked. "It's Friday night. Shouldn't you be out on the town?"

Ignoring her invitation to make small talk, I got right to the point. "Can I get a peek at the police report for Lyle Kincade's murder?"

"Lyle?" she said. "You sure you don't mean Zachary?"

"I'm sure."

"Well," she said, elongating the word, "that's not usually done. Privacy issues, security concerns, you understand. Allowing you access could impede our progress on the case."

"It's been thirteen years."

"Murder cases are never closed, and this one's active again," she countered. "You know our focus."

I held my breath. "I know."

"Why do you want to see the old file?" Tank asked. "What do you expect to find?"

I hesitated. "I have a hunch."

Tank was silent. "A hunch," she said finally. "Care to share?"

"Not over the phone. But I think I'm right."

"Everybody who has a hunch thinks she's right. Until she's not."

I waited.

She gave a resigned sigh. "You got time now? Come down to the station. You and I will look over it together."

"I'll be right there."

THE EMBERSTOWNE POLICE STATION WAS housed in a former raised-ranch single-family home in the middle of a small subdivision that had probably cropped up about the same time the Embers' home had. The blue-sided structure was freshly painted and featured new windows, but the building still resembled a house more than it did a hub of law enforcement, despite the parked squad cars surrounding it.

I'd been inside before but had never gotten used to the smell. The new indoor-outdoor carpet's freshness did little to mask the sour and stale odors that permeated the building's pine-paneled walls, and the dropped ceiling that had yellowed with age and who-knows-what else.

Just inside the front door, visitors were faced with the choice to go up or down. Down the short flight were interrogation rooms and the lockup. If you could call it that. Lockup consisted of a scarred bench and handcuffs attached to either end. I'd often wondered what would happen if the police arrested more than two people at one time.

Tank stood at the top of the entrance steps. She tilted her head to her right and disappeared, leaving me to follow.

Upstairs, in a tiny office with one equally tiny window, I took a seat at her metal desk. "Where are Rodriguez and Flynn?" I asked.

"Home for the weekend. With me being from out of town, I don't have much to do here other than work, and we have a murder on our hands. I like keeping busy."

"Me, too," I said.

Atop the desk in front of her, was a thick expandable file covered in heavy blue cardboard. "Before I let you see this, I need to know what you hope to find."

I chose my words carefully. "If my hunch is right, Jack is innocent." I pointed to the blue folder. "Of Lyle's murder." I met her gaze.

"Uh-huh," she said. "You weren't here when this murder happened. Neither was I."

I sensed I was in for a lecture.

She tapped the blue cover. "It's not written here in black and white because it can't be. But every cop who was on duty thirteen years ago says the same thing: All their manpower was devoted to this case. They investigated hard. Yet Jack Embers was the only suspect they came up with. They all believe he's guilty. Unfortunately, knowing something and proving it are two different things. They couldn't make it stick, so they let it go. I trust these people. I trust their judgment."

"Which may have been clouded," I said, gauging her reaction. "I have another theory. I can't prove it, not yet, but there may be something in the file—something that confirms what I suspect."

"This file could just as easily prove you wrong. Are you willing to risk that?"

I nodded.

She came around to my side of the desk and took the seat next to mine, repositioning the book so we could both read it at the same time. She placed her hand atop the cover, fingers spread. "I'm doing you a favor, you have to do me a favor."

I knew what was coming and sucked in a breath.

"Before I open this," she said, "no more dancing around

the issue. You're going to tell me right now. Who do you think killed Lyle Kincade?"

I let out the breath I'd been holding. Very quietly I said, "Gordon Embers."

She stared at me, expressionless, then got up and shut the door. As she reclaimed her seat, she said, "This better be good."

I TRIED TO AVOID LOOKING TOO LONG AT THE pictures of the crime scene but the full-color images imprinted themselves on my brain faster than I could pass them to Tank. "Gruesome," she said, echoing my thoughts. "You sure you want to do this?"

"I'm sure," I said.

"What exactly are you looking for?" she asked. "Detectives from this department went over this file hundreds of times. They could never get enough evidence to stick against anyone. Not even Jack."

"Because Jack didn't do it. According to the guy who delivered his pizza, Jack was in his college apartment at the time of the murder. Far enough away that he couldn't have made it to Lyle's home and back. He couldn't have done it."

"Pretty flimsy alibi."

I looked at her. "Not if it's true. Which it is." I turned to the reports filed and to statements taken from everyone who had been interviewed. "I think there's a chance Gordon's alibi won't hold up."

Tank was shaking her head. "I've been talking to some of the older guys on the force here. They all swear Gordon was laid up with a back injury. He couldn't move."

I sifted through more pages. "Where's the doctor's report?"

Tank frowned and joined me in my search.

"If your alibi is a back injury, don't you think you'd have a doctor's report?" I asked.

"You think he made it up?"

"Gordon Embers supposedly hurt his back during an altercation with Lyle a week before the man was murdered. Here's something." I tapped a report. Tank read over my shoulder.

Frances had been wrong in this instance. Gordon Embers had most definitely been present the week before the murder when Jack and brother Keith went to "visit" Lyle. A complete list of injuries to all parties was included in the report. Jack's gashed face and Lyle's broken knee. Keith had apparently suffered a punch to the kidney and a broken nose. According to the report, Gordon had sustained no injuries.

Beneath this report was a statement issued by the police department to the press claiming that Gordon Embers had arrived on the scene just as his sons and Lyle Kincade started fighting. He was credited with breaking up the violence before it escalated further, and had been commended for his involvement.

"Nice way to get him off the hook," Tank said as she skimmed another page. "Here, I found the doctor's report. Take a look."

She handed me a statement from Gordon Embers's doctor dated several days after the altercation. Dr. Pfinster diagnosed Gordon with a severely pinched nerve in his back. He had recommended bed rest for a month and prescribed a combination of powerful painkillers.

"Those would choke a racehorse," Tank said. "Gordon must have been down for weeks."

"*If* he took the meds," I said, skimming the reports. I knew what I was looking for.

Tank stared at me. "Why wouldn't he?"

"What if he made it all up? What if there was no back injury? What if he faked all this to provide himself with an alibi?"

"Do you realize what you're suggesting?" Tank's expression was grim. "You're talking about premeditated murder."

"I know," I said. "I think Gordon got the idea to kill Lyle after the altercation in Lyle's home. They left the guy with a broken knee. He wouldn't have been able to put up much of a fight. It was now or never, in Gordon's mind. So he came up with the back injury idea, acted the part for the doctor's benefit, and came home to recuperate with a hefty supply of meds that served as his alibi."

She tapped the report. "Gordon's wife didn't work. She was home all day."

I pointed farther down. "Except not the day of the murder. Here, look."

Tank read what I'd been skimming—Eileen Embers's statement. When she finished, she said, "Okay, so the wife went out with her friends for the whole day."

"Right. Because, in her words, Gordon insisted that she get a day off from 'hovering over him.'"

"I see where you're going, but you forgot one important detail."

I hadn't but I let her talk.

"The son Davey was still in high school. An emergency at the school sent all the kids home early that day. Gordon couldn't have anticipated that. Davey says his dad was home when he got there, and that he never left. In fact, he said his dad never even got up off the couch the whole day."

"Uh-huh."

"What?" Tank asked. "You doubt the kid?"

"What if," I said, "Davey Embers came home from school and his father *wasn't* there? His father who was supposed to remain immobile? What if Gordon returned with no explanation, but when the cops came to interview the family he pressed Davey into swearing he'd been there the whole time?"

Tank sat silent for a moment. "The kid was about fourteen at the time?"

I nodded.

"Something like that would screw up a kid but good." She pursed her lips and stared away. "If you're right, and that's a big 'if,' there's no way to prove it. The kid would have been carrying the secret for half his life. He's not going to turn Dad in now."

"I know."

Tank didn't look at me as she continued to sort through the file. "Gordon Embers retired immediately after his medical leave was over."

"Is that significant?"

She met my gaze. "I've only met Gordon a couple of times but he strikes me as a man with strong convictions. And from what I understand around here, he was highly respected. He epitomized what police officers should be." She chewed her bottom lip. "How can a man who upheld the law for so many years ever reconcile himself with taking another human life? If you're right—and I'm not saying you are—he murdered Lyle in cold blood."

"To protect his family."

"To protect his family," she admitted. "He probably saw giving up police work as the price he had to pay for his deed." Tank scratched her forehead, then continued, "If Gordon Embers really did kill Lyle thirteen years ago, that throws a new light on Zachary's murder."

"How so?"

She waved a hand. "I'm not suggesting Gordon killed Zachary, but what I told you about it getting easier the second time, is true. With the entire PD convinced Jack was guilty of Lyle's murder . . ."

"Jack became the target of your suspicions," I finished. "I get it." My mind raced. Should I share any of this with Jack? Telling him I suspected his father of murder would surely put an end to our burgeoning relationship. But how could I *not* tell him?

Tank read my thoughts. "Do not say a word to anyone."

I started to open my mouth.

"Not a word, do you understand?" She brought her face closer and kept her voice low. "All you'll do is open a can of worms that you can't handle. If you're right, Gordon Embers killed once to protect his family. Do not put a target on your back by threatening him."

"But what if it is true? Doesn't Davey deserve a chance at a better life? Wouldn't bringing the truth out into the open help him face reality? Maybe give him the opportunity to grow up?"

Tank held up a finger. "Not your concern. Not now. Give me a couple days to sort this out. Let me make some discreet inquiries, okay? That's the key here—discretion. If I start asking questions about this old case, no one will think twice. Heck, I've been doing that already. But if you start poking around . . ." She let the thought hang. "Don't."

I gave a huff of frustration. I wanted to do something.

"Give me your word," she said.

I stared up at the older woman. For the first time, I noticed that her eyes were a pale gray rimmed in dark blue. Piercing, and more than a little unsettling. I didn't give my word lightly and I wasn't ready to do so now.

"Grace," she said, startling me with her force.

I knew I wasn't getting out of this room without agreeing to keep quiet. "Okay."

"Say it."

"I won't share my suspicions about Gordon Embers with anyone." After a pause, I added, "I give my word."

She nodded acknowledgment. "And I give my word I'll keep you posted on developments."

I called Jack on my way home just to let him know I was there for him. Got his voicemail again. "Jack," I said, "talk to me. You can't crawl into a hole like this. If you and I are ever going to have a relationship, we have to learn to work together. Give me a try. If we make it through this . . ."

I wanted to say that we'd make it through anything, but

that was cliché and melodramatic. Instead I simply said, "Trust me, okay?"

When I got in I saw a blinking light on my answering machine. Jack had left me a voicemail on the house phone. "I got your messages," he said haltingly, "and even though I know you're right I just can't talk right now. I can't see anyone. It's all happening again and this time I don't think . . ." There was a pause. "Just give me time, Grace. Please. I promise that when I'm ready I'll get in touch." He made a sound like he wanted to say more, but hung up instead.

I stared at the phone for a long time.

Chapter 24

SATURDAY AFTERNOON, I MET FRANCES AT the office. "Sorry to infringe on your weekend," I said, "but I appreciate you helping me out."

"I should take this next week off just to make up for all my playacting," she said with a frown, "but I know I'm going to have piles of work waiting for me." Heaving a deep sigh, she added, "I expect you're keeping track of the time off I'm owed."

"Of course."

"Good. So am I."

Of that I had no doubt.

Today's visit to the Civil War camp was of utmost importance to me. Not only would the camp be open to the public for most of the afternoon as drills and battles were re-enacted, but tonight was the celebratory ball signaling the official end of the event. Although I had a passing interest in seeing some of these things, what I wanted most of all was to talk with Davey again. I had a feeling that he would open up to me if I could get him alone again for just a little while.

Clearing Jack of the first murder wouldn't automatically clear him of the second, but it would be a good start. I wanted Frances along today because I was convinced that one of Zachary's Civil War colleagues did him in, most likely Jim Florian. If we were to learn anything of importance about Zachary's murder from these people, it would have to be today or not at all.

Frances, clad in her 1860s-era working shift with her ball gown draped over one arm, took a final look at her watch before removing it from her wrist. Giving me a pointed stare she wiggled a finger at my blue jeans and tank top. "You better get changed. We should get down there ASAP."

I planned to slather on sunscreen after I donned my Civil War getup, but as I dug through my bag, I couldn't seem to find it.

"Can't you move a little faster?" she asked. "You're not even changed yet."

"Why are you in such a hurry?"

"No reason," she said stiffly. Then added, "It's just that I told someone I'd meet them down there before it opened to the public."

I looked up. "Who?"

"Hennessey."

My eyebrows arched.

"Get your mind out of the gutter, missy. The only thing I want from him is information. Last time we talked, he seemed a lot more tuned in than I'd given him credit for. We have about a half hour before I told him I'd be there."

"So he's more of a kindred spirit than you originally thought."

She made a noise of disdain. "Do you want to help figure out who killed that Zachary fellow or not?"

I grabbed my day outfit and started for the nearest washroom on this floor. "I'll be right back," I said.

Although the facilities in this part of the mansion had

been upgraded when converted into an administrative wing, the last time this section had seen any renovation had been in the early 1960s. Pink tile floors and walls, high ceilings, and black-seated toilets between pink stalls kept the room bright, though severely dated. With everyone in this area off for the day except me and Frances, I opted to avoid a cramped stall, and instead started changing clothes in the middle of the room.

I'd just pulled the dress over my head when I heard the bathroom door open. "Eep!" I screamed, scrambling to pull the fabric down past my face, to see who had come in.

Frances held my cell phone out to me. "Sorry," she said, "it's for you. I thought it might be important." She gave me a funny look. "Your dress is on backward."

I hated that she was right and that I looked stupid. Forgoing the bodice, I jerked the garment down to my waist, and stood there in my contemporary cami with a poofy blue skirt cocked unevenly at my hips. "Thank you," I said, reaching for the phone. "Hello?" I said into the little receiver.

"Grace?"

"Tooney?" I said, recognizing his voice. "What did you find out?"

"I need more information first," he said. "Couple of dead ends so far. This guy you want me to investigate, where's he from?"

For a half-second I couldn't come up with it, then remembered what Frances had told me about Florian being a big shot at NASA. "He lives in Florida," I said.

"Great. I'll be in touch."

When he hung up, Frances asked, "What did he want?"

"Just wanted to know where Florian lived. That must be a more popular name than I expected."

WHEN WE ARRIVED, MOST OF THE RE-enactors were gone. An elderly woman was seated outside her tent under an improvised awning. Perched on a small stool, she shucked corn on top of a wooden box that had been turned on its side and wobbled on the uneven ground. Her skirt was pulled up, exposing bony knees she kept spread wide around her makeshift table. "Where is everyone?" Frances asked her.

"Hot one today, isn't it?" the woman asked with a toothy smile.

"Very hot," Frances agreed, fanning herself.

They weren't kidding. Although it was still only midmorning, the sun beating down on us was making me doubly glad I'd eventually found my sunscreen. Perspiration gathered at my hairline and I felt bright beads hover before tracing their hot path down my back. The tight bodice wasn't helping matters. I glanced down and noticed a small damp patch of sweat forming just below my neckline.

"Gonna get hotter before it gets cooler," the woman added.

I'd been busy looking around. "Over there. Way down past the last Confederate tents," I said. "Looks like that's where everyone is gathered."

"Sure enough," the woman said, tossing the cleaned ear of corn into the pot next to her and grabbing a fresh one to shuck. "That there is the practice for this afternoon's battle. Gotta get it all right, you know. Don't want the wrong side to win this time." She chuckled at her own joke.

"Thank you," I said as Frances and I set off.

"You'd be smart to stay up here, where it's nice and cool," the woman said. She winked at me and beckoned me to come closer.

Frances gave me the eagle eye as I obliged the old lady.

"Lookie what I got," she said triumphantly, leaning back so I could peer into the upturned wooden box. An electric fan, its cord covered by debris to keep it hidden, whirred quietly inside. "They ain't getting me to come down to that sweltering meadow. No way."

I grinned at her. "I don't blame you a bit."

We started off again and she raised a hand to wave good-bye. "Hope you find what you all are looking for."

I waved back. "Me, too."

"Are you like that with everyone?" Frances asked.

"Like what?"

"So . . . insufferably cheerful."

I turned to catch a look at her face, to see if she might be kidding. She wasn't. I shrugged. *Not with you*, I thought.

BY THE TIME WE MADE IT TO THE BATTLE-ground, the final scripted attack was under way. "We missed him," Frances said, clearly miffed. "He wanted to meet me before the last battle began."

"I'm sorry, Frances."

She waved off my apology. "It is what it is," she said. "Let's go watch."

Ropes laid out on the grass separated the participants from the onlookers. Frances and I fell in behind the families gathered there, watching husbands, brothers, and friends wage war.

A cry went up and hundreds of soldiers leapt into action, both on horse and on foot. Reverberations from the galloping hooves trembled the ground beneath my feet. Men shouted and screamed. Some fell, clutching their sides, writhing to the ground in mock pain.

Sweat popped out from every pore in my body. The heat and brutality combined to make me light-headed, and a quick glance at Frances told me she was feeling the same. "This is more real than I expected," I said in a hushed voice.

Frances nodded but stayed silent.

Standing next to me, a mother leaned over one of her kids and whispered, "This your first time?"

I told her it was.

"It still hasn't gotten old for me. I've been doing this for years, but I remember the first time I came to one of these with my husband. Never expected to be as . . . moved . . . as I was."

She was exactly right. I'd never experienced war first-hand and I certainly hoped I never would, but this event, though pretend, was having an effect on me I hadn't antici-pated. Men charged and fought and died on the field in front of me. I swallowed. "This is intense," I said.

The woman smiled and tousled the hair of the young boy next to her. "It is," she said.

Frances hadn't said anything for a long time. Her face was unreadable.

Someone called a halt, and all the "dead" soldiers got to their feet, coming to join their families and grab a drink of water. Frances tapped me on the arm. "Let's find Hennessey."

It didn't take long. We walked along the outer perimeter of the battleground and found him grabbing a long drink of water from an upturned canteen. The liquid dribbled down his beard as he gulped and when he finally opened his eyes, his face lit up when he saw us standing there. "Well, there you are," he said, pleased. "Did you see me in action?"

I smiled. "Pretty impressive." But Hennessey was more interested in what Frances had to say.

She backed away from him, waving her hand in front of her nose. "Don't you ever bathe?"

Not at all insulted, Hennessey guffawed.

"I'm sorry we were late," I said. "We hoped to talk with you before the battle."

He was shaking his head before I got the apology out. "Change of plans. Last night we got the final schedule. Everything got shifted."

"Oh," I said, "what about the events for tonight?"

"You mean like the ball?" he asked, wiggling his eye-brows at Frances. "You going to save me a dance, honey?"

"Not unless you fumigate yourself first."

"Hoo-wee," he said, "that's a date."

My eyebrows shot up, but Frances refused to look at me.

"What about voting the new general in? When will that take place?" I asked.

"Just past sundown and right before the ball. We get all dressed up in our best finery"—another lurid glance at Frances—"and just after sundown we take a vote. But with Florian running unopposed, that shouldn't take more than a minute or two. Then it's party time." He examined the sky. "We don't have that much longer to go. I'd best go wash up, right, Frannie?"

Frances had been fanning herself ever more quickly as he'd talked. A thin sheen of perspiration gathered on her upper lip and her face had lost all color.

"Frances," I said, grabbing her arm, "are you okay?"

She started to answer, but her eyes fluttered then rolled back in her head. She pitched forward, dead to the world. Fortunately Hennessey grabbed her from the other side. "Medic!" he shouted to the crowd. "We need a medic."

I turned Frances onto her back and loosened the collar of her dress. Hennessey splashed water onto his hands and patted Frances's face. Less than a minute later a medic ran up, but Frances's color had begun to return. She opened her eyes. At first confused, she looked around, saw me and Hennessey crouched on either side of her, and her expression flashed to fury. "Oh for heaven's sake," she said, trying to boost herself up.

"Stay down, Frances."

"I will not allow myself to be a spectacle . . ."

"Just relax," I said sharply. "It's brutally hot out here, you're wearing layers and layers of clothing, and you passed out. It's completely normal."

"Not for me it isn't," she said, but when she tried to sit up again I could tell it took too much effort. "If I can get to a chair, maybe . . ."

The medic's tent was all the way back in the center of camp, near the sutlers' area. "We'll get you there," I said, "just take your time. Have some water."

She did, and after drinking a little she was able to sit up in the grass. "Everyone is staring at me," she said. "Get me out of here."

"I don't think you're ready . . ."

Through clenched teeth she repeated, "Get me out of here."

"Give the lady what she wants," Hennessey said as he and I helped Frances to her feet. "I gotcha, honey."

She didn't fight him. Even more surprising, she didn't fight me.

The three of us, with the medic trailing, made our way slowly back toward the camp. The few times I thought Frances might go down again, she surprised me by continuing to put one foot in front of the other by sheer force of will, until we made it all the way to the medic's tent.

"Go back to your group," I said to Hennessey when we'd gotten Frances stretched out on a cot. Rules against farby didn't apply here. The white tent was clean and smelled of disinfectant. There was an oscillating fan blowing from the far corner, and the medic pulled out a bottle of lemon-lime Gatorade from a nearby cooler.

He handed it to Frances. "This should help."

"Don't you have purple?"

"The patient is feeling better, I see," he said with a smile. "Purple, coming right up."

As the medic exchanged flavors, Hennessey dragged over a stool and positioned it next to the cot. "I don't need to go back," he said. "I think I'll just stay here awhile."

Frances took a deep swig of her purple Gatorade. "Much better," she said. Before taking another drink she turned to glare at me. "What are you waiting for?"

My mouth opened, but I didn't know what to say.

"Go," she said, making a little scooting gesture with her

free hand. "You have work to do. It will be sundown before you know it. Get going."

MOST OF THE RE-ENACTORS WERE RETURN-ing to camp from the far battleground. From their conversations, it was obvious all were preparing to change into their evening wear. I hadn't seen Davey, nor Florian, and I didn't want to waste time hoofing it all the way back to the car in this heat just to don my ball gown. Being properly dressed for the ball was nowhere near as important as talking to Davey alone. Where could he be?

For a moment I wondered if Gordon had succeeded in dissuading his son from participating. I hoped not. For some reason I couldn't quite understand, this activity had struck a chord with Davey. It was obvious the young man needed focus. If this was where he found it, then Gordon shouldn't stand in his way.

Of course, Gordon might not be as concerned about Davey finding a creative outlet as he was worried that his youngest son might find a confidante. That, I believed, was what terrified Gordon most of all. And was what kept him hovering over his son, watching every move like a daddy hawk.

Davey had obviously never confided in Jack. I wondered why I believed he might confide in me. I didn't know, but I knew I had to try. Too many lives were hanging in the balance.

Making a second circuit of the camp at the southern edge of the Union side, I was starting to feel a bit self-conscious. All the other women had put on their ball gowns, and the entire feel of the encampment had changed. This was more *Gone With the Wind* barbecue at Twelve Oaks than a collection of wannabe soldiers in grubby duds. The men, changed into dress uniforms, offered their arms to hoop-skirted companions as they strolled about the grounds. The mood was cheerful and festive as participants meandered, laughing and sharing drinks.

I wandered about in my cotton work dress, which clung to my skin like hot butter on popcorn. As desperately as I wanted to peel it off and change clothing, I knew this was no time for vanity or even comfort. Sliding hair away out of my eyes, I continued to scan the crowd, desperate to find Davey. I would never be welcome at the Embers home again and I didn't know when else I'd ever have the chance to speak with him. Much hinged on him finally coming clean with the truth. Would he?

Deep within my cavernous dress pocket, my cell phone vibrated against my left leg. I'd had the presence of mind to turn the ringer off when I came down here, but I stopped short of leaving the device behind. I'd refused to give up my sole connection to the real world. Not today.

There was no way to answer it without causing a farby commotion, so I hurried up the nearby incline, hoping to scurry down the other side before whoever was calling hung up. I made it to the top of the rise on the phone's third ring and nearly froze in my tracks at the crest. Directly below me was the spot where Zachary had been killed.

My heart thrummed in my throat, but I bit my lip and continued down toward the ravine, plucking the phone from my pocket and answering it the moment I was out of sight.

It was Tooney.

"Grace?" he said.

"Talk fast."

"Okay." He took a breath, then began, "Your guy is squeaky clean in the real world. Well, sort of."

"Is he, or isn't he?"

"Let me start again. He's held the same job for thirty years."

Thirty years? I didn't think Florian was old enough to have been working that long.

Tooney kept talking. "Same apartment, too. Has a routine he follows. No deviation. Spends every lunch hour at a library near his office researching the Civil War, and stops at his local bookstore twice a week on the way home to see if any new Civil War books have come in. Lives alone, spends all his downtime on research."

This did not sound at all like Florian. He had a family. I'd met one of his kids. None of this fit.

"Tooney, are you sure? How could you find this out? How would you know his routine? It's not like you could have shadowed him. He's been here the whole time."

"That's where it really gets interesting," he said. "Hang on."

"Don't play games with me. Just spill it."

"No, wait, listen. There's more. He logs onto Civil War sites all the time: chat rooms, LISTSERVs, you name it."

"Hurry up, Tooney."

"The guy has at least three dozen different screen names and he comments from each of them as though they're different individuals."

"So?"

"So there's a lot of chatter on these sites. Civil War re-enactors discussing plans, ideas, the future. Your guy is a dyed-in-the-wool purist. A vanishing breed, it seems. He's one of the few left fighting against . . ." Tooney hesitated.

"Farby?"

"Yeah, exactly. So he puts his views out there under his real screen name then assumes these other online personas to voice support for his own agenda. Pretty clever."

"Are you making all this up?"

"No." Tooney sounded hurt. "How could you even think that?"

So far there wasn't much to indicate that Florian was hiding something. "I don't understand how you suddenly came across all this great intelligence," I said. "It's not as though people's daily schedules are available on the Internet."

"I told you, that's where it gets interesting."

"Quit dancing around. Just tell me."

"I got most of this information from a private investigator. Great guy. I could learn a lot from him." Just as I was about to ask what any of this had to do with Florian, Tooney continued. "This PI was hired by a family named Sutherland to look into their father's sudden death."

"I'm not following."

"The death was ruled suicide, but the family didn't believe it. Sutherland was in great shape, healthy, happy. In fact, he was running for election as top man of his Civil War group." Tooney paused. "Starting to sound familiar?"

"Go on."

"Sutherland was the man to beat, but just before the election, he killed himself. Supposedly."

"Okay . . ."

"The family asked this PI to conduct a private investigation—and it's ongoing. They keep this PI on retainer and he shadows your guy a couple times a month. We did a little professional reciprocity. He shared some of his findings with me and I gave him a heads-up about what's been going on here."

My head spun. Sutherland. That name was familiar. Pierpont and Florian had mentioned him when we were eavesdropping the other day. But what had been said? I couldn't remember exactly.

"Pretty good work, if I do say so myself," Tooney said.

"Couple of things aren't making sense."

"Like what?"

"Why would Sutherland's family think Florian had anything to do with their father's death? As far as I know, this is the first time Florian is running for election."

Silence.

"Tooney?"

"Uh . . ." I thought I heard Tooney swallow. "Florian? I thought you wanted me to check out Pierpont. Remember, *P-i-e-r* like the dock?"

"Are you telling me you wasted all this time investigating the wrong man?" Frustrated, I fought for control. Closing my eyes for a count of five, I took a deep breath and opened them again.

"I'm sorry . . ." he said. "I could have sworn . . ."

I rubbed my hand along my forehead, immediately sorry I'd done so when it came back sticky with sweat. "Okay," I said, staring at the ground, "give me a minute." My brain needed time to recap everything Tooney had just told me, replacing Florian with Pierpont. The conversation Frances and I had overheard now fit. Pierpont had referred to precedent being set when he had to step in for Sutherland after the man's sudden death.

I must have been quiet for too long because Tooney asked, "Grace?"

"Yeah," I said, finally looking up.

Davey stood on the rise, right above me.

"Gotta go, Tooney," I said, and slapped my phone shut.

Chapter 25

DAVEY DIDN'T WAVE, NOR DID HE SEEM pleased to see me. The moment we made eye contact, he turned away and headed back down the other side of the hill.

I ran after him. "Davey!"

By the time I'd crested the rise, he was gone. With the sun beginning to set, re-enactors were gathering in the center, where the sutlers' tents had been broken down and removed, and where a makeshift stage was being set up next to a giant campfire. The bright yellow flames drew people in like moths as the evening light eased from orange to purple. I stood atop the hill wishing for just a little more light, wishing I knew why Davey had run.

Tooney's report was playing over and over in my mind. Pierpont suspected of foul play? Could Tooney have gotten it wrong? Could Florian have killed Sutherland? Was that what Pierpont held over the other man's head?

"Grace!"

I turned. "Jack?"

"Hurry," he said, waving impatiently. "We need help."

I was down the hill in a heartbeat.

"Come on," he said falling into a brisk jog. "We have to get back to the Confederate side."

I joined him, running. "Wait, why?"

Jack kept turning his head from side to side as he ran as though looking for someone. "I don't have time to explain it all, but my brother Keith just texted me from the Confederate camp. Somebody there might have seen Davey. We need to find him."

I pointed back the way we'd come. "*I* just saw him."

Jack stopped. "You did? Was he okay?"

"Yeah. I called to him, but he took off."

"He's going to the Confederate side, come on."

I followed him past the Union's western boundary, where Jack pointed to the right, guiding us around the crowd that was gathering at the camp's center. His lips were tight and his face was pale.

Out of breath I asked, "What happened?"

"Davey left a suicide note."

I stopped in my tracks.

He grabbed my arm but I pulled away. "We don't have time for this," he said. "We have to keep moving."

"No." I thought back to where I'd seen him. "Suicide?" Staring suspiciously, people navigated around us. I grabbed Jack's arm and pulled him out of the traffic pattern. "What was in the note?"

Jack's eyes were wild. He tried to pull away but I held tight.

"This is important," I said.

"He claims to be guilty of killing both Lyle and Zachary and said that this was the only place—this re-enacting camp—where he felt a sense of honor. He wants to die here." Jack's eyes tightened. "But that can't be . . ."

"Did you call the police?"

"My dad did. They're on their way. Maybe they're already here."

I let go of Jack's arm and started back the way we'd come. "I know where he's going."

"No, he's over on the Confederate side. Keith said so."

I took another few steps east. "No," I said, "he's going to be where Zachary was killed. He'll think it's symbolic. Trust me."

"He's over there." Jack pointed westward, then backed away, hands up. "I can't risk being wrong. Davey's life is at stake."

"I know," I said, "that's why I have to go back."

I WISHED I HAD ON RUNNING SHOES INSTEAD of these Civil War clodhoppers. My feet pounded the ground, beating a staccato rhythm that echoed in my head and my heart. I whispered, "Don't, Davey. Please don't," as I ran. A new crop of sweat burst out over the dried and crusty residue that was already there, causing my clothing to stick to every inch of my skin. Temperatures had cooled and the brisk breeze I generated by running chilled me to the bone. The very definition of a cold sweat.

I finally reached the far edge of the Union camp. Quiet and empty because everyone had gravitated to the center, I was completely alone, hearing only the pulse of my heart in my ears, the heaving of my every breath, and crickets chirping in the night.

Just a little farther.

Panting, I scrambled up the familiar hill yet again, my thighs burning with exertion, my hands scraping the dry grass, seeking purchase. I finally made it to the top and looked down.

"Davey?" I called.

No answer.

I looked back the way I'd come. What if I was wrong?

Darkness was settling quickly now and I could make out very little beneath the heavy canopy of trees. Not for the first time did I think that whoever had picked this location to kill Zachary had chosen well. One thing I would bet, though—it wasn't Davey.

I started down the other side, moving as quickly as I could without being able to see the ground clearly enough to know where to step. I half slid to the bottom, much the way I did the morning Zachary's body was found. The similarities were too eerie. "Please," I whispered to the dark sky above, "don't let Davey be dead."

Davey could be fifty feet in front of me and I wouldn't know it. The line of trees that had sheltered Zachary's murder so effectively could be providing cover for him as well. "Davey?" I called, more quietly this time, like I was afraid of scaring him off. "I know you're here."

My breathing was deep and ragged from my sprint and I shuddered, both from the evening chill and from the ominous shadows around every tree. Nearby, a branch snapped and I jumped, suddenly remembering my vow to keep out of danger. But Davey wasn't dangerous. Not to anyone but himself, at least.

"Please, Davey. I know you're here. Talk to me."

Leaves rustled far to my left.

I tried again. "I hear you breathing, Davey." I didn't, but it sounded plausible. "Just come out. You can trust me."

Another couple of twigs snapped, closer to me this time. "I thought you went off with Jack," Davey said, and stepped out of the foliage into what little light remained.

I'd been holding my body tense but now relaxed ever so slightly. "Jack thinks you're hiding on the Confederate side of the camp."

He was close enough now for me to see his face. Disappointment flittered across his features as he stared westward. "Jack has never understood me." Turning to me, he asked, "How is it you do?"

I didn't know, and said so. "Kindred spirits, maybe." He

didn't say anything, so I inched closer. "Don't do this, Davey. You're not helping anyone."

"Jack told you about the note."

It wasn't a question.

"You didn't kill Lyle," I said, "and you didn't kill Zachary either."

"Sure I did," he said flippantly. "And once I'm dead, they can close both cases. My family won't have to live under the constant suspicion anymore. I want to do this for Jack."

I stepped a little closer, then noticed he had a gun in his hand. "And for your father?"

He looked away.

"Lyle lived in a different town. You were fourteen," I said. "You couldn't drive."

"Yeah well, that doesn't mean I didn't do it."

I pointed. "Is that one of your father's guns?"

Davey nodded.

"Don't kill yourself to cover up for him."

His face tightened in pain. "No one knows. How did you figure it out?"

I thought about Tank's assessment of Davey being damaged goods. The same could have been said about me just about a year ago. "Like I said, kindred spirits."

He didn't answer, so I went on, "You came home that day but your father wasn't there. Is that right? Did he force you to cover for him?"

"No, never," Davey said quickly. "He didn't have to ask. I took one look at his face and I saw . . . something terrible. Grief, I guess. Hard, raw, intense grief. Once I heard Lyle was dead it didn't take much to figure out what had happened." Davey worked his teeth over his bottom lip. "I saw what it had done to him—to my dad, I mean. He was broken. I might have only been a kid, but I understood everything in that minute. I couldn't turn him in. He was just protecting our family. Protecting Calla. It destroyed him to do what he did. And I'm just as guilty as he is. Lyle's dead. That can't be changed. Turning my dad in wouldn't do anyone any good."

Davey's voice grew bolder as he spoke as though finally sharing the memory had given him strength.

"Now it's my turn to protect my family," he said. "You have to understand that. Just walk away."

"You know I can't do that."

Davey turned the gun over and over in his hands as he spoke. I thought about trying to make a grab for it, but knew such a move would not only be dangerous, but would ruin any trust we'd built. "Grace, please. Let me do this. Otherwise, what am I besides useless? I have no life. I have nothing to live for. I don't know why I didn't think of this sooner."

"Stop a minute, Davey. Think." Buying time, I reasoned with him. "Put Lyle's murder aside for a moment. You didn't kill Zachary. Neither did Jack. So . . . why take the blame for that one? You're letting the real murderer off scot-free."

He shrugged. "Except everybody *thinks* Jack did it. If I confess and then kill myself, they'll close the cases and Jack will have his life back."

"It doesn't work that way."

Noises, voices from behind me. Davey flinched. I turned.

"Oh my God," Davey said, staring upward.

There was enough ambient light up there for us to make out a group of about seven gathering at the top of the rise. Jack, his father, another man who had to be Keith Embers, Tank, and several uniformed officers. Jack had his hands out as though asking, "Where?"

Tank pointed right at us, but I could tell we couldn't be seen.

"Don't move," Davey whispered, close to my ear.

"You can't hide forever," I whispered back.

"I don't intend to hide anymore," he said softly. "This is my life, Grace. For once, let me make my own decision."

I swallowed around what felt like wadded-up sand-paper.

He gripped my arm with his free hand and again spoke close to my ear. "As soon as they go back down, you follow them," he said. "Don't look back."

I tried to turn, but he shook me to face forward.

"No argument."

"Davey, please."

But my words were lost as Gordon Embers shouted his son's name at the exact same time. "Davey," he called again, his voice cracking, "are you there? Please, son, an-swer me."

Davey gripped me harder, and pointed the gun at his own head. We stayed very still. I wanted to call out, to scream. To alert them to our location, but deep inside I knew that any quick movement would be disastrous for us all.

"Please son, I'm begging you." Gordon's voice broke and we both heard him stifle a sob. "I'll do anything. Just please, don't hurt yourself."

Davey's fingers tightened around my upper arm, and I could feel his body trembling. I heard him swallow three times in rapid succession.

"I told the detectives," Gordon continued, shouting into the confessional of the dark night, "I told them what really happened. They know the truth now, Davey. You don't have to protect me any longer."

A sharp intake of breath and Davey swallowed again.

"You mean the world to me, son. I'm so sorry for what I've done to you all these years. I never realized . . . Please don't hurt yourself. Please, son."

Struggling to keep his emotions in check Davey made an incomprehensible noise. He blinked away tears.

"He loves you, Davey," I whispered. "Take a chance. Take back your life. Can't you see your father needs your forgiveness? And you need to give it to him."

"Davey," Gordon shouted again. "Please, forgive me."

Davey stared up at the group. He swallowed again.

"Okay, Dad," Davey shouted in a voice thick with emotion. "Everything is okay. Grace is with me."

The group on the ridge reacted, but I was more concerned with Davey. He choked back tears and let go of my arm. "He did it," he whispered. "He did it for me."

I put my arm around him. "Yes, he did."

Davey lowered the gun. "Thank you."

As the group began to make their way gingerly down the hillside, I placed both hands around the weapon, easing it away from him and into my deep dress pocket. "You did good, Davey."

"But will they still think Jack killed that other guy?" he asked. "I don't want Jack to go to jail." He looked at me forlornly. "Being part of this re-enacting group made me feel like I could really do something important. Honorable. I thought that by taking the blame I would be doing right by Jack." He glanced away. "Sounds stupid now, doesn't it?"

"Misguided, maybe," I said. "But in this case you wouldn't have been serving justice, you'd be impeding it."

"Yeah." The group was close now and our time alone was just about up. "I guess I shouldn't have listened to Pierpont."

"What?" I asked. "This was his idea?"

"No," Davey said quickly. "It was always about doing the right thing. Always about working for the greater good. About putting others first. He talked a lot about dying an honorable death. He knew how upset I was about Jack being arrested. He knew how much it meant to me to clear Jack's name. Pierpont wasn't trying to get me to take the blame for Zachary's murder for his sake . . ." He looked at me with dread in his eyes. "Was he?"

When the Embers men and police escort made it to our position, I saw an expression on Jack's face I'd never seen before. He stayed as far from his father as possible and wouldn't make eye contact with the man, even as Gordon reached out to embrace Davey. "I'm so sorry, son," he said pressing his face into Davey's shoulder. "I am so sorry."

They broke apart, Davey looking miserably conspicuous, and Gordon trying without success to keep his emotions in check. He lowered himself to the ground and dropped his head into his hands.

Jack exchanged a look with Keith and walked away.

Tank took control immediately, frisking Davey. When she came up empty, she asked, "Where's the gun?"

I was about to answer that I had it when Gordon cried out. He clutched his chest, falling forward, gasping for air. Tank was next to him in a moment, crouching low, issuing orders. To the uniforms: "Get help. They must have a medic here. You," she pointed to another cop, "call for an ambulance." She loosened Gordon's collar as she barked her commands. Two of the officers ran off.

"There is a medic," I said. "I know what he looks like. I'll go."

I ran off before anyone could stop me, racing up the hill yet again. The gun bounced against my inner thigh and as I made it to the top of the rise I saw Frances hurrying my way. Having changed into her hoop-skirted gown, she reminded me of a bell, tolling with every step she took.

"Frances," I said, "I'm so glad to see you." The surprise on her face was probably very similar to mine. I never would have expected to be saying those words. "Gordon Embers is having a heart attack. Down where Zachary was killed. Where's the medic?"

"He went to the election," she said. "Come on, I'll show you where I saw him."

Frances couldn't run as fast as I could, so I reluctantly slowed my pace and hoped the uniformed officer had already found the doctor and that they were on the return trip. No way to count on that, however. I pressed on.

Holding her skirt up as she tried to keep pace, Frances asked, "What happened down there?"

"Should you be running?"

"It's cool out now. I'm fine. What happened?" she asked again.

"Too much to explain."

We kept running and had just made it to the edge of the gathering when sirens blared behind us. Everyone stopped what they were doing, turning to see what was going on. An ambulance bounded over the far hill and bounced along the rough terrain following the path the coroner's van had taken less than a week ago. I hoped that wasn't a bad omen.

"That was fast," I said.

I heard a woman murmur, "What's going on?"

"No idea," her husband said. "Pierpont will know." He turned toward the stage. "Hey, Pierpont!"

"They've kept an ambulance on-site all day today," Frances told me. "The doctor got very chatty while I was in there with him. He said that over the years they've learned to anticipate a few emergencies when the partying gets out of hand on the last night."

"Lucky for Gordon," I said.

"What was he doing here anyway?" she asked.

I was about to answer, but Pierpont had stepped onto the makeshift stage. "What was the question?" he asked into a microphone.

"A microphone?" I asked. "They must have some sort of generator. I'm surprised Pierpont's using it."

"Once the election is over they can officially return to the twenty-first century with all its wonders," Frances said. "Pierpont's rule."

"Convenient."

We were within five feet of the stage, but Pierpont didn't

see us. He was gazing out over the crowd, one hand up, answering the man's query. "Everything is under control," he said. "One of our visitors didn't leave at the prescribed time and suffered an unfortunate accident, but the local authorities are handling it. Nothing we need to be concerned about."

Frances gave me a skeptical look. "He's making that up, isn't he? He has no idea what's going on over there."

As she spoke, I thought about Pierpont's assertion about the back gate having been left unlocked the night of the murder, and it being mysteriously secure when the police checked it out. "I bet that's not all he made up," I said. I hadn't shared my suspicions with anyone, and I had no intention of confronting Pierpont myself. With him onstage addressing his troops, I felt safe. As soon as this event was over, however, I planned to share everything I'd learned about Pierpont with Tank. I was about to start back, intent on talking with her, when Pierpont's speech stopped me.

"Thank you all for your support," the little man was saying, "especially in the wake of all the unpleasantness we experienced this week. Additionally, I'm sorry that my friend Jim Florian had to give up his candidacy. That was a very moving speech you gave, Jim." He sent a meaningful glance to his right, where Jim Florian leaned sloppily against the stage, looking wretched and very drunk. Addressing the crowd again, Pierpont said, "Jim would have made an excellent general. His father and I were friends from way back when and I remember watching Jim grow up, go to college, and get his great job at NASA."

Pierpont sent another meaningful glance toward Florian, who was attempting to right himself. He scratched the back of his head, took a few shaky steps away from the stage, then stopped. Nodding to no one in particular, he turned back.

Pierpont continued to address the audience. "The truth is, with our Gettysburg event coming up next month, I'm particularly delighted to remain in the position of general . . ."

With drunken determination, Florian boosted himself onto the stage. "Now just you wait a minute," he said.

Pierpont stuttered as Florian advanced. He sent a panicked look toward the crowd. "Another round of applause for Jim, everyone?"

The audience complied. Florian turned, blinking at the burst of noise, then shook off his confusion and yanked the microphone out of Pierpont's hand.

"Somethin' I forgot to add . . ." he said.

Pierpont reached to grab it back. "Maybe later, Jim."

Dulled reflexes notwithstanding, Jim lifted the microphone out of Pierpont's reach, grinning. "Uh-uh," he said, "my turn, shorty."

The look on Pierpont's face sent a chill up the back of my neck. Unable to drag my attention away, I whispered to Frances, "This could get ugly."

She nodded.

Catcalls ranging from: "Sit down, Florian!" to "Had enough to drink?" bubbled up from the audience. He ignored them.

Waving a finger, he said, "Here's what you all *don't* know. I didn't step down from the election because I wanted to . . . Oh no."

Pierpont made another lunge for the mic, but Florian stumbled sideways, keeping it out of the other man's reach. He stepped up to the very edge of the stage and I worried he might pitch forward, but he seemed to be looking out, searching. "Any of you got kids still hanging around, you better take them back to your tent."

Nobody moved.

"I mean it," he shouted, making us wince. "This isn't going to be a PG-rated show. Not tonight." Backing up to the middle of the stage, he chuckled to himself. "Pretty funny, huh? PG?" He pointed to Pierpont. "Nobody in the

Civil War would have heard about PG. That would be
farby." He elongated the word. "And old Pierpont over
there is probably having a hissy fit right now. But you all
notice how it's okay we have a microphone here tonight?
How come? Because it suits the little general's pursp . . .
pruspi . . . purposes." He shrugged. "You know what I
mean." He cupped his eyes. "Now get the kids out of here."

Some of the parents, looking confused, complied.

Apoplectic, Pierpont started toward Florian again, but
Hennessey had come up behind him and grabbed Pierpont
by the arm. From where we stood it looked like Hennessey
said, "Let him talk."

Pierpont continued to struggle. I hoped Hennessey held
on for the rest of the night.

"Okay, so here it is, folks," Florian said. He pointed to
Pierpont. "I hate that guy. Probably even more than the rest
of you do. Know why? Not because I can't have a cooler in
my tent. Nope. Something bigger. Waaay bigger. He made
me step down." Nodding, slurring his words, he went on.
"Blackmail. Yep. You heard right. Mr. Dictator knows how
much you all deps . . . dssip . . . despise him. Knows it full
well and knew his days were numbered. That's why he
wanted me to be the new general. So I would be the face,
but he would still be in power. You understand this yet?"

I was beginning to.

"But when he found out I was planning to relax the rules
from his dictatorial standards, he took it all back. Told me
I had to give up."

The crowd had gone utterly silent.

"And I did. Because of what he was holding over me."
Florian stared out, looking morose. "But not anymore.
Nope. I'm here to tell you that I lied. Okay? Got that? This
won't mean squat to any of you, but I lied a really long time
ago. I got my job at NASA based on a little, itty-bitty false-
hood." He held his index finger and thumb very close together, then moved them apart, then spread his arms wide.

"Maybe not so itty-bitty. You see, I didn't graduate from MIT like I told them. I had a friend who worked in admissions though. He fudged the records and that got me the job. That was years ago, y'understand. But if it ever got out even now, I'd never work in my field again." His eyes widened. "You getting all this? I would be ruined. Like I am now."

I didn't know exactly what I'd expected, but it hadn't been this.

"Pierpont's known me since I was a kid. We were neighbors and he worked with my dad. Pierpont knew I didn't go to MIT. Didn't know I lied to NASA, though, until I told him once when I was drunk. Ever since, he's made me his little puppet." He seemed to find that funny. "Kinda ironic that I'm drunk again and telling all of you." Growing serious again, he shouted, "But no more!"

Wild-eyed, Pierpont struggled against Hennessey, but was clearly outmatched.

Florian was rambling now. "I'll tell you how bad it got. He made me lie for him all the time. He told me he saw someone here at our camp the day of Zachary's murder. But he said it would look fishy if *he* went to the police so he told *me* to do it. I didn't want to, but . . ." He shrugged. "Blackmail is a real killer," he said. "For all I know, Pierpont made the whole thing up and I was just being his puppet again."

Florian hung his head down for a breathless moment. I wondered if he was about to pass out, but then he looked out at the crowd again. "So now you know the truth. And now you know that my career with NASA is shot. My life is shot. Just like I'm about to be shot."

With that he pulled a handgun out from his pocket and raised the barrel to his head.

Everyone screamed and I started toward the stage, knowing I would be too late to stop him. But Hennessey wasn't. Dropping his hold on Pierpont, he hit Florian in a flying tackle, the pair falling to the ground with a heavy double *thud*. The gun went off, but I saw them both move.

I didn't stop to see if they were okay. I figured with all those people around, someone would take charge. I had to move because Pierpont was taking advantage of the chaos. He ducked behind the stage, making a break for a clean escape.

"Call the cops," I said to Frances as I scooted through the crowd to follow him. I didn't shout, didn't warn, I just followed, trusting that my long-legged strides would outpace his before he got to the parking area. A heavy weight bounced against my leg as I ran. I still had Davey's gun.

Although it was dark, the meadow was wide open and there was enough light from the moon to keep him in sight. He glanced back and saw me, redoubling his speed, but I was younger and taller. Now I did yell, "Stop, Pierpont. You know you can't get away."

I didn't have a plan, unfortunately. The parking lot was still a long way off and by this time we were far away from any other people. No one would see us here. Too late I realized I'd rushed headlong into danger, yet again.

But this time I had a gun. He had nothing.

To my surprise, Pierpont stopped. "Okay," he said, bending over, pressing his hands to his knees. He wheezed, then crouched and rocked in place. "I can't run anymore."

"No you can't," I said, easing my hand into the pocket of my dress and wrapping my fingers around the grip of the gun. It never hurt to be prepared. "It's over."

We were about fifteen feet apart in the center of the meadow. He stood up slowly. "You should have stayed out of it."

In that breathless silence after he spoke, I heard the *snick* of a switchblade. Moonlight slid along its metal edge. Instinctively, I backed up. "Don't," I said.

"I may be small, but if I took Kincade down, I can certainly handle you."

"Kincade was drunk," I said, "you couldn't have done it otherwise."

He came at me, slicing the air with his knife. I dodged the blade but in my haste to jump away, I'd caught my foot on a branch and tumbled left.

I managed to get up, scrambling away from him as I did so. The moment I was back on my feet, I pulled the gun from my pocket. Relief made me glib and I pulled a line from memory, "It's a mistake to bring a knife to a gunfight, Pierpont."

The moment he saw the weapon he froze in place. He looked back the way we'd come. I knew what he was thinking: that it could be quite a while before anyone thought to look for us out here. "You know how to use one of those?" he asked as he started to circle clockwise around me.

"Point and shoot," I said, keeping the gun trained on him. "Just like a camera."

"That's a semiautomatic," he said conversationally, still moving—edging closer as he did so.

"Stand still," I said.

"Why? Are you planning to shoot me? I sincerely doubt you will, Ms. Wheaton. You don't have the stomach for it."

"Don't bet on it," I said with far more nerve than I felt.

Still circling, he pointed to the gun. "You need to chamber a round before it will fire."

I moved with him. "So?"

"Did you?"

I had no idea if Davey had chambered a round before he'd handed the gun to me. I assumed he had. I blustered, "Only one way to find out, isn't there?"

Pierpont chanced a look back. I didn't waver an inch.

I knew Frances would notice my absence the minute she returned to the group with the cops. With Pierpont missing, too, she'd be on our trail like a hound dog.

"It's not going to be much longer," I said.

"I agree with you, Ms. Wheaton. Not much longer. For me at least. But for you, it will be forever."

Pierpont became a blur as he leapt at me, switchblade slashing. I ducked to my right, out of harm's way, and pulled the trigger.

Nothing.

I didn't know how I'd been knocked to the ground but I got up fast. My left forearm was suddenly scalding and wet, like I'd fallen against a searing hot stove. I still had the gun in my right hand, and although I willed my left arm to come up, it was reluctant to behave as ordered.

Pierpont, just as surprised as I was by the gun's dry-fire, had backed away when I'd tried to shoot. He came at me again, screaming and hacking the air like a madman.

I took off running with him right behind me. "Help!" I screamed into the darkness, hoping someone would hear. Picking my feet up as I ran, I prayed to avoid any roots or stones that might cause me to stumble like women always did in slasher movies. "Help!" As I ran, blood—my blood—dripped down my arm, and landed on the front of my dress with heavy splatters I could feel. I managed to grasp the gun's slide and, with enormous effort—my left arm screaming with delayed pain—pull it back until I felt the satisfying *chink* of a round being chambered.

I angled away, turning to face him. "It's chambered now," I said breathlessly. "Don't move."

He hesitated, looked back toward the camp, then back at me. We were close enough for me to see his wild expression. "This is my battlefield," he said, inching closer, "but your blood."

I backed away.

In the distance I thought I heard someone call my name. But all my attention was on the little man with the knife in his hand and hatred in his eyes.

"Don't do it, Pierpont. Please."

"You've taken my life. Now I will have yours."

When he came at me again, I pulled the trigger, aiming center mass. A burst of fire shot from the barrel of the gun. The recoil sent my arm flying back. The noise made me scream.

I couldn't see him, couldn't hear anything, so I backed away, calling for help. I closed my eyes for a precious second to try to reestablish my night vision. "Help!" I shouted. Why was my voice so muffled?

When I opened my eyes, I saw Pierpont on the ground. He grasped his leg, writhing in pain. I backed away. "Here! Over here!"

Maybe I was shouting to no one. But I had to try.

Pierpont was up on all fours now, crawling toward the parking area, moving like a broken toy. I pulled my finger away from the trigger into the safe position, but kept the gun aimed at him as he wheezed and crept away. I stayed far enough behind to feel secure, hoping someone would come to my rescue. Pierpont turned and spoke to me. I couldn't make out what he was saying. I couldn't even read his lips.

I chanced a look back toward the camp. Someone was coming. Finally. From the looks of it, a lot of someones.

Pierpont saw them, too. Finally giving up, he turned onto his back, raised his hands to his face, and began to weep.

IT DIDN'T TAKE LONG FOR THE POLICE TO ASsume control and call for another ambulance. With the cops arriving en masse with flashlights, it looked like we were about to be attacked by a giant swarm of lightning bugs. I couldn't have been happier.

The medic—who was probably having the busiest night of his re-enactment life—tossed me a roll of bandages and began ministering to Pierpont.

I sat in the damp grass, attempting to roll the gauze around my arm. Not having much luck.

"How is Gordon?" I asked Rodriguez when he showed up.

"Mr. Embers is stable," he said. "Where's the gun?"

It was lying next to me on the grass. I pushed it toward him. He picked it up, removed the magazine, racked back the slide, and dumped the remaining round into his hand. "All better now," he said.

Giving my bandaging efforts a scornful look, he pushed my right hand away and took control, proceeding to wrap my arm snugly and quickly with confident expertise.

"There you go," he said. "But you better have that looked at as soon as possible. You're going to need stitches."

He was about to say more, when Tank strode over. "Weren't you supposed to stay out of this one?" she asked.

"I tried to," I said. "What are you doing here? I thought you'd be at the hospital with Gordon Embers."

"He's too weak to give an official statement yet, but he's going to be okay. Guards are watching him round-the-clock."

"You think that's necessary?" I asked.

"Procedure." She pointed at my arm. "Nice field dressing."

"Thanks to Detective Rodriguez."

He waved my comment away as an ambulance bounced over the grass, headlights glaring. I started to shield my eyes with both hands, thought better of it, and used only my right. One of the uniformed officers trotted over as the paramedics spilled out of the vehicle.

"It appears the victim sustained a gunshot wound to the thigh. The doctor here was able to staunch the blood loss, but his pressure's dropping and he may go into shock."

Tank nodded. "Thanks."

Rodriguez patted my shoulder.

A shrill voice blared from the darkness. "Where is she?"

I turned toward the sound. "I'm over here, Frances."

She made her way toward us, tolling bell dress gripped in both hands, held high as she gingerly chose her footing. Hennessey trailed behind her. "For heaven's sake," she said, "you could have at least told me you were planning to run off like that."

"It was a surprise to me, too."

She came close, inspected my bandaged arm and said, "You just can't help getting into the middle of these things, can you?"

"I guess not."

Frances sniffed, then turned to Hennessey. "Told you she's nothing but trouble. She's just lucky she has me to back her up."

I laughed. "That I am, Frances. That I am."

RODRIGUEZ ACCOMPANIED ME TO THE EMER-gency room and stayed in the tiny examining area while I waited to be seen. "You want to talk about it?" he asked.

I found that I did. We sat behind a striped ceiling-mounted curtain that was pulled closed to provide privacy and I told him everything that had happened since I ran off to find the medic.

He nodded and took notes. "I know I don't need to tell you not to talk to the media," he said. "There's already a bunch of reporters outside asking what new excitement Marshfield Manor is up to."

I groaned. "We only have one local paper. How come the news media seems to expand whenever we have a crisis?"

"Human nature," he said. "Know how we pull from other departments to arrange a task force? They must do the same thing. Cover the big stories that way. And not much happens around here." He gave me a dire look. "Well not until recently, that is."

"I guess."

"Anybody I should call?" he asked.

"No, I'll be going home soon enough. Can I hitch a ride with you?" I asked. "No need to get my roommates riled up."

"You got it."

"Why don't you go get a cup of coffee or something, I think it's going to be a while."

He stood up, clearly relieved. "You want anything?"

"No thanks."

"You sure? I've been here enough times. I can get the cafeteria ladies to whip you up something special."

"I'm fine. You go ahead."

Five minutes after he left, I was trying to make pictures out of the dots scattered across the ceiling tiles. I had just come up with two smileys and a cat's face complete with whiskers when I heard, "Knock, knock."

Jack?

"Come in," I said.

He pushed the curtain aside, looking sheepish. "I didn't know how else to get your attention. They said you were in here and I thought I should stop by. How's your arm?"

"I'll live," I said, "and I'm hearing Pierpont will, too."

Jack nodded, then stared at the ceiling. I wondered what pictures he saw up there. After a moment he said, "Wow. This is awkward."

"Why don't you sit for a minute?"

He took the rolling stool Rodriguez had vacated. "I don't know where to begin."

"How's your dad?"

He bobbed his head. "Good. Stable. Should make a full recovery." Jack's eyes got suddenly shiny. "He's got a lot ahead of him . . ."

"How's Davey?"

"Okay, considering the rough night he's had." Then, as though hearing his own words, Jack amended, "What am I saying? He's had it rough for a lot longer than that." He blinked several times. "Calla's here with her husband. She knows Dad had a heart attack. She doesn't know the rest. Not yet. She thinks the guards outside his room are because he's a retired cop."

"Your family is strong. You'll get through this."

"I lived with them my whole life and I never suspected," he said. "How did you know?"

I had no answer.

He was silent for a long time. "Thank you for all you did for Davey. I just wish . . ."

More silence. I couldn't stand it anymore.

"I understand," I said. "Now, why don't you get back to your dad? I'm sure he needs his family close by."

"Yeah." At the curtain, he turned back. "I know we just went out on one date, but I think it may be a while before I'm ready to go out again."

"I get it, Jack. Take your time."

"Thanks, Grace."

The doctor arrived a few minutes later. She examined my wound, asked me about my last tetanus shot, made small talk, and with crisp efficiency, left me with a neat line of fourteen stitches. "Should heal up nicely," she said, and handed me a sheet of instructions for at-home care. "You got lucky. It wasn't deep."

When she left, I pondered her words. I *had* gotten lucky. Again. I hoped this was the last time I'd have to depend on good luck to survive.

Rodriguez returned with Tank in tow. "They say you're ready to go," Tank said.

"Can't wait to get out of here."

Rodriguez gave me a sorrowful look. "One problem," he said as I lowered my feet to the floor, "about that ride."

My heart sank. "You can't drive me?"

"Somebody else muscled me out."

I knew he wasn't talking about Jack. Please don't let it be Tooney. "Who?" I asked.

Bennett walked into the curtained area, concern narrowing his eyes. "Are you all right?"

"I'm fine," I said, enormously cheered to see him. "Good as new."

"Terrence briefed me," he said. "Gracie, you have to be more careful."

"I thought I was."

Tank cleared her throat. "Not Grace's fault, Mr. Marshfield. She kept us updated at every step. This shouldn't have happened. But it did. She's a tough cookie, this one."

I blushed. "Nice to know you don't think I messed you guys up."

Rodriguez held open the curtain for me. "Not this time, kiddo."

"ARE YOU ABLE TO WALK?" BENNETT ASKED. "Do you want to hold onto my arm?"

I was perfectly capable of making my way to the hospital's front door, but Bennett seemed so earnest, his eyes bright with worry, that I couldn't refuse. "Thanks," I said, tucking my hand into his elbow.

He straightened and smiled. "Good. Nice to see you safe and sound, Gracie. When Terrence came to tell me, I was out of my mind with worry."

"I didn't mean to get into trouble this time. In fact, I believed I was steering clear."

"You need to try harder."

Outside, the night was crisp and breezy. "Beautiful," I said as I drew in a deep breath of damp, cool air.

"Only because you're still with us." Bennett placed a hand over mine and said, "I was very concerned about you."

I didn't know what to say, but Bennett didn't seem to need an answer. "Grant will be here any moment," he said.

He wasn't kidding. Less than a minute later, Grant drove

up. That in itself wasn't surprising, as Bennett rarely drove himself anymore. What was surprising was *what* he was driving.

"The Packard?" I asked.

Bennett was grinning, clearly pleased to have surprised me. "Nothing but the best to take you home in style."

Grant stopped the car in front of us, got out, and handed us into the huge vehicle's rear seat. "Would you like the top up, miss?" Grant asked.

I looked up at the moon. "No, this is perfect, thank you."

Bennett sat next to me. I was on the driver's side with Bennett to my right. I wanted to put my left arm out to catch the wind as we drove, but after getting fourteen stitches, that wasn't a viable plan. Even though I knew Grant wouldn't be able to hear a word we said if we talked, Bennett and I were silent for the first mile or so. His mention of taking me "home" made me wonder if he planned to take me to my house, or if he hoped I'd spend some time at Marshfield under his watchful eye and that of his staff. I'd spent one night there once before and although it was glorious being waited on hand and foot, I really wanted to be in my own house tonight.

Bennett must have read my mind because he cleared his throat and said, "About you moving into Abe's cottage . . ."

I took a deep breath, but he continued before I could say anything.

"I was thinking about rescinding my offer. Temporarily, that is."

I looked at him. The wind lifted his white hair as he stared out, straight ahead.

"Rescind?" I repeated.

"Only temporarily." He turned to face me. "I can't advocate what that Embers boy did protecting his father all these years, but I do understand it. What a burden that boy placed on himself. No wonder he's been in trouble for so long."

"He needs a fresh start."

"Exactly my thought. Seems to me that living with Jack hasn't been the right answer. And I can't see how going back to the family home—full of all those memories—is going to do him much good, but the boy needs a place to live if he's going to make anything of himself."

"And you want to offer him Abe's cottage?"

Bennett nodded. "If that's all right with you."

Not for the first time did it occur to me that Bennett was one of the most thoughtful, generous people I'd ever met.

"I think it's a wonderful idea."

He nodded. "One more thing," he said. "I still want to help you with your repairs. Your house needs work, Gracie. And you haven't been able to keep up."

"That wouldn't be fair," I said. "You were only going to do that if I took the cottage."

"This is a condition of our agreement—our new agreement. Davey comes to live at the cottage, and you allow me to help out from time to time. Beyond that, no strings attached."

I tucked my right hand in the crook of Bennett's elbow again. "You're a good man," I said. "Thank you."

Chapter 26

SUNDAY MORNING WAS SO RAINY AND OVER-cast that I barely knew that it had dawned. I was up early having coffee in the kitchen, sneezing from having had Bootsie sleep with me all night when Bruce bounded downstairs. "Did you see the weather? Good thing your re-enactors finished up last night." He stopped and stared. "What happened?"

I glanced around, then realized he was talking about my arm. "Oh, this," I said. "Long story."

"That's a pretty professional bandage job," he said, taking a closer look at my arm. "Who did it?"

"Emergency room."

"What?" Bruce said. "Talk to me." He turned to Scott who had just ambled in. "Did you hear that? Our Grace was in the emergency room last night." To me, "Why didn't you call us?"

"I got a ride home. It was no big deal."

Bruce looked unconvinced. "Spill it. Or no more chocolate-covered strawberries for you."

I took a deep breath. "Okay . . ."

When I was done, the two had their mouths open. They'd peppered me with questions throughout my recitation, but now they hit me with the big one. "Why didn't you tell us that Bennett offered you a home on his property?"

"Because I didn't plan to ever take him up on it."

The two exchanged a look. Bruce asked, "Because you felt responsible for us?"

"No," I said, "because I didn't want to leave you two."

Scott reached for my right hand and squeezed. Bruce knew better than to grab my left, but he laid his hand across the top of my fingers. "I'm glad," he said.

Bootsie jumped into my lap and gave a tiny yowl.

"I think she's glad, too," Scott said.

FOUR HOURS LATER, THE DOORBELL RANG and Bootsie scurried out of the room. We both knew who it was before I looked. My heart sank as I plodded to the front door and opened it.

"Tooney," I said.

He stood there hat in hand. A cat carrier sat on the stoop next to him.

"Hi there, Grace. It's okay if I call you Grace, right?"

I sighed and stepped aside to let him in. "After all we've been through lately, yeah. Sure." Right now I didn't care. He was here to claim Bootsie and that was all I could think about. We went into the parlor, where I offered him a seat and looked for her. She usually came to see what the humans were doing. But she was not in the room.

"I screwed up," he said as he sat, placing the cat carrier on the floor next to his chair. "On that Florian-Pierpont thing."

"Yeah."

"You mad?"

"How can I be? Turned out we should have been investigating Pierpont all along. I told the police what you found out and they're launching an investigation into that Sutherland's death now, too. So the guy's family should be happy about that, at least."

"Grace," he said, leaning forward, "I know I'm not exactly your favorite person, but I have to say I'm a little concerned."

I'd been staring at the cat carrier. Thinking about Bootsie's future life in Westville with those cute kids. I should be happy for her. But I was too sad for me.

"What about?"

"You just solved a thirteen-year-old murder as well as the one that happened last week. You took down the bad guys and came out smelling like a rose."

"Your point?"

"Shouldn't you be a little happier today? Feeling you did some good in this world?"

Tooney giving me life advice? "Maybe," I said, "but not today."

"I'm sorry to hear that." He stood, and picked up the cat carrier. "Because I have more bad news for you."

I remained seated. If he was such an amazing PI, let him figure out where Bootsie was. I didn't want to be Dorothy handing Toto over to Miss Gulch. "Yeah?" I asked not even looking at him. "What's that?"

"I screwed up again."

"How so, Tooney?"

"That cat, Mittens? The one with the reward?"

"Yeah?"

"She found her way home while I was checking out Pierpont."

Now I glanced up. Tooney was grinning, looking particularly proud of himself. "Yep. The real Mittens is back safe home with her family." He pointed under my seat. "Looks like that one—Bootsie, is it?—is all yours."

"You're not just saying that, are you, Tooney?"

He shook his head. "Turns out there were a couple of extra markings not visible in the photos. When they got their cat back they noticed. They *thought* Bootsie was theirs. But she isn't."

I was confused. I pointed at the cat carrier. "But . . . but . . . you brought that."

He handed it to me. "A gift," he said, "for having faith in me."

Bootsie poked her nose out from under my chair, as though she'd understood exactly what was going on. She stood next to my leg and cried up at me.

I felt my throat grow warm as I bent down to pick her up. "Thanks, Tooney," I whispered. "You're okay."

"I'll see myself out." He placed his hat on his head and winked. "You take care."

"You, too," I said. And sneezed.